George Lovett Bennett

Second Latin Writer

containing hints on writing Latin prose with graduated continuous exercises

George Lovett Bennett

Second Latin Writer
containing hints on writing Latin prose with graduated continuous exercises

ISBN/EAN: 9783337369569

Printed in Europe, USA, Canada, Australia, Japan

Cover: Foto ©Andreas Hilbeck / pixelio.de

More available books at **www.hansebooks.com**

SECOND LATIN WRITER

CONTAINING HINTS ON WRITING LATIN PROSE
WITH GRADUATED CONTINUOUS
EXERCISES

BY

GEORGE L. BENNETT, M.A.

HEAD MASTER OF THE HIGH SCHOOL, PLYMOUTH

SECOND EDITION

Boston

JOHN ALLYN, PUBLISHER

MDCCCLXXXII

PREFACE

My object in writing this book is to endeavour to teach boys who have mastered the elementary rules to write Latin Prose without cramming them with rules and examples. My main idea has been to insist on a careful comparison of the English with the Latin, and to let the pupil learn by steady practice, drawing his attention to the fact that the only way to learn to write good Latin is by trying to appreciate the Latin authors he is reading.

With this end in view I have given some hints on the difference between English and Latin in idiom and in style. There are in addition some notes on the commoner difficulties, with a table of differences of idiom.

I have also insisted strongly on the careful use of the analysis, which will teach English as well as Latin.

The pieces for translation are mainly selected from MSS. sources—school and college exercises. I have to thank Mr Arthur Sidgwick for his kindness in revising the Introduction, and for many most valuable suggestions. I am also indebted to several of my old colleagues at Rugby for some of the materials of the Exercises.

GEORGE L. BENNETT.

High School, Plymouth,
December 1879.

CONTENTS

Contents.

CHAPTER I

INTRODUCTORY.

THE USE OF LATIN PROSE COMPOSITION.

WITHOUT enlarging on the advantages that have been claimed for the study of Latin prose composition, it may be fairly asserted that the habits of attention and accuracy which are absolutely essential to pass muster (not to speak of higher aims) must have a direct and real educational value on the mind. There is no other means whereby we can combine the accuracy required in the study of the exact sciences with the literary refinement that is indispensable to a liberal education. It is considered that to know a modern language one must be able to translate it and converse in it. Admitting that as a conversational language classical Latin is dead, Latin prose writing is the nearest approach to conversation in Latin. Why not try to know Latin as well, or nearly as well, as we try to know French or German? Latin is the most *logical* of all languages. From its study we get a habit of expressing ourselves logically and tersely. Latin words enter largely into the English language; how can we know our own language if we neglect nearly a third of it? Latin prose writing teaches us our own language as well as Latin; it explains many an idiom that we should otherwise use without understanding it. Perhaps one may never have occasion to write any Latin after one's school days, but the mental discipline this study entails will always be of lasting service; its effects will never disappear. If it is nothing else, it is a mental gymnastic that must benefit our reasoning faculties, just as fresh air and exercise benefit our bodies.

A

THE COMPARISON OF ENGLISH WITH LATIN.

1. A full appreciation of the meaning of the English is absolutely necessary before we can attempt to put it into Latin. Read and re-read the *whole* passage till you thoroughly understand it, and then attempt your task. But remember you have to give the *sense* in your translation, so do not fall into the error of supposing that you have done so because you have given grammatically correct Latin equivalents for the English words. Thus you must not translate ' Rome is on the Tiber ' by *Roma in Tiberi est*, which would mean 'Rome is in the Tiber,' but by *Roma ad Tiberim sita est.*

THE LATIN VERB.

2. Perhaps the greatest difficulty is in the correct use of the Verb. First the rules for the Moods and Tenses must be mastered. Then we find that the Latin Verb has more to do than the English one. It has to take the place of and express abstract ideas, many—indeed most—of which we express by Substantives, generally derived from the Latin, but often with meanings widely differing from their classical use. Thus, 'A longer occupation of the city' is not *Longior urbis occupatio*, but *Diutius in urbe manere.*

CLEARNESS OF EXPRESSION.

3. If on reading your translation there is any obscurity, you may be sure that it is not good Latin. Rewrite it. Be sure that any boy in your own form could construe it as easily as he would an ordinary piece of Latin before you are content with your work. Neglect of the proper stops is a frequent cause of obscurity. In reading Latin authors it is usually easy for a fairly advanced student to see the general drift of any passage, though it may be difficult to translate it into good English. Let then the *meaning*, at all events, of your Latin prose be quite evident.

THE USE OF THE DICTIONARY.

4. A golden rule is: **Use your English-Latin Dictionary as little as possible.** In the case of Verbs especially a little thought will generally show that you do know a Verb that will convey the idea, though at first sight you are at fault. For instance, in translating the sentence, 'He made up his mind to go,' if you do not know what the Latin for 'to make up one's mind' is, you probably do know words meaning 'to resolve' or 'determine.'

Again, in the case of Substantives, and particularly abstract ones, you find them often rendered in the dictionary by Latin equivalents which have a widely different classical usage. Such words as *persona*, *officium*, *statio*, etc. have special uses, and would often be wrongly used to translate the English words derived from them.

An English-Latin dictionary that would repay one for the trouble of looking up every word would have to be in many volumes.

Purely modern ideas and inventions have of course no corresponding Latin. For instance, you could not put 'a breech-loading rifle' into classical Latin. You must call it a weapon simply. So with proper names. Use Latin names instead, unless you can give them a Latin form. Remember, also, dictionaries are not supplied in examinations. But when you look up a word in your Latin-English dictionary, get into the habit of reading the whole article right through, with all the examples. You will soon find that the number of words you have to look up will decrease.

ANALYSIS.

5. By means of a careful analysis you may absolutely ensure accuracy, and be as certain of using the right Mood as you would be of finding the product of two and two. You have probably been taught to use the analysis and rules given below. If so, so much the better. If not, pay the strictest attention to them now. There is no other way of being accurate.

CHAPTER II

ANALYSIS.

I. THE SIMPLE SENTENCE (ORATIO RECTA).

6. (1) STATEMENT,—Verb in Indicative (of facts)—

> Civis Romanus sum.   *I am a Roman citizen.*

Or in Conjunctive (of possibilities)—

> Dixerit aliquis.   *Some one may say.*

(2) COMMAND,—(*a*) Positive : Verb in Imperative or Conjunctive—

> Parce victis.   *Spare the conquered.*

(*b*) Negative : Verb in Conjunctive—

> Hoc ne feceris.   *Do not do this.*

(*a*) In Positive commands use the

> Present Imperative of Second Person.
> Present Conjunctive of First and Third Persons.

So in English we say, 'Let me go,' 'let him go,' 'let us go ;' but in the Second Person 'Go.'

The Future Imperative is seldom used except in legal language, or in oracular responses.

(*b*) In Negative commands use

> Aorist (Perfect) Conjunctive of Second Person.
> Present Conjunctive of First and Third Persons.

(*c*) The Conjunctive Mood has two uses—

> (I.) Pure, or not dependent on another Verb. It often has Auxiliary Verbs (*may, might, can, could, would, should*) for signs in English.

(II.) Dependent on another Verb (when it is called the Subjunctive). It is generally to be translated as an Indicative.

(3) **QUESTION,**—Verb Indicative (Fact) with Interrogative word—

     Quis es ?   *Who are you?*

Or in Conjunctive (Deliberation) with Interrogative word—

     Quid faciam ? *What am I to do?*

Interrogative words—

     Quantus, uter, qualis, quis, quot, quotus, unde, ubi, quando, Cur, quoties, quare, quam, quomodo, num, ne, ut, an, utrum.

Nonne expects the answer *yes;* *num* the answer *no;* *ně* simply asks for information; *an* often implies surprise and expects the answer *no.*

Nonne canis similis lupo est ?	*Is not a dog like a wolf?* / *A dog is like a wolf, is it not?*
Num feles similis lupo est ?	*Is a cat like a wolf?* / *A cat is not like a wolf, is it?*
Potesne mihi respondere ?	*Can you answer me?*
An tu me tristem esse putas ?	*Do you really think me unhappy?*

DOUBLE QUESTIONS.

     Utrum—an.
     Num—an.
     Ně—an.

Are you an Englishman or a Frenchman? { Utrum Anglus / Num Anglus / Anglusne } an Gallus es ?

Translate 'or not' by *annon.*
The Interrogative word is sometimes omitted.

II. THE COMPOUND SENTENCE.

7. A Compound Sentence consists of a Principal Sentence with Dependent Clauses.

NOTE.—Dependent Clauses are also called Subordinate. Sentences or Clauses independent of one another are called Coordinate.

III. SEQUENCE OF TENSES.

8. In Dependent Clauses the Tense of the Subjunctive is regulated by that of the Verb on which it depends.

Like follows like.   So—

> Primary Tenses follow Primary.
> Historic Tenses follow Historic.

1. In narrative what is called the Historic Present takes the Historic Sequence.

Primary Tenses $\begin{cases} \text{Present} \\ \text{Perfect} \\ \text{Future} \end{cases}$ are followed by $\begin{cases} \text{Present.} \\ \text{Perfect.} \end{cases}$

So—

I ask	*what you are doing.*	Quaero	quid agas.
I have asked	*what you have done.*	Quaesivi	quid egeris.
I shall ask	*what you are going to do.*	Quaeram	quid acturus sis.

Historic Tenses $\begin{cases} \text{Imperfect} \\ \text{Aorist} \\ \text{Pluperfect} \end{cases}$ are followed by $\begin{cases} \text{Imperfect.} \\ \text{Pluperfect.} \end{cases}$

I was asking	*what you were doing.*	Quaerebam	quid ageres.
I asked	*what you had done.*	Quaesivi	quid egisses.
I had asked	*what you were going to do.*	Quaesiveram	quid acturus esses.

2. The poverty of Latin in Tenses only allows one form, *quaesivi*, to translate 'I asked' (Aorist), and 'I have asked' (Perfect).

3. There is no Future Subjunctive, so its place has to be supplied by the Future Participle conjugated with *sim* (after Primary Tenses) and *essem* (after Historic Tenses).

TENSES OF THE INFINITIVE.

The Present refers to the same time as $\left. \vphantom{\begin{matrix}1\\2\\3\end{matrix}}\right\}$ the Verb on which it
The Perfect refers to the time before
The Future refers to the time after   depends.

Remember that there is but one form for the Present and Imperfect, and also but one for the Perfect and Pluperfect.

IV. DEPENDENT CLAUSES. •

9. Dependent Clauses are called Substantival, Adjectival, or Adverbial, according as they take the place of a Substantive, Adjective, or Adverb.

SUBSTANTIVAL CLAUSES (ORATIO OBLIQUA).

10. Substantival Clauses are used—

(*a*) As Subject.

Constat multos interfectos.esse.	*It is well known that many were slain.*
Humanum est ut erremus.	*Error is common to mankind.*

(*b*) As Object to a Transitive Verb.

Dixit se civem Romanum esse.	*He said that he was a Roman citizen.*
Rogat quis adsit.	*He asks who is present.*

(*c*) In Apposition to a Noun or its equivalent (Pronouns, etc.).

Docebat Caesar hanc Romanorum esse consuetudinem ut amicos honore auctiores velit esse.	*Caesar proceeded to point out that the custom of the Roman people was to resolve that its friends should be increased in honour.*

They are divided into Indirect Statement, Indirect Command, and Indirect Question.

Hence it is clear that Simple Sentences can be changed into Substantival Clauses by making them depend on a Verb.

I. INDIRECT STATEMENT.

11. (*a*) Accusative with Infinitive depending on Verbs of saying (stating, affirming, promising, etc.) and feeling (perceiving, thinking, hoping, etc.).

Verbs of hoping and promising naturally take the Future of the Infinitive, as the subordinate clause is Future.

(*b*) *Quod* with Indicative, implying a fact, especially after words that express emotion, as—

Gaudeo quod venisti.	*I am glad you are come.*

Or when the clause stands in Apposition, as—

Id Caesar inhonestum ratus, quod pugnare nolebant, convocatos milites in hunc modum allocutus est,	*Caesar, thinking their disinclination to fight discreditable, assembled the troops and addressed them as follows,*

This use of *quod* is really not very far removed from its usual Causal force, though it introduces what is logically a Substantival Clause.

II. INDIRECT COMMAND.

12. (*a*) Ut, ne, after Verbs and expressions of ordering (entreat, ask, persuade, forbid, law, duty, expediency, necessity, etc.).

　(*b*) Similarly after expressions of allowing, caring, endeavouring, effecting.

　(*c*) Somewhat similarly after expressions of preventing.

(*a*) The Conjunctions *ut* and *ne* are often omitted. Veto (*I forbid*) and iubeo (*I order*) take the Infinitive when used affirmatively—

　　　　　Iubeo te abire.　　*I order you to go.*

But—

　　　　　Iubeo ne abeas.　　*I order you not to go.*

(*b*) Conor (*I endeavour*) takes the Infinitive.

III. INDIRECT QUESTION.

13. Interrogative words with Subjunctive after Verbs of asking, doubting, telling, finding, knowing, deciding, deliberating.

(1) But in a continuous reported speech questions in the First and Third Persons, not depending on any word in the speech itself, can be asked in the Infinitive. This is Livy's general practice. Caesar, however, prefers the Subjunctive.
　Questions that require an answer *must* be in the Subjunctive.

Ex militibus quaesivit quidnam sibi　*He asked the soldiers what they* vellent. Ecquem dubitare posse?　　*meant. Could any one hesitate?*

(2) The Interrogative word is often omitted.

(3) 'Or not' can be translated by *necnĕ*, as well as by *annon*, in Indirect Questions : or often it can be omitted.

PECULIAR CONSTRUCTIONS.

14. We have left two classes of Verbs that take peculiar constructions. They may be regarded as logically Substantival, though *perhaps* not so grammatically.

1. Verbs of fearing.

(*a*) Vereor ne veniat.	*I fear that he will come.*
(*b*) Vereor ut (ne non) veniat.	*I fear that he will not come.*

2. After words expressing a consequence (restat, sequitur, accidit, contingit, etc.) we find clauses introduced by *ut* which may be taken as Substantival (Indirect Statement), though grammatically Consecutive.

ADJECTIVAL CLAUSES.

15. Indicative with the Relative and its particles, *unde, ubi,* etc.

1. The Relative often has an Adverbial force, and requires the Subjunctive.

(*a*) **Final.**

Gladium strinxit quo se necaret.   *He drew a sword to kill himself with.*

(*b*) **Consecutive.**

Facit quod omnes turbet.   *He acts in a manner to disturb every one.*

(*c*) **Causal.**

Irascor tibi qui hoc facias.   *I am vexed with you for doing this.*

(*d*) **Concessive.**

Lorica, quae densa esset, perforata est.   *In spite of its thickness the breast-plate was pierced.*

(*e*) **Limitative.**

Solus omnium, quos quidem noverim, ita agit.   *He is the only man I know who acts in this manner.*

2. Clauses introduced by *quin* (=qui non) after negative expressions and interrogations expecting a negative answer are Adjectival.

Nemo fuit quin fleret.	*There was no one who did not weep.*
Numquis fuit quin fleret ?	*Was there any one who did not weep?*

ADVERBIAL CLAUSES.

16. Adverbial Clauses modify the Principal Sentence like Adverbs, showing how, why, or when a thing is done.

They are divided into—

1. FINAL.

Ut, ne (ne quis, ne ullus, ne quando, etc.), or Relative words (see *Adjectival Clauses*, 1 (*a*)), with Subjunctive (including quominus=ut eo minus). Remember that if there is a Comparative in the clause, *quo* (=ut eo) takes the place of *ut*.

Final Clauses only use the Present and Imperfect Tenses.

2. CONSECUTIVE.

Ut, ut non (ut nemo, ut nullus, ut nunquam, etc.), or Relative words, with Subjunctive. (See *Adjectival Clauses*, 1 (*b*).)

(*a*) Consecutive Clauses only use the Present and Imperfect Tenses.

Exception.—The Aorist is used in Narrative (especially in Livy) when it is desired to lay special stress on the fact itself.
So—

Tam catus erat ut nihil diceret.	*He was so shrewd as to say nothing.*
Tam catus erat ut nihil dixerit.	*He was so shrewd that he said nothing.*

(*b*) Under the head of Consecutive Relative Clauses comes the use of *quin* (qui, old form of Ablative—non) in negative sentences.
So—

Facere non possum quin ad te mittam. *I cannot refrain from sending to you.*

There seems to be a Demonstrative word implied in the Principal Sentence, 'I cannot (so) do how I should not send to you,'

3. TEMPORAL.

Cum, quando (*when*), quoties (*as often as*), simul, simul ac, simul atque (*as soon as*), ut (*when, since the time*), ubi (*when*), postquam (*after that*), dum, donec, quoad (*whilst, as long as*), with Indicative.

Dum, donec, quoad (*until*), antequam, priusquam (*before that*), with Indicative when the action is completed; with Subjunctive if the action is not completed; thus—

Cenavi priusquam huc veni.	*I dined before coming hither.*
Cenabo priusquam huc veniam.	*I shall dine before coming hither.*

Note the following idioms—

(a) Cum (*when*, denoting the occasion), with Imperfect or Pluperfect Subjunctive. This use seems to imply a Causal notion, as cum (*when*), *purely Relative*, generally with antecedent expressed, must take the Indicative.

Zenonem, cum essem Athenis, audiebam frequenter.	*I used often, when at Athens, to attend Zeno's lectures.*
Heri, cum Romæ fui, morbo sum oppressus.	*Yesterday, when at Rome, I was taken ill.*

(b) Dum (*whilst*) is often found with an Indicative Present, even of a thing past, and in Oratio Obliqua.

4. CAUSAL.

Quod, quia (*because*), quandoquidem, quando, quoniam, siquidem (*since, inasmuch as*), with Indicative. Cum (*since*), and Relative, with Subjunctive. (See *Adjectival Clauses*, 1 (c).)

5. CONDITIONAL.

Si (*if*), nisi (*unless*), with Indicative or Subjunctive.

A complete Conditional Sentence contains a Principal Sentence (Apodosis = result), and a Conditional Clause (Protasis = condition).

We may divide Conditional Sentences into three classes:—

	Condition.	*Result.*
(1)	Indicative.	Indicative.
(2)	Present Perfect } Subjunctive.	Present Perfect } Conjunctive.
(3)	Imperfect Pluperfect } Subjunctive.	Imperfect Pluperfect } Conjunctive.

(1) Si vales, bene est.   *If you are well, it is well.*
Si fecisti, interficieris.   *If you have done it, you will be slain.*

(2) Si { abeam / abierim } merces { vendam. / vendiderim. }

If I were to go away, I should sell my wares.

(3) Si { abirem / abissem } merces { venderem. / vendidissem. }

If I had been going, } *I should have been selling* } *my wares.*
If I had gone, } *I should have sold* }

(*a*) Modo, dum, dummodo, modo ut (*provided that*), with Subjunctive, are practically Conditional, though they have a Final or Concessive force implied.

(*b*) In turning Conditional Clauses into Indirect Statement, the Apodosis, or result, being the Principal Sentence, will of course be in the Infinitive.

6. Concessive.

Quanquam (*although*), utut (*however*), with Indicative. Licet, quamvis, ut, cum (*although*), with Subjunctive. Etsi, etiamsi, tametsi, (*although, even if*), with Indicative or Subjunctive. Relative with Subjunctive. (See *Adjectival Clauses*, 1 (*d*).)

7. Comparative.

Tanquam, velut, ceu, quasi (*as if*), with Subjunctive.

ADJECTIVAL AND ADVERBIAL CLAUSES IN ORATIO OBLIQUA.

17. All Adjectival and Adverbial Clauses in Oratio Obliqua must take the Subjunctive, and are called Sub-oblique. We sometimes find an Indicative, but it is then independent of the Oratio Obliqua, being put in as an explanatory remark by the speaker or writer.

VIRTUAL ORATIO OBLIQUA AND VIRTUALLY SUBOBLIQUE CLAUSES.

18. Oratio Recta (Simple Sentences) may be virtually Oblique; that is, may state a thought, decision, or declaration. Conse-quently an Adjectival or Adverbial Clause, depending on such virtual Oratio Obliqua, will be virtually Suboblique. Thus—

Laudat Africanum Panaetius, quod   *Panaetius praises Africanus for his*
fuerit abstinens.   *temperance.*

We cannot account for the Mood of *fuerit* (for *quod* governs the Indicative, and the Principal Sentence is Oratio Recta), except by saying that *laudat* (=dicit laudandum esse) is virtually Oblique, and that the Subjunctive depends on the implied Oratio Obliqua.

In other words, Adjectival or Adverbial Clauses containing explanations *other than those of the writer* are virtually Suboblique, and require the Subjunctive.

NOTE.—The most usual form of virtually Suboblique Clause is introduced by *quod* (=on the ground that).

CHAPTER III

SOME COMMON DIFFICULTIES.

THE INDEFINITE ARTICLE.

19. There is no Indefinite Article in Latin, but the English *a* or *an* is sometimes definite, and must be translated by a Latin Adjective or Pronoun ; *e.g.*—

He sold the book for a penny.	Librum uno (*one*) denario vendidit.
Did not Scaevola lose a hand ?	Nonne Scaevola alteram (*one of two*) manum amisit ?
He was of a courage that could not be resisted.	Eius (*such*) erat virtutis, cui resisti non posset.
A man told me this.	Quidam (*a certain*) hoc mihi narravit.

THE DEFINITE ARTICLE.

20. There is no Definite Article in Latin, but the English *the* must often be translated by a Demonstrative Pronoun ; *e.g.*—

Ten commissioners were chosen for the purpose.	Decem viri ad eam rem delecti sunt.
They said they were not the persons to do this.	Negabant se eos (*such*) esse qui hoc facerent.
Disturbances took place at Rome, Caesar at the time being absent.	Tumultus Romae fieri, Caesare eo tempore absente.

The want of the Definite Article compels us in like manner to supply its want by the use of a Substantive.   Thus—

The brave Hercules.	Hercules, vir fortissimus.
The silly sheep.	Ovis, animal stultissimum.

'IT,' 'THAT.'

21. *It* and *that* are often redundant in English, and are not to be translated into Latin. So—

It is said that Socrates was very wise.	Ferunt Socratem sapientissimum fuisse; or, Socrates sapientissimus fuisse dicitur.
It was Caesar that said this.	Caesar hoc dixit.
He divided his own share and that of his officers among the troops.	Suam legatorumque partem militibus divisit.

'MOST,' 'MOST OF,' 'ALL OF,' 'WHOLE OF.'

22. *Most* is to be translated by *plurimi* when it means 'very many' or 'more than any one else:' by *plerique* when it means 'the majority.'

Most of is to be translated by *plerique*, which agrees with Substantives, but takes the Genitive of Pronouns.

Most of the ships.	Pleraeque naves.
Most of whom.	Quorum plerique.

All of, whole of, are to be translated by *omnis* and *totus* in agreement with their Substantives.

All of you.	Vos omnes.
The whole of the booty.	Tota praeda.

'HIS OWN,' 'THEIR OWN,' ETC.

23. *His own, their own,* etc., will be generally translated by *suus*, as they usually refer to the Subject. If they do not, you must translate them by *ipsius* or *ipsorum*. Thus—

He said he would not have deserted his own post if he had not been told to do so by one of their own officers.	Negavit se stationem suam deserturum fuisse nisi id sibi ab uno ex ipsorum legatis imperatum esset.

'SE,' 'S US,'

24. *Se* and *suus* refer to the Subject of the sentence—

He loved his wife.	Uxorem suam diligebat.
They said that they were afraid.	Aiebant se timere.

In a sentence like this, 'Caesar asked his soldiers why they distrusted their own valour or his energy,' there are two Subjects,

Caesar and *they*. If we translate *their own* and *his* by *suus*, it might lead to confusion. So we make *ipse* refer to the principal Subject, and *suus* to the second Subject. The sentence will run thus in Latin : 'Caesar ex militibus quaesivit cur de sua virtute aut de ipsius diligentia desperarent.'

THE SUBSTANTIVE.

25. As the Grammar says, 'Abstract Nouns are those which you can neither touch nor see.' As a rule, avoid translating English Abstract Nouns by Latin Abstract Nouns. In the first place, there are few that have Latin equivalents ; in the next place, the simple and direct nature of Latin prefers Concrete Nouns. Often, however, further turning is required. Sometimes a Verb has to be used—

His sufferings were very great.   Permulta passus est.

Sometimes you have to use a combination of words—

Agriculture is useful.   Cultus agrorum utilis est.

Of course there are proper equivalents for such common abstract ideas as love, hate, fear, etc.

THE ABLATIVE ABSOLUTE.

26. This invaluable construction makes the want of the Perfect Participle Active to be felt less often—

Caesar having conquered the Gauls returned to Rome.   Caesar victis Gallis Romam rediit.

It takes the place of the English Participle 'being'—

Tullus being king.   Tullo rege.

Accessory ideas or facts are constantly rendered by it. Remember that 'Absolute' means 'absolved, or freed from agreement.' This will prevent you from making the serious mistake of using it when the words are the Subject or Object of the sentence. Thus—

Pompeius having been conquered fled to Egypt.   Pompeius victus in Aegyptum se contulit (*Subject*).

Having taken the town he burnt it.   Captam urbem incendit (*Object*).

THE LOCATIVE CASE.

27. When we have the word 'town' in Apposition to a name of a .town in the Locative Case, the question naturally arises, What case must 'town' be in, for *urbs* or *oppidum* have no Locative Case? The answer is, It cannot really be in Apposition, so use the Preposition *in* with it.

In the celebrated city of Athens.   Athenis, in urbe praeclarissima.

ENGLISH PREPOSITIONS.

28. Sometimes the English Prepositions can be rendered correctly by Latin Prepositions : even then the varying meaning of the English may require several Latin Prepositions to meet its different usages. But there are vast numbers of English phrases introduced by Prepositions which require a different treatment. Get the *meaning* of the phrase, and translate it, putting all idea of necessarily using a Latin Preposition out of your head. The difficulty will disappear with practice. Notice such sentences in your reading. The only other way is to get by heart long lists of such prepositional phrases and their Latin translations. The difficulty of this plan will appear from an examination of some of the different renderings of a single Preposition. Let us take *Without—*

Without hope.	Sine spe.
Without the city.	Extra urbem.
He is without courage.	Virtute caret.
He went away without shutting the door.	{ Abiit, nec portam clausit. { Ita abiit ut portam non clauderet.
He was condemned without a hearing.	Causa indicta condemnatus est.
You cannot read well without study.	Bene legere non potes nisi studes.
I never saw him without calling him.	Nunquam eum videbam quin compellarem.
He would not go without consulting his general.	Ire noluit nisi prius ducem consuluisset.
His management was without success.	Rem male gessit.

And so on *ad infinitum.*

B

THE AUXILIARY VERBS.

29. No rule can be given for the translation of the Auxiliary Verbs. It depends entirely on the *meaning* whether they are to be represented in Latin by a Mood, or translated separately.

A few examples may be useful :—

Licet tibi ludere.	*You* MAY *play.*
Fieri potest ut interfectus sit.	*He* MAY *have been killed.*
Ede ut vivas.	Eat that you MAY *live.*
Si des, neget.	*If you* WERE *to offer it he* WOULD *refuse it.*
Potuit respondere sed noluit.	*He* MIGHT *have answered, but* WOULD *not.*
Quotidie in foro ambulabat.	*He* WOULD *(used to) walk daily in the forum.*
Hoc facere debuisti.	*You* SHOULD *have done this.*
Utinam thesaurum reperiam !	WOULD *that I* MIGHT *find a treasure!*
Pace tua dixerim.	*With your leave I* SHOULD *say.*
Hoc sese facturum confirmavit.	*He asserted that he* WOULD *do this.*
Facerem si vellem.	*I* COULD *have been doing it if I had chosen.*
Infelici arbori reste suspendito.	*You* MUST *hang him to the gallows with a rope.*
Ludendum est iis.	*They* MUST *play.*
Non potuit hoc non facere. } Fieri non potest quin hoc fecerit. }	*He* MUST *have done this.*

ACTIVE AND PASSIVE.

30. Often you ought to change the English Passive Verb into a Latin Active. The Latin Passive is much less commonly used than in English. Thus, in such sentences as ' Caesar was killed by a friend,' the Latins prefer to say, *Caesarem interfecit amicus,* though of course *Caesar ab amico interfectus est* is perfectly good Latin. So in French (in which Latin lives again), ' Les Anglais l'ont battu,' where we should say, ' He has been beaten by the English.' Yet the Passive is often used in Latin where we should use the Active. Impersonal Passives are very frequent: *pugnatum est* is generally preferable to *pugnaverunt.*

VERBS GOVERNING DIFFERENT CASES.

31. A very common mistake is to forget that Latin Verbs do not all govern the same case, and to treat them as if they did. Thus, in the sentence 'The rebels were commended for their timely submission, yet were not altogether forgiven,' we must remember that *laudare*, to commend, is Transitive, while *ignoscere*, to forgive, governs a Dative, and can only be used impersonally in the Passive. The sentence will run thus : 'Laudantur rebelles quod tempori in officium rediissent, neque tamen iis omnino ignoscitur.'

'QUIN.'

32. We have given above two separate uses of this anomalous word. It may be useful to compare them side by side.

1. In Adjectival Clauses, quin = qui non.

Nemo fuit quin (*or* qui non) fleret.   *There was no one who did not weep.*

Use, however, *non* with the other cases in preference to *quin.* So—

Nemo fuit quem non laudaret.   *There was no one he did not praise.*
Quis erat cuius non misereretur?   *Who was there he did not pity?*

2. In Consecutive Adverbial Clauses, quin = qui (old form of Ablative)—non.

Facere non possum quin ad te mittam.   *I cannot (so) do how I should not send to you ; i.e. I cannot refrain from sending to you.*

Nihil dubium est quin gaudeam.   *There is no doubt how I should not rejoice ; i.e. There is no doubt that I rejoice.*

Quin can only be used after—

    a. Negatives.
    b. Words expressing doubt or ignorance.
    c. After a question expecting a negative answer.

3. There is a third use of *quin* worth noticing—

| Quin equos conscendimus ? | *Why not mount our horses ?* |

Here *quin* is merely an Interrogative. So with Imperative, the interrogative meaning being lost,—

| Quin sic attendite ! | *But attend to this !* |

4. Hence the adverb *quin*, 'moreover.'

'WHETHER—OR.'

33. A doubt often arises with beginners as to how they should translate 'whether—or.' All doubt will disappear if you analyse the clause. If it is a question, use of course *utrum—an*. If it is not a question, use *sive—sive (seu)*.

| *Whether he was an Englishman or a Frenchman, he was a brave man.* | Sive Anglus *erat* sive Gallus, vir fortissimus erat. |
| *It does not appear whether you are an Englishman or a Frenchman.* | Utrum Anglus *sis* an Gallus non liquet. |

LETTER WRITING.

34. A Roman's letter did not begin with 'Dear Sir,' etc., nor did it end with 'Yours truly,' etc. The dedication and signature head the letter. Thus, suppose Cicero is writing to his brother Quintus from Athens, the heading of the letter will be *M. T. Cicero Quinto fratri S. D. (salutem dicit)*. If the date is mentioned, it will either be put at the end or introduced as part of the letter; as—

| *I am writing from Athens on the 28th of March.* | Scribebam Athenis (*Locative*) a.d. V. Kal. Ap. |

The *Imperfect* Tense is used because the action is *past* to the recipient of the letter. This is another of the many instances which show the exactness of the Latin language. So, if Cicero meant to say 'I was writing,' he would write *scripseram*. But if he wanted him to answer the letter, he would say *oro rescribas*, not *orabam*, because the request remains *present* to the recipient.

THE RELATIVE USED AS A LINK.

35. We have been taught that in Adjectival Clauses the Relative is followed by the Indicative or Subjunctive. Yet in reported speeches we find Relatives in the Accusative case with an Infinitive following. How is this? Why, the Relative in such a case is not a true Relative, but a Pronoun with a connecting link (*et is, nam is*, etc.). Relatives at the beginning of a Principal Sentence belong to this class, and must be resolved into their elements, as we have shown. 'And he' is generally rendered by *qui*, not by *et is*. So—

Nam illorum urbem ut propugnaculum oppositam esse barbaris, apud quam iam bis classes regias fecisse naufragium.	*For their city was opposed to the barbarians like a bulwark, on which the royal fleets had twice been wrecked.*

Here *apud quam* = *nam apud eam.*

Anseres non fefellere, quibus sacris Iunoni in summa inopia cibi tamen abstinebatur. Quae res saluti fuit.	*They did not escape the notice of the geese, who were still being spared as sacred to Juno, though the scarcity was so great. This piety was their salvation.*

The Latin *quae* is merely the English 'this,' plus a connecting-link.

STRICT CORRECTNESS IN WRITING.

36. English is much more loose and inaccurate than Latin. Thus we say, 'They fought on horseback;' in Latin it is, *Pugnabant ex* EQUIS. The Latins were very careful in all these, to us apparently, trifling points. Note all such in your reading. The superior strictness of Latin is still more noticeable in their use of the Tenses of the Verb. Mistakes in the use of Tenses are very serious. The looseness of the English may lead you into trouble. Attention to the following rules will save you from many pitfalls.

a. The Present Tense. In such sentences as these the English use what is apparently the same Tense, but really not so.

He is loved.	Amatur.
This letter is written.	Haec epistola scripta est.

An English Present must often be translated by a Latin Future or Future Perfect.

I shall come if I can.	Veniam, si potero.
He will stay here till you go.	Hic manebit, dum abieritis.

b. The Perfect Tense.

When I have dined I shall set out.	Cum cenavero proficiscar.

c. The Present Participle is never used in Latin except of an action that is taking place at the time described; so you must render—

Hearing of the flight of the enemy, he hastened to London.	Audita fuga hostium (*or*, cum hostium fugam audivisset) Londinium contendit.

Even when the use of the Present Participle is appropriate the Latins prefer using a Deponent Participle if there is one. So write *ratus* instead of *putans*, *veritus* instead of *timens*, etc.

CHAPTER IV

STYLE.

WHAT IS STYLE?

37. STYLE in Latin prose writing means ability to write Latin like the great Latin writers. Style does not mean filling a piece with the mannerisms of an author. The main characteristics of Latin are—

> **Clearness.**
>
> **Simplicity.**
>
> **Directness.**
>
> **Melodious sound.**

The great Latin writers are never intentionally and rarely accidentally obscure. They express themselves easily and naturally, and never strive at effect by the use of elaborate phrases or redundant epithets. A Latin epithet is never used except for a good and sufficient reason. Their object is not to see how much they can write on a given subject, like our penny-a-liners, but how they can best explain their meaning. They express themselves tersely and directly, and avoid as far as may be the use of abstract words. Their accounts and explanations are always logical: their sentences follow each other in their true and logical order. Good Latin prose is always satisfying to the ear, and never unmusical. There is one way, and one way only, to attain style—read Latin carefully and intelligently. If you can appreciate good Latin, you will be able to write it.

ORDER OF WORDS IN THE SENTENCE.

38. There are two emphatic places in a Sentence—the beginning and the end.   Of these the latter is most emphatic, and so we generally find the Verb there, as the Verb is the most important word.

The Subject should come at first, unless you wish to lay great stress on it by putting it at the end.

Negatives and Interrogatives should come as early as possible.

Adjectives and governed Genitives follow their Nouns usually, unless they are intended to be emphatic.

Indirect Objects precede Direct Objects.

Adverbs and Adverbial expressions usually come early in the Sentence.

So we may say the usual order is—

    1. Subject (with or without Negative or Interrogative).
    2. Adverb or Adverbial expression.
    3. Indirect Object.
    4. Direct Object.
    5. Verb.

Strict adherence to this rule will cause stiffness.   Notice in your reading the constant departures from it for the sake of variety, and you will soon learn when you can change the order with propriety and effect.

CONTRAST BETWEEN ENGLISH AND LATIN IN STYLE.

39. English prefers Co-ordinate Sentences, Latin Subordinate. This being the case, when several English Sentences have the same Subject or Object, you should generally form them into a Latin Period, the main idea being the Principal Sentence, and the rest Dependent Clauses.

THE PERIOD.

40. A Period (περίοδος) is so called because the reader must go round the whole Sentence (including its Dependent Clauses) to grasp the full meaning.   A Period then is a Compound Sentence containing a Principal Sentence with Dependent Clauses.

THE CONSTRUCTION OF THE PERIOD.

41. Suppose that on reading through your English you find three main conceptions, the remaining sentences containing merely accessory ideas. There will then be three Periods. Make each of the three leading ideas into a Principal Sentence, and group with it the accessory ideas logically connected with it as Dependent Clauses. Be careful in your choice of links to use an appropriate one. See that the connection in words between the clauses is obvious. Avoid a collection of Verbs at the end of a Period. Avoid ending a Period with the end of a verse, such as *esse videtur; dicere nonvult.*

ORDER OF CLAUSES IN THE PERIOD.

42. The arrangement of Clauses in a Period should resemble the usual arrangement of words in a Simple Sentence. But as a collection of Verbs at the end of a Period is to be avoided, we often find the Principal Verb preceding Substantival, Final, and Consecutive Clauses.

43. EXAMPLE OF A LATIN PERIOD.

Numitor inter primum tumultum hostes invasisse urbem atque adortos regiam dictitans, cum pubem Albanam in arcem praesidio armisque obtinendam avocasset, postquam iuvenes perpetrata caede pergere ad se gratulantes vidit, extemplo advocato concilio, scelera in se fratris, originem nepotum, ut geniti, ut educati, ut cogniti essent, caedem deinde tyranni seque eius auctorem ostendit.

When the disturbance began Numitor exclaimed that the city was entered by enemies, who had assailed the palace. He hurried away with the men of Alba to man and defend the citadel. When he saw the youths, after they had killed Amulius, approaching joyfully, he summoned a council forthwith. He proceeded to tell of the wrongs he had suffered at his brother's hands, the parentage of his grandsons, their birth, their bringing up, and how he had recognized them. Finally, he related how they had slain the tyrant, and that they had done so at his suggestion.

Here the main idea is how Numitor told his story, so Livy gives the whole passage as a single Period. It is unnecessary to multiply examples, for the periodic style is the usual one, and is not abandoned except for some good reason.

DETACHED STYLE.

44. *The use of the Period is not always appropriate.* Where the Sentences are distinct from each other, and consequently of equal weight, we must use the detached style. It will be found appropriate in the following cases—

a. In rhetorical prose. To express all emotions (anger, astonishment, etc.) in argument, and in denouncing wrong.

Qua re secedant improbi, secernant se a bonis, unum in locum congregentur, muro denique, id quod saepe iam dixi, discernantur a nobis : desinant insidiari domi suae consuli, circumstare tribunal praetoris urbani, obsidere cum gladiis curiam, malleolos et fasces ad inflammandam urbem comparare ; sit denique inscriptum in fronte unius cuiusque quid de republica sentiat.

So let the evil stand· aside, and be separated from the good. Let the wall, as I have often said, be between them and us. Let them abandon their plots against the consul in his own house, cease thronging round the judgment-seat of the praetor urbanus, desist from surrounding the senate-house arms in hand and preparing torches and faggots to burn the city. In fine, let every one have his political sentiments written on his face.

Velut haec tota fabella veteris et plurimarum fabularum poetriae quam est sine argumento ! quam nullum invenire exitum potest !

Here you have an instance of what I have said. How entirely without plot is the whole story of this old scandalmongeress ! How utterly it fails to get to any issue !

Hoc teneo, hic haereo, iudices,.hoc sum contentus uno ; omitto ac neglego cetera ; sua confessione induatur ac iuguletur necesse est.

I press this, my lords, this is the .point I stick to ; I don't care for anything else ; by his own admission he must be hopelessly entangled and undone.

b. In familiar letters.

Ad ceteras meas miserias accessit dolor e Dolabellae valetudine et Tulliae. Omnino de omnibus rebus, nec quid consilii capiam, nec quid faciam, scio. Tu velim tuam et Tulliae valetudinem cures. Vale.

To add to my other troubles comes the anxiety I feel about Dolabella's and Tullia's indisposition. I am utterly at a loss on all points, what to plan or what to do. I hope you will take care of yourself and Tullia. Farewell.

c. In narratives of exciting events, such as battles or panics.

Multi sequi, fugere, occidi, capi.

Many were going in pursuit, many were fleeing, some were being slain, others taken prisoner.

Hostes postero die multo maioribus coactis copiis castra oppugnant, fossam complent. Eadem ratione, qua pridie, ab nostris resistitur. Hoc idem reliquis fit diebus. Nulla pars nocturni temporis ad laborem intermittitur.

Next day the enemy, with largely increased forces, attack the camp, and fill the ditch. Our men resisted as before; and this went on during the remaining days. Our labours were protracted throughout the whole of every night.

d. In detailed descriptions.

Hominum est infinita multitudo, creberrimaque aedificia, fere Gallicis consimilia: pecorum magnus numerus. Utuntur aut aere aut talcis ferreis, ad certum pondus examinatis, pro nummo. Nascitur ibi plumbum album in mediterraneis regionibus, in maritimis ferrum; sed cius est exigua copia; aere utuntur importato.

The country is densely populated, and dwellings are of very frequent occurrence. These resemble the huts in Gaul. There is also much cattle. The inhabitants supply the place of coin either by bronze or iron ingots of a certain fixed weight. Tin is found in the southern districts, and small quantities of iron on the seaboard. They import what bronze they use.

Hic non solum proximo regi dissimilis, sed ferocior etiam quam Romulus fuit. Tum aetas viresque tum avita quoque gloria animum stimulabat. Senescere igitur civitatem otio ratus, undique materiam excitandi belli quaerebat.

The latter was not only unlike the late king, but was even more warlike than Romulus. The vigour of youthful manhood and the glorious traditions of his house were urging him to action. Thus, thinking that peace was enervating his people, he began to look about him for a pretext for war.

SOUND AND RHYTHM.

45. In Latin, as in English, it is quite possible to write a piece that is utterly disagreeable to the ear, although grammatically correct, and showing ingenuity in turning the English by appropriate phrases. Beyond the caution to avoid closing a sentence by the end of a verse, there are no rules that will enable a beginner to avoid this fault. He must educate his ear as he

would in learning music.   The only way is to read good
Latin till the ear insensibly detects a want of rhythm.   What is
rhythm?   Rhythm means balance of words, clauses, and periods,
the result being a measure or time that satisfies the ear.   It is
excellent practice to learn short pieces of Livy and Cicero by
heart after translating them into English.

METAPHORS.

46. When a word appropriate to one idea is transferred to
another it is called a Metaphor (μεταφέρω).   So in the line 'How
sweet the moonlight sleeps upon this bank,' 'sleep' (appropriate
to a living creature) is transferred from its proper idea to 'moonlight.'   This ornamental figure is common in Latin as in English.   Be careful in translating an English metaphor.   What is
English may not be Latin.   An English metaphor may often be
translated by a different Latin one.   For instance, 'What a sea of
evils' is not *Quantum miseriarum mare*, but *Quanta miseriarum
incendia*.   Notice all metaphors and differences of idiom in your
reading.   Most English metaphors, however, will be rendered
without any metaphor in Latin.

CHAPTER V

CAUTIONS.

47. 1 Do not attempt to translate a piece of English into Latin until you understand the *whole* of it, not merely the first sentence.

2. Be very careful in punctuating your translation.

3. Remember that English prefers Co-ordinate Sentences, and Latin Subordinate Clauses.

4. Connect your Sentences by the proper links (Conjunctions, both Copulative and Disjunctive; Adverbs and Relatives).

5. Epithets must often be translated by Subordinate Clauses.

6. Avoid the use of Abstract Nouns as much as possible.

7. Be careful in translating words derived from the Latin by the words from which they are derived. The classical meaning is often widely different from the English one.

8. Avoid using Pronouns, except when absolutely necessary for clearness, or to give emphasis.

9. The Present Participle is used more strictly than in English. It can only be used to denote a simultaneous action.

10. Do not use short Co-ordinate Sentences, except for effect (*i.e.* when you wish to denote rage, astonishment, hurry, fear, etc.).

11. Ne—quidem, *not even*, has the emphatic word or words between the Particles.

Not even you can do this.   Ne tu quidem hoc facere potes.

12. Quisquam, ullus, unquam, usquam, are only used with a Negative, or a Particle that implies doubt (si, num, etc.), or in comparisons, as—

Fortior erat quam quisquam e mili- *He was braver than any of the*
 tibus.   *soldiers.*

13. In Consecutive Clauses write ut non, ut nemo, ut nullus, ut nunquam, ut nusquam.

14. In other clauses write ne, ne quis, ne ullus, ne quando, ne usquam.

15. For et nemo   write neque quisquam.
    „   et nihil   „   neque quicquam.
    „   et nunquam „   neque unquam
    „   et nusquam „   neque usquam.
    „   et non   „   neque (nec).
    „   dico non   „   nego.

16. Non nihil, *something;* nihil non, *everything;* non nunquam, *sometimes;* nunquam non, *always.*

17. *Omnis* does not mean *every.*

18. Instead of *neminis* and *nemine,* write *nullius* and *nullo.*

19. In Oratio Recta translate 'he said' by *inquit,* putting it after the first emphatic word in the speech.

20. Translate 'do not love' by *ne amaveris, noli amare, cave (ne) ames;* not by *ne ama* or *ne ames.*

21. If there is a Comparative in the clause translate 'in order that' by *quo.*

22. Few Present Participles can be used as Adjectives. (*Sapiens, potens,* and a few others, are regarded as Adjectives, not Participles.)

23. Do not use two Adjectives with a Noun without a Conjunction.

24. Caius, Balbus and Julius; either Caius, Balbus, Iulius, or Caius et Balbus et Iulius.

25. You ought often to translate an English Passive Verb by a Latin Active one.

26. Remember that Latin Verbs which govern a Dative can only be used impersonally in the Passive. 'I am being answered' is *respondetur mihi,* not *respondeor.*

27. *Nostrum* and *vestrum* can only be used after Partitive words.

28. The English Present must often be translated by a Latin Future,—

I shall do it when I come.   Faciam cum venero.

29. 'I ought to have gone' is *debui ire,* not *debui ivisse.*

30. Write mecum, tecum, secum, nobiscum, vobiscum, quocum (quicum), quacum, quibuscum.

31. The Ablative of Manner can only be used instead of the Nominative or Accusative with *quam*. So 'nihil est amabilius virtute' is right; but 'exstinctus est siti potius fame' is wrong.

32. After a Past Tense *will* and *shall* become *would* and *should*.

33. Write *si quis, num quis*, not *si aliquis, num aliquis*.

34. Write *dicitur amare* in preference to *dicitur eum amare*.

35. There is no Perfect Participle Active in Latin. Use a Deponent Participle whenever you can.

36. The years in dates must be expressed by Ordinal Numbers. So—

In the year 1879.   Anno post Christum natum mille-simo octingentesimo septuagesimo nono.

37. Distributive Numerals are used with Substantives that have no Singular or that have a different meaning in the Plural. In these cases *singuli-ae-a* cannot be used: *uni-ae-a* is used instead. 'One camp,' 'two camps,' *una castra, bina castra*. 'Two letters,' *binae literae; duae literae* would mean two letters of the alphabet.

38. *Interest* and *refert* take a Genitive, except with the words mea, tua, sua, nostra, vestra, cuia.

39. The Prolate Infinitive (carrying on the meaning) is used with only a few Adjectives, *paratus, assuetus,* etc.

40. The Ablative of Manner without an epithet requires a Preposition (except in a few phrases, such as *vi, fraude, iure, iniuria,* etc. These are regarded as Adverbs): thus—

I speak with grief.   Cum dolore loquor.

CHAPTER VI

MISCELLANEOUS IDIOMS.

48.

You and I.
Ego et tu.

The brave Caesar.
Caesar, vir (*or,* ille) fortissimus.

A thousand cavalry and two thousand infantry.
Mille equites et duo millia peditum.

The top of the mountain; the bottom of the river.
Summus mons ; imum flumen.

I fear that he will come.
Vereor ne veniat.

I fear he will not come.
Vereor ut (*or,* ne non) veniat.

He addressed those present.
Eos, qui aderant, allocutus est (*not* eos praesentes.)

One—another; some—others; the one—the other.
Alius—alius; alii—alii; alter—alter.

They were so far from fearing.
Tantum aberat ut timerent (*not* aberant, *as it is impersonal*).

He was more cruel than brave.
Crudelior erat quam fortior.

What o'clock is it ?
Quota hora est ?

He is twenty-one years of age.
Viginti unum annos natus est.

Yes or No.
Etiam aut Non.

He went to his mother in Rome.
Romam ad matrem profectus est.

He got his son taught.
Filium docendum curavit.

The celebrated poet.
Poeta ille.

The French were defeated by the Germans.
Gallos vicerunt Germani.

The city of Thebes was taken.
Thebae oppidum captum est.

A friend of mine.
Quidam ex amicis meis.

He was not the man to do this.
Non is erat qui hoc faceret.

Henry was succeeded by his son.
{ Henrico successum est a filio.
{ Henrico filius successit.

The quicker the better.
Quo citius eo melius.

In the consulship of Cicero and Antonius.
Cicerone et Antonio consulibus.

A desperate fight took place.
Atrociter pugnatum est.

A young man should respect his seniors.
Est adolescentis maiores natu vereri.

He was blind of an eye, and his sister was lame of a foot.
Ille altero oculo captus, soror autem altero pede clauda erat.

The fierce lion.
Leo, animal saevissimum.

Caesar subdued the Gauls.	Caesar Gallos suae ditionis fecit.
Quicker than was expected.	Opinione celerius.
Philosophy teaches manners.	Philosophia morum magistra est.
Then and not till then was I persuaded.	Tum demum mihi persuasum est.
He sent the most faithful slave he had.	Servum misit quem fidelissimum habuit.
Atrocities were committed on the inhabitants.	In incolas saevitum est.
It is my interest to see him; but it is his and Caius' to avoid me.	Mea interest ut illum videam; illius autem et Caii interest ut me vitent.
In the year of Rome 231.	Anno urbis conditae ducentesimo tricesimo primo.
He is of an ambition that nothing can satisfy.	Eius est ambitionis cui nihil possit satisfacere.
These apples cost me two denarii apiece.	Haec poma mihi binis denariis steterunt.
Her head was struck off at a blow.	Caput ei uno ictu abscissum est.
I cannot but go.	Facere non possum quin eam. Non possum non ire.
He is the bravest soldier in France.	Miles est fortis, qualis in Gallia nemo. Militum Gallorum, si quis alius, fortissimus est.
Such was his foresight.	Ut erat providus. Quae eius erat prudentia. Cuius erat prudentiae. Qua erat prudentia. Pro eius prudentia.
Some good.	Aliquid boni, *or*, aliquod bonum.
I shall come if I can.	Veniam si potero.
This will be the result if the captives are foolishly spared.	Hoc fiet si captivis stulte parcetur.
All the men in the city.	Quicquid hominum in urbe erat.
What did you give for the horse?	Quanti equum emisti?
Not much.	Parvo.
At daybreak.	Ut illuxit, *or*, prima luce.
Towards evening.	Sub vesperum, *or*, cum advesperasceret.
The battle of Cannae.	Proelium Cannense.
All the wisest men.	Sapientissimus quisque.
The day after the battle.	Postridie pugnam, *or*, postridie quam pugnatum est.
As far as I know.	Quod sciam.
Every ten years.	Decimo quoque anno.
A citizen of Rome.	Civis Romanus.
This is in our favour.	Hoc a nobis facit.
I was unwilling to go to Marseilles or Africa.	Massiliam aut in Africam ire nolebam.

C

He made the same reply as before.	Idem quod antea respondit.
He fell at the head of his men.	Dum pugnam princeps ciet interficitur.
He came to receive it.	$\left\{\begin{array}{l}\text{Ut acciperet}\\\text{Ad accipiendum}\\\text{Accipiendi causa}\\\text{Acceptum}\\\text{Accepturus}\end{array}\right\}$ venit.
They went away without effecting their purpose.	Re infecta abierunt.
He has pains in his feet.	Ex pedibus laborat.
Two miles off.	A millibus passuum duobus.
I must go.	$\left\{\begin{array}{l}\text{Necesse est}\\\text{Oportet}\end{array}\right\}$ me ire, *or,* eam.
I ought to go; I ought to have gone.	Debeo ire; debui ire.
He did not know what she would have done.	Nesciebat quid factura fuisset.
When I come I shall inform you.	Cum venero te certiorem faciam.
The crew jump overboard.	Qui in nave erant in mare desiliunt.
He was honoured as a god.	Aeque ac deus honoratus est.
The future of India will be different to its past.	Alia erit India atque olim fuit.
He was so far from praising me as not even to thank me.	Tantum aberat ut me laudaret ut ne gratias quidem ageret.
They did not know when he was likely to come.	Nesciebant quando venturus esset.
Perhaps he will stay.	Nescio an mansurus sit.
Perhaps he will not stay.	Nescio an non mansurus sit.
I wrote yesterday from London; I write to-day from Dublin, and beg you to answer by return of post.	Heri dederam Londinii; has literas Eblanae dabam atque oro ut quamprimum rescribas.
Caesar decimated that legion.	Eius legionis decimum quemque supplicio affecit Caesar.
The Parthians fight on horseback.	Parthi ex equis pugnant.
I was the last to be asked for my opinion.	Ultimus rogatus sum sententiam.
They threw themselves at the king's feet.	Regi se ad pedes proiecerunt.
He is in debt.	In aere alieno est.
He cannot possibly come here.	Fieri non potest ut huc veniat.
In this state of gloom and apprehension.	In hoc tam tristi metu.
Not long afterwards.	Haud ita multo post.
Many large vessels were sunk.	Multae et magnae naves depressae sunt.
The horses were up to their necks in the water.	Equi capite solo ex aqua exstabant.

He went to Samos as quickly as possible. — Samum adit { summa celeritate. / quam celerrime.

A plot was hatched at the instigation of Histiaeus. — Auctore Histiaeo seditionem ineunt.

The soldiers began to encourage each other. — Milites alter alterum hortari.

It happened that I met a lion while walking. — Forte ex itinere leoni obviam factus sum.

This temple is near the citadel. — Haec aedes ab arce prope abest.

Each will finish his own business. — Suum quisque negotium conficient.

Some were running one way, others another. — Alii alio currebant.

It is all up with the Turks. — Actum est de Thracibus.

His death took place thirty-one years after the capture of Troy. — Triginta uno annis post captam Troiam mortuus est.

None of you pity us. — { Nemo vestrum nostri miseretur. / Neminem vestrum nostri miseret.

He pitched his camp at the foot of the mountain. — Castra ad imum montem posuit.

Ingratitude is abhorred by all men. — Omnes immemorem beneficii oderunt.

Cicero was appointed consul for the second, and Genucius for the third time. — Cicero iterum, tertium Genucius consules designati sunt.

All the Greeks in the city were ordered to leave it. — Graecis, siqui in urbe erant, ut abirent imperatum est.

A man's riches are in proportion to his strength. — { Quo quis fortior eo ditior fit. / Ut quisque fortissimus ita ditissimus est.

He seemed too strong to be resisted. — Fortior videbatur quam cui resisti posset.

I made no reply to Caius' questions, nor did I give him anything. — Interroganti Caio respondere nolui neque quicquam dedi.

If you come, I shall give it you; if not, I shall send it. — Si veneris, hoc tibi dabo; sin minus, ad te mittam.

He is too wise to believe you. — { Sapientior est quam qui / quam ut } tibi credat.

I am delighted at your coming. — Gratum est quod venisti.

He sent two letters to each of the six generals. — Ad unumquemque sex legatorum binas literas misit.

A truce was made on condition that the prisoners should be spared. — Ea conditione foedus ictum est ut captivis parceretur.

Agesilaus died after coming into harbour. — Decessit Agesilaus cum in portum venisset.

During my stay at Athens I used often to attend Socrates' lectures. — Socratem, cum Athenis essem, audiebam frequenter.

I am aware of the kindly feelings you had towards me. — Scio quanto in me studio usus sis.

He lived at the celebrated city of Miletus. — Mileti in urbe praeclarissima habitabat.

I shall have much pleasure in doing this for you, as you have done much for me.
: Hoc pro te libenter faciam qui, *or,* ut qui, *or,* quippe qui, multa pro me feceris.

He was within an ace of being killed.
: Minimum abfuit quin interficeretur.

The plan is a useful one, but by no means honourable.
: Consilium ut utile, ita nequaquam honestum est.
: Consilium ita utile est ut nequaquam honestum sit.

I am on the point of setting out.
: In eo sum ut proficiscar.

Enough of this.
: Sed haec hactenus.

The consul gave the signal for retreat.
: Consul receptui cecinit.

There are many admirable passages in Homer which are translated into Latin in Vergil's Aeneid.
: Multi et praeclari loci sunt apud Homerum qui in Vergilii Aeneide Latine redditi sunt.

I shall now offer a few remarks on virtue.
: Quod attinet ad virtutem nunc pauca dicam, *or,* de virtute.

I said this once and once only.
: Semel neque amplius hoc dixi.

These islands are opposite Marseilles.
: Hae insulae sunt e regione Massiliae.

I heard of her singing at Naples.
: Neapoli cantare illam audivi.

I heard her singing at Naples.
: Neapoli illam cantantem audivi.

What on earth are you doing?
: Quid tandem agis?

I shall be drowned and no one will save me.
: Mergar, neque quisquam mihi subveniet.

I knew he would pity us.
: Sciebam fore ut nostri miseresceret.

This is the third year I have been visiting London.
: Tertium iam annum Londinium adeo.

He became so cruel as to be unwilling to spare even women.
: Eo saevitiae venit ut ne mulieribus quidem vellet parcere.

Caesar was opposed by his friends.
: Caesari adversati sunt amici.

Everything in the town was sold by auction.
: Quicquid in oppido erat sub corona venditur.

Again. (In arguments, etc.)
: Quid multa? *or,* quid quaeris? *or,* quid?

In the open air.
: Sub divo.

I don't choose to stay here, much less fight.
: Hic manere nolo, nedum pugnare.

To be insolvent.
: Solvendo non esse.

By your leave.
: Pace tua dixerim.

You would think. You would have thought.
: Putes. Putares.

He went away without shutting the door.
: Abiit nec portam clausit.

EXERCISES.

1. *The Extreme of Laziness.*

A certain king had three sons, and said that he would leave his kingdom to that son who could show that he was the idlest. So the eldest came to his father and said, 'Let not my brothers vex themselves *with idle hopes,*[1] for I am *sure to gain*[2] the kingdom : for lately, when I was very cold, I ordered a fire to be made ; and having sat down too close to it, my legs were burned by the heat ; but so great was my sloth that I did not remove them.' Then the second observed *with a chuckle,*[3] 'I once was standing by a wall, to which my sword was hanging ; and when I had pushed it by accident, I saw that it was about to fall and wound me, unless I moved away : but still I stayed there and suffered myself to be wounded.' But the third brother said that he was the laziest of all, for although he heard his two brothers *telling*[4] lies in order to get the kingdom, he was so lazy that, although he was able to lie much better, he was unwilling to say a word. Then the king said that he indeed ought to receive the kingdom.

1. by hoping in vain.   2. future participle.   3. not without laughter.
4. not infinitive.

2. *Regulus.*

War subsequently broke out between the Romans and Carthaginians, for Hiero, King of Syracuse, and an ally of the Carthaginians, attacked *by force of arms*[1] the Mamertines who dwelt at Messina. The latter implored the help of the Romans, who hastened to the island of Sicily, and there against Hiero commenced the war, *the fortune of*[2] which proved for a long time doubtful, the Carthaginians *having the best of it*[3] by land and the Romans by sea. Of all the leaders the most worthy of mention was M. Atilius Regulus. He, after defeating the enemy by land and sea, refused to grant peace except on *very hard*[4] conditions, and was completely defeated by Xanthippus, the Carthaginian leader. 1015 Romans were taken prisoners and 30,000 slain, and Regulus fell into the power of the enemy. Being afterwards sent to Rome by the Carthaginians to *treat*[5] of an *exchange*[6] of prisoners, Regulus strongly dissuaded *such a course,*[7] and on his return to Carthage he was put to death with tortures.

1. by force and arms.   2. omit.   3. think what this means.   4. iniquus.
5. agere.   6. exchanging, *gerundive.*   7. this.

3. *Joseph's Perils.*

Joseph was especially beloved by his father Jacob, *as being*[1] the eldest son of Rachel. This *unfair partiality*[2] and a dream which the lad himself related to his brothers, *signifying*[3] that he was *destined to be*[4] greater than they, caused him *to be envied and hated*[5] by them. *One day*[6] while feeding their flocks, *they saw him approaching and*[7] formed a plan to put him to death. Being however persuaded not to shed his blood, they stripped him of a coat *of many colours*[8] which his father had given him, and threw him into a pit; but seeing certain merchants who *through God's guidance*[9] were passing by at the time, they took him out and sold him to them, as if he were a slave or one of the animals they were pasturing. To *conceal*[10] their brother's fate from their father, they stained his coat with blood, and took it to the old man, who thereupon *concluded*[11] that his son had been devoured by a wild beast. Meanwhile Joseph was carried away into Egypt and sold to Potiphar, one of Pharaoh's generals.

> 1. since he was, *quippe qui*. 2. amor iniquus. 3. by which it was signified. 4. futurus esse. 5. to come into envy and hatred. 6. quondam. 7. get rid of the 'and' by saying 'when they had seen.' 8. versicolor. 9. abl. abs. 10. *celare*, with double accusative. 11. colligo.

4. *The Gauls in Rome.*

When the Gauls rushed in, and found no one in the city except these old men, who sat in silence, they were astonished. At last one of the Gauls began to stroke the long white beard of Marcus Papirius, who was one of the priests. He in anger struck the Gaul with his ivory sceptre which he held in his hand. Then the Gauls rushed upon them, and killed them all, and set fire to the city. Next the Gauls tried to take the Capitol, but they could not find any way up to it, because the rock was steep. At last they found a path, and one night a band of Gauls climbed up so secretly that no one of the Romans heard them. But there were in the Capitol some geese, which were sacred to the goddess Juno; and as the Gauls reached the top, these geese began to cackle, and awoke a brave Roman, Marcus Manlius, who *was just in time*[1] to find the foremost Gaul clambering over the edge of the rock. He pushed him back with his shield, and the Gaul fell : as he fell he knocked over many of those who were following him, and the Romans *had time*[2] to awake and drive the rest back. So the Capitol was saved ; and after a while the Gauls went back to their own country, carrying their plunder with them.

> 1. having awoke in time (*tempori*). 2. it was allowed.

5. *Unity is Strength.*

When his soldiers had for some time been asking for a battle, and their eagerness could not be restrained, Sertorius placed two horses before them : one a stout animal, and the other a *gaunt,*[1] weak creature ; he then ordered a sturdy youth to pull off the tail of the weak horse *in one piece,*[2] and a weak old man to pluck off one by one the hairs of the strong horse's tail. The ineffectual efforts of the youth *caused*[3] *universal*[4] amusement, but the old man accomplished *his task*[5] with the greatest ease. As the soldiers were at a loss to comprehend *the meaning of this,*[6] Sertorius turned to them and said, 'The enemy's army is like a horse's tail. *If you*[7] attack it *piecemeal*[8] it can easily be defeated; but all efforts to destroy it while united will be fruitless.'

1. exilis. 2. totus. 3. movere. 4. to all. 5. turn this by an adjectival clause. 6. what this meant (*sibi velle*). 7. he who, etc. 8. parts.

6. *The Fall of Troy.*

When the war had been *protracted*[1] up to the tenth year, the *distress*[2] of the Greeks was so great that it seemed that nothing could be added thereto. A fearful pestilence raged in their camp ; a violent quarrel arose between Agamemnon and Achilles, the bravest of the Grecian leaders. Achilles, with his Thessalians, withdrew from the army of the Greeks ; the Trojans *took advantage of*[3] the distress of their antagonists, attacked their camp, and in most encounters were conquerors. In these *straits,*[4] the leaders of the Greeks besought Achilles, with his warriors, to return. He flatly refused, but sent them his friend Patroclus, who was killed by Hector, a son of Priam, in single combat. The death of his beloved friend summoned the Thessalian *hero*[5] to avenge him ; Hector fell by his sword, and with him the hope of Troy, which was now subdued, *either*[6] by stratagem *or*[6] by the superior force of the Greeks. The old king, Priam, was slain at the foot of the altar, his sons slaughtered, his wife and daughters carried into slavery, the city burned, and entirely demolished.

1. producere. 2. calamitas. 3. abuti. 4. angustiae. 5. that very brave man. 6. sive—sive.

7. *Patient Grissel. I.*

Gualterus, the *prince*[1] of the Salassi at this time, was a young man who was so fond of *hawking*[2] and hunting that he neglected the cares of the state. Nevertheless his people were obedient to his rule, being proud that a young and courteous prince should reign over them; one thing only displeased them—that he remained unmarried. So the elders of the tribe came to him and begged him to *take to himself*[3] a wife; else, *said they,*[4] should anything happen to him, he would leave no heir and they would be without a chieftain. If he *consented*[5] to their request, *they added,*[6] they would find a lady of good birth worthy to be his wife. Gualterus thanked them *for their care of him*[7] and promised to do *as*[8] they wished, intimating at the same time that he preferred to choose his own wife.

There was in a village near the chief town of the Salassi an old man, with one only daughter, named Griselda. She was fair to look upon, and her *affection for*[9] her father, as well as the *neatness*[10] of their home, had often attracted the notice of the prince when he was returning from his hunting. Griselda had heard that he was about to marry, and on the day appointed for the ceremony had *risen early*[11] and performed all the duties of their *little farm,*[12] that she might have leisure to witness the marriage procession.

1. regulus. 2. aucupari. 3. ducere. 4. omit. 5. annuere. 6. omit. 7. *virtual oratio obliqua,* because they cared so for him. He actually said, 'I thank you,' etc. 8. what. 9. pietas erga. 10. munditiae. 11. matutino expergisci. 12. agellus.

8. *Patient Grissel. II.*

As she stood at the door to watch the *procession*[1] pass, and was wondering whither it *was bound,*[2] the prince suddenly stopped and called for her father. He took him aside, and told him that he *was minded*[3] to marry his daughter, provided she would *bow*[4] herself unto his will. The maiden was sent for, and in reply to the prince's questions, promised to do whatever should please him, and although it might bring her pain, not to show herself discontented in look or word. When she had made this promise the ladies that *were in attendance*[5] clad her in costly attire, and brought her to the prince's palace, where the marriage was celebrated. Her gentleness won the love of all the prince's subjects, for she was always ready to lighten their distress and to settle their *differences.*[6] At the end of a year a daughter was born, and the prince resolved to try his wife whether she would be true to her word. So he sent one of his officers with instructions to carry off the babe, and commit it to the charge of his sister who lived in Bononia, but to tell his wife that he had orders to kill the child. Griselda asked that she might give it a *farewell*[7] kiss, and then surrendered it without a murmur, only asking that its body might not *be exposed*[8] to birds or wild beasts.

1. pompa. 2. was going. 3. wished. 4. flectere. 5. adesse. 6. simultas. 7. for the last time. 8. proicere.

9. *Patient Grissel. III.*

Four years afterwards a son also was born to them, but him too the prince sent away, telling his wife that the people were discontented with his marriage, and would not endure that the grandson of a peasant should reign over them. Nor was this sufficient for him. When his daughter was already *of a marriageable age,*[1] he formed another plan to test his wife's constancy. He ordered *forged*[2] letters to be prepared, by which the Pontifex allowed him to *put away*[3] his wife and to marry another, in order to quiet the minds of his people and to secure to him his power. Having done this he sent messengers to Bononia, to ask his sister to send him his children on a certain day, *without telling*[4] any one whose children they were, but to give out that the maiden was to be married to the chief of the Salassi. He then went to his wife, and told her that a new spouse was on her way, and bade her return as she had come to her father's house. She went forth with bare head and feet, accompanied by a crowd of the people that bewailed her fate, and returned to her home, where her father received her *with open arms,*[5] for he had always expected some such end of his prince's *caprice.*[6] There she dwelt a little space, giving no sign by word or look that any offence had been done to her.

1. nubilis. 2. fictus. 3. renuntiare (with dative). 4. and not to tell. 5. gladly. 6. libido.

10. *Patient Grissel. IV.*

On the appointed day the prince's brother-in-law arrived with the two children. Before their arrival the prince had sent for Griselda, and[1] bidden *her*[1] get everything ready *for the reception of his guests.*[2] When the people saw the new bride, as they imagined, *in their fickleness*[3] they praised *the prince's choice,*[4] for the maiden was fairer as well as younger than Griselda. The latter *did not fail to commend*[5] her rival, and to wish her and her husband a happy union; but she begged him at the same time not to vex and torment his new bride *as he had tormented her.*[6] She was more tenderly fostered, she said, and could not bear such treatment like one who had been bred in poverty. She had hardly finished these words when her husband clasped her in his arms and told her that she only was his wife—he would have none other. *These, he added,*[7] are the children you suppose to be dead, but whom I sent away that I might *try*[8] the steadfastness of your mind. *Now*[9] receive your reward; for prince and people will honour such faith as yours.

1. get rid of these words by making Griselda the object of bidden. 2. that his guests might be received. 3. as they were of fickle (*mobilis*) mind. 4. her whom the prince had chosen, concrete for abstract. 5. freely (*ultro*) praised. 6. the very thing (*id quod*) he had done towards her. 7. omit; these, &c., oratio obliqua. 8. pertentare. 9. proinde.

11. *Hannibal's Address to the Campanians.*

Hannibal's only fear was that on his departure the Campanians would forthwith surrender. He therefore *induced*[1] a Numidian—a man ready to do and dare anything—to take a despatch, enter the Roman camp as a deserter, and so reach Capua *unsuspected.*[2] In this despatch he thus addressed the citizens: 'With your courage and endurance, O Campanians, I am greatly pleased, nor am I ignorant what great evils you have suffered; at the same time I am grieved that you have to endure so many and so great hardships. Be not down-hearted: be mindful of your former valour. I am *convinced*[3] that by my departure I shall draw off both the Roman generals and their armies from the siege of Capua to the defence of Rome. In that case, *who can refuse*[4] to believe that your troubles will be over, and your city will be saved?'

Throw the words of the despatch into oratio obliqua if you can. In that case the vocative 'O Campanians' must be omitted.

1. persuaded. 2. inopinatus. 3. persuaded. 4. continuous questions in oratio obliqua are in what moods?

12. *The Story of Constance. I.*

Some merchants of Syria came to Rome and there heard of the fame of Constantia, the emperor's daughter, whose beauty and goodness *won*[1] all hearts. On their return they reported to their king what they had seen and heard, for he loved to hear tidings of foreign lands; and amongst other things they told him of the fair princess, and set forth her virtues in such a way that the king *vowed*[2] that he would have her for his wife. He called together his council, and having laid before them *his intention,*[3] begged of them, *if they cared for his life,*[4] to find some means of *carrying it into execution.*[5] They tried to dissuade him from his plan: no Christian king, they said, would give his daughter to one who followed another law. But the king was ready to forsake his law *rather than*[6] abandon his design; so ambassadors were sent to Rome to ask the maiden in marriage. The emperor, *hoping*[7] that thus a great nation would turn away from false gods, consented to their request *on condition that*[8] the king and all his subjects should embrace the Christian faith; and the *bride,*[9] with costly presents and a numerous *train,*[10] was sent to her new home.

1. conciliare. 2. iurare. 3. avoid the abstract idea by turning it into a clause. 4. if his life was (for) a care to them. 5. of carrying out (*exsequi*) his desire. 6. *potius quam* with subjunctive. 7. not the present participle. 8. ea conditione ut. 9. sponsa. 10. comitatus.

13. *The Story of Constance.* *II.*

But the king's mother, who was unwilling to forsake the law of her fathers, sent for the chief men of the state, and when they were come together, she showed them in how great danger they were. They swore to *stand by*[1] her, in whatever plan she should *devise*.[2] So she went to the king her son, and told him that she also wished to *worship*[3] these new gods ; and begged that she might receive the young maiden at her coming. The king heard gladly that his mother did not *oppose*[4] his marriage, and bade her *entertain*[5] the strangers as she would. So the queen went forth to meet the bride and her train, and prepared for them a *sumptuous*[6] banquet, and invited to it the king and all his *counsellors*.[7] But when they were all gathered in the queen's palace, and they were present who were *privy*[8] to the plot, the doors were shut, and the king and all the Christians slain, Constantia only being left. Her they took and *set on board*[9] a ship without rudder, to sail back again to Italy. But they gave back to her the treasure which she had brought, with clothes, and great store of food. So she sailed forth on the wide sea.

1. adesse. 2. struere. 3. colere. 4. adversari. 5. hospitio accipere. 6. lautus. 7. qui a consiliis erant. 8. conscius. 9. imponere.

14. *The Story of Constance.* *III.*

The ship was carried by wind and tide past the pillars of Hercules, and after being long tossed *on*[1] the ocean, was *stranded*[2] on the shore of Britain. The maiden was brought *before*[3] the prefect, who, wondering at her fortunes, asked her who she was and whence she came. But the princess pretended that she was so *dazed*[4] by her recent danger that she had lost all memory of her past life. The prefect *introduced*[5] her to his wife Cornelia, who entertained her kindly. After some time the prefect *went on*[6] a journey. During his absence, a young man, who was angry because Constantia would not be his wife, determined to bring her to a shameful death. Accordingly he made his way into the chamber where the maiden and her hostess were lying, and having slain the latter, placed the *blood-stained*[7] knife by Constantia's side. The prefect returned, and Constantia was accused of the murder, and brought before Ella, the king of the country. The young man came forward as a witness against her, and was bidden to swear upon the sacred books that his witness was true ; but no sooner had he sworn than an unseen hand smote him on the neck and felled him to the ground, and at the same time a voice was heard, declaring that he had slandered an innocent maiden. So Constantia was saved, and the young man punished as he deserved.

1. per. 2. appelli. 3. coram. 4. obstupescere. 5. tradere. 6. undertook. 7. cruentatus.

15. *The Story of Constance. IV.*

Awestruck[1] at this great miracle, the king determined to worship
the God who thus protected His servants, and made Constantia his
wife. A few months after the Picts *invaded*[2] the land, and Ella
went out with his army to drive them back, *leaving his wife in the
charge of*[3] the prefect of the city. During his absence she bore a son,
and the prefect sent a messenger to the king *to carry*[4] the glad news.
Now the king's mother was jealous of Constantia's influence and
resolved *to put her out of the way.*[5] So she stayed the messenger, and
while he slept *substituted*[6] a forged letter, telling her son that his
wife had given birth to a monster so horrible that none durst look
upon it; that she was plainly *some elvish*[7] creature, unfit for the
society of men. The king, in his reply, bade the prefect keep
mother and son with all care till his return; he himself would decide
what was to be done. But his mother again detained the messenger,
and took from him his letter, putting another in its place, which bade
the magistrate put Constantia and her child on the ship in which
she came and send them out to *sea.*[8]

1. attonitus. 2. bellum inferre. 3. committere. 4. use relative clause.
5. amovere. 6. supponere. 7. ex Lemurum genere. 8. in altum.

16. *The Story of Constance. V.*

When King Ella returned from his journey, he was not a little
surprised[1] to find his palace deserted, and his wife and child gone.
The prefect showed him the letter that he had received, and told
him how he had executed his commands. Thereupon the king
commanded the messenger to be *brought,*[2] and inquired of him with
whom he had *stayed,*[3] and in what place he had slept each night of
his journey. He at once suspected who was the author of the
mischief,[4] and was so enraged that he ordered his mother to be put to
death, because she had been treacherous to the king. But some years
afterwards he bitterly repented him of his deed, so that he went as
a *pilgrim*[5] to Rome, *to pay the price*[6] of his crime. Meanwhile
Constantia had been *cast up*[7] on the Italian shore, and was rescued
by a Roman senator, who took her to his home. It so happened that
this senator was chosen to *entertain*[8] King Ella *on his arrival,*[9] and
in his house the king met his own child, who was so like to Constantia that he began to hope that she might still be alive. Soon after
this she *declared*[10] herself to her husband, and they went together to
the emperor to announce to him that his *long-lost*[11] daughter was
in safety.[12] His grandson, Maurice, afterwards became emperor in
his place : Ella and his wife returned to Britain, and lived in peace.

1. mirabundus. 2. arcessere. 3. commorari. 4. malum. 5. supplex.
6. luere. 7. deferre. 8. hospitio accipere. 9. arriving.
10. patefacere. 11. adjectival clause. 12. adjective.

17. *The Windbags of Aeolus.*

Nine days they sailed smoothly, favoured by the *western wind,*[1] and by the tenth they *approached so nigh*[2] as to discern lights kindled on the shores of their native land ; when *by ill fortune,*[3] Ulysses, overcome with fatigue of watching the helm, fell asleep. The mariners seized the opportunity, and one of them said to the rest: '*A fine time has*[4] this leader of ours : wherever he goes he is sure of presents, when we come away empty-handed ; and see what King Aeolus has given him, store no doubt of gold and silver.' A word was enough to those covetous wretches, who *quick as thought*[5] untied the bag, and instead of gold, out rushed with mighty noise all the winds. Ulysses with the noise awoke and saw their mistake, but too late, for the ship was driving with all the winds back far from Ithaca, far as to the island of Aeolus from which they had parted, in one hour measuring back what in nine days they had scarcely tracked, and *in sight of home too!*[6] Up he flew amazed, and raving doubting whether he should not fling himself into the sea for grief of his bitter disappointment. At last he hid himself under the hatches for shame. And scarce could he be prevailed upon, when he was told he was arrived again in the harbour of King Aeolus, to go himself or send to that monarch for a second succour ; so much the disgrace of having misused his royal bounty (though *it was the crime*[7] of his followers and not his own) weighed upon him.

1. Zephyrus. 2. tam prope abesse. 3. casu. 4. nimirum bene se habere. 5. not literally. 6. when they were in sight even of home. 7. do not use *crimen*, which means an accusation.

18. *Strange Ways of Burying.*

The Egyptians were in the habit of embalming their dead, and *after the operation,*[1] keeping them in their homes in cases. The Persians, too, used to cover the bodies of the dead with wax *to retard decomposition.*[2] It was a rule with the Magi in Media (a *caste*[3] which superintended the worship of certain deities, a thing forbidden to all else) not to bury the bodies of their friends before they had been mangled by wild beasts. It is also related that the Hyrcani kept dogs at the public charge to lacerate the bodies of their dead relatives, considering this to be the best mode of sepulture. Herodotus also, who has been called the 'Father of History,' tells an almost incredible story of a certain Indian tribe whose members used to eat their fathers. They thought it the duty of a *dutiful*[4] son to perform *this astounding rite,*[5] and on the other hand looked upon a wish to bury or burn the dead as an impious and utterly abominable crime.

1. when embalmed. 2. that they might be preserved longer. 3. gens. 4. pius. 5. qualify 'astounding' by the adverb *tam*. The Latins did not like an unqualified adjective after a demonstrative pronoun.

19. *Ulysses and the Cyclops.*

He drove his flock to the interior of the cave, but left the rams and the he-goats without. Then taking up a stone *so massy*[1] that twenty oxen could not have drawn it, he placed it at the mouth of the cave, to defend the entrance, and sat down to milk his ewes and his goats ; which done, he lastly kindled a fire, and *throwing*[2] his great eye round the cave, by the *glimmering*[3] light he discerned some of Ulysses's men. 'Ho, guests, what are you? merchants or wandering thieves?' he bellowed out in a voice which took from them all power of reply, it was so astounding. Only Ulysses summoned resolution to answer, that they came neither for plunder nor traffic, but were Grecians who *had lost their way*,[4] returning from Troy ; which famous city they had sacked, and laid level with the ground. Yet now they prostrated themselves humbly before his feet, whom they acknowledged to be mightier than they, and besought him that he would *bestow*[5] the *rites*[6] of hospitality upon them, for that Jove was the avenger of wrongs done to strangers, and would fiercely resent *any injury which they might suffer*.[7] 'Fool,' said the Cyclops, '*to come*[8] so far to preach to me the fear of the gods. We Cyclopes *care*[9] not for your Jove, whom you *fable*[10] to be nursed by a goat, nor any of your *blessed ones*.[11] We are stronger than they, and dare bid open battle to Jove himself, though you and all your fellows of the earth join with him.'

> 1. of such huge size. 2. looking. 3. uncertain. 4. viam deviam sequi. Yet now, etc., continue in oratio obliqua. 5. use. 6. ius. 7. an injury, if they suffered any. 8. use a causal relative. 9. rationem habere. 10. fingo. 11. divus.

20. *Canute.*

Who has not heard the story of the wise King Canute? One day he was sitting on the sea-shore, surrounded by his *courtiers*,[1] and watching the tide which was coming in at his feet. One of the courtiers, wishing to flatter him, remarked that nothing could resist his commands. At first he seemed not to hear, and only commanded the waves not to rise beyond a certain mark. Still the water rose higher and higher, and at last touched the king's feet. Then the king *turned*[2] to his courtiers, who were wondering why he sat so unmoved, and made them observe that the waves would not obey him, and *called upon them to confess*[3] that God alone is omnipotent.

> 1. optimates. 2. conversus. 3. let them forthwith (*proinde*) confess.

21. *Scylla.*

Ulysses *went*[1] *up and down*[2] encouraging his men, one by one, giving them good words, telling them that they *were*[3] in greater perils when they were blocked up in the Cyclop's cave, yet, heaven assisting his counsels, he had delivered them out of that extremity. That he *could not believe but*[4] they remembered it; and wished them to give the same trust to the same care which he had now for their welfare. That they must exert all the strength and wit which they had, and try *if*[5] Jove would *not*[5] grant them an escape even out of this peril. In particular he cheered up the pilot who sat at the helm, and told him that he must show more firmness than other men, *as*[6] *he had more trust committed*[7] to him, and had the sole management by his skill of the vessel in which all their safeties were embarked. That a rock lay hid within those boiling whirlpools which he saw, on the outside of which he must *steer*,[8] if he would avoid his own destruction, and the destruction of them all. They heard him, and *like men*[9] *took to*[10] the oars; but little knew what opposite danger, in shunning that rock, they must be thrown upon. For Ulysses had *concealed*[11] from them the wounds, never to be healed, which Scylla was to open: their terror would *else*[12] have robbed them all of all care to steer, or move an oar, and have made them hide under the hatches, *for fear*[13] of seeing her, where he and they must have died an idle death.

1. use the frequentative. 2. hither and thither. 3. versari. 4. facere non posse quin. 5. num. 6. quanto. 7. they trusted more. 8. cursum regere. 9. pro virili parte. 10. incumbere. 11. *celo* takes two accusatives, one of the person, the other of the thing. 12. alioquin. 13. lest.

22. *The Greeks and Phoenicians.*

Formerly the Greeks, broken up into small *groups*,[1] inhabited Greece itself, the islands of the Aegean sea, and also the *seaboard*[2] of Asia Minor. The rich men owned flocks and herds, corn-lands and vineyards; the poor had only little farms of their own, or worked *as hired labourers*.[3] But on the coast a new *manner*[4] of life was beginning: there the Greek met the Phoenician merchant, who had long before been visiting unknown lands *for trading purposes*.[5] The Phoenicians had an *alphabet*,[6] and a *scale*[7] of weights and measures in use from ancient times. They were skilled in many arts which they had either learned themselves or brought from foreign parts: they had long been accustomed to work mines and *smelt*[8] silver, iron, and copper. Subsequently they visited Greece in great numbers, and in exchange for their own wares brought home timber, wool, and slaves. In consequence of this the Greeks of the coast, taught by the Phoenicians, began to use letters and these new arts and customs.

1. societas. 2. orae maritimae. 3. hired with a reward. 4. ratio. 5. for the sake of trading. 6. literarum ordo. 7. ratio. 8. conflare.

23. *The Crossing of the Danube by the Russians.*

General Dragimiroff, who was in command of the Russian forces, assembled his men, *intending to cross*[1] the Danube near Sistova. Having found a convenient place where an island prevented the enemy from *watching*[2] his movements, he ordered his troops to lie hid among the *brushwood*.[3] A large number of boats and rafts had previously been assembled for the purpose of bringing the soldiers across. At last the signal was given. The Russians embark, and *under the cover*[4] of night commence the crossing, using the *utmost*[5] caution lest the Turks should become aware of the attempt. They failed, however, in eluding the vigilance of the Turks, who *opened a heavy fire*[6] on them. Many of the boats were sunk, but *the survivors*[7] pressed bravely on and at length reached the opposite bank. A large number of armed men were standing there ready to receive them as they landed. An officer of the *guards*[8] leaped on shore first, crying with a loud voice, 'Follow me, *my lads!*'[9] The soldiers obeyed him, and sprang boldly into the water. A desperate struggle ensued, but the Turks were soon thrown into confusion and put to flight.

1. future participle. 2. servare. 3. virgultum. 4. hidden. 5. summus. 6. crebro tela conicere. 7. adjectival clause. 8. praetoriana cohors. 9. commilitones.

24. *A magnanimous Brigand.*

The leader of a gang of *banditti*[1] in Corsica, who had long been famous for his exploits, was at length taken, and committed *to the care*[2] of a soldier, from whom he contrived to escape. The soldier was condemned to death. *At the place of execution*[3] a man coming up to the commanding officer said, '*Sir*,[4] I am a stranger to you, but you shall soon know who I am. I have heard that one of your soldiers is to die *for having suffered*[5] a prisoner to escape. He was not at all to blame; besides, the prisoner shall be restored to you. Behold him here! I am *the man*,[6] I cannot bear that an innocent man should be punished for me, and have come to die myself; *lead*[7] me to execution.' '*No!*'[8] exclaimed the French officer, who *felt*[9] the sublimity of the action as he ought; 'thou shalt not die; and the soldier shall be set at liberty. Endeavour to reap the fruits of thy generosity. Thou deservest to be henceforth an honest man.'

1. latrones. 2. that he might be guarded. 3. when they were going to execute (*supplicium sumere de*). 4. omit. 5. who (*causal*) suffered. 6. is. 7. deducere. 8. immo. 9. aestimare.

25. *Delos.*

The island of Delos, situated *in the middle*[1] of the Cyclades, is said formerly to have floated about the Aegean Sea, and after many centuries to have become fixed and immovable. *It was deemed*[2] a place of peculiar sanctity by the Greeks, on account of its having been the birthplace of Apollo and his sister Diana. There was in the island a famous oracle of Apollo, and also a fountain of great celebrity, at which sacrifices used to be offered in honour of the god. There were *many magnificent*[3] buildings, the most renowned and splendid of which was the temple of Apollo, which according to the account given by ancient writers, was of great antiquity and so wonderfully built as to deserve a place among the wonders of the universe. As both the god and goddess were averse to death and pain, *no one*[4] was allowed to die in Delos; and if any one suffered from any serious illness, orders were at once given by the chief men for his removal from the island.

> 1. remember the use of adjectives of position. 2. translate by an active verb. 3. do not use two adjectives without a conjunction. 4. neque quisquam; remember the negative should come as early as possible in the sentence.

26. *Presence of Mind.*

I once heard a traveller relating an instance of his presence of mind in danger, and how he had rebuked a cowardly companion. *He went on to say*[1] that once when travelling with an acquaintance they fell in with an immense bear. His companion *made the best of his way*[2] up the nearest tree, but he lay down and feigned death. The bear after sniffing at him as he lay and trampling on him, went off, leaving him unharmed. When the brute had retired the *tree-climber*[3] came down and asked him *what on earth*[4] the bear had been saying while he was whispering in his ear. The other merely remarked, that the bear had advised him not to put any further confidence in men who abandoned their friends in a moment of danger.

> 1. imperfect. 2. give the plain sense of the expanded English. 3. adjectival clause. 4. quidnam.

27. *Bravery of Caesar's Soldiers.*

Such, moreover, was the affection of his soldiers, that they who under other commanders *were*[1] nothing above *the common rate*[2] of men, became invincible where Caesar's glory *was concerned.*[3] *To give an instance.*[4] In Britain some of the vanguard happened to be entangled in a deep morass, and were there attacked by the enemy, when a *private*[5] soldier, in the sight of Caesar, threw himself into the midst of the assailants, and, after prodigious exertions of valour, beat off the barbarians, and rescued the men. After which, the soldier, with much difficulty, partly by swimming, partly by wading, passed the morass, but in the passage lost his shield. Caesar, and those about him, astonished at the action, ran to meet him with acclamations of joy ; but the soldier, in great distress, threw himself *at Caesar's feet,*[6] and, with tears in his eyes, begged pardon for the loss of his shield.

1. dared.　2. consuetudo.　3. agi (*impers.*) de.　4. that I may adduce (*subicio*) something as (*in*) an instance.　5. legionarius.
6. Caesari ad pedes.

28. *Literature under Augustus.*

During the reign of Augustus learning was made much of. At this time lived most distinguished writers in whose works the emperor is highly praised. It was in his honour *that*[1] Vergil, a most famous poet, wrote the exploits of Aeneas, from whom the Julian gens or family was descended. Horace and Ovid, poets of great reputation, also flourished at this date, and T. Livius wrote the history of the Roman republic. Young men paid great attention to all kinds of learning and especially to the literature of the Greeks, *and they*[2] used frequently to visit Athens *to attend the lectures*[3] of the philosophers. On their return the love of study became so general that *ignorance*[4] of the Greek language was held as a great reproach.

1. notice the redundant 'that' in English, which of course is not to be translated.　2. use the relative, which forms a very convenient link.　3. to hear.　4. if any one was ignorant.

29. *Clemency rewarded.*

The city of Cajeta having rebelled against Alphonso, was invested by that monarch with a powerful army. Being sorely distressed *for*[1] want of provisions, the citizens put forth all their old men, women, and children, and shut the gates upon them. The king's ministers advised his majesty not to permit them to pass, but to force them back into the city ; by which means he would speedily become master of it. *Alphonso, however, had too humane a disposition to hearken to counsel, the policy of which rested on driving*[2] a helpless multitude into the jaws of famine. He suffered them to pass unmolested ; and when afterwards reproached with the delay which this produced in the siege, he feelingly said, 'I had rather be the preserver of one innocent person than be the master of a hundred Cajetas.' Alphonso was not without the reward which such noble clemency merited. The citizens were so affected by it, *that repenting of their disloyalty,*[3] they soon afterwards yielded up the city to him of their own accord.

1. ob.　2. Alphonso, however, was of a more humane disposition than who (*qui = ut is*) could hearken to those who counselled him to drive.　3. that it repented them that (*quod*) they had been disloyal (*infidelis*).

30. *Ionides.*

There was once a man at Athens, by name Ionides, who was so gentle in his disposition that he never was angry with any man. Accordingly his friends were wont to say of him, that if any one were to tread on his foot, he would ask for pardon because he had been in the way. In the same city there lived a lawyer, who had to examine Ionides in the presence of the judges; for his brother *was on his trial,*[1] and Ionides was a witness. But as Ionides gave evidence that his brother had done no wrong, the lawyer tried by abuse to enrage him, in order that he might speak hastily before the judges, *and*[2] so might be convicted of false-witness. He, however, being naturally so gentle, disregarded the abuse, and answered whatever he asked truly and quietly. So the lawyer, perceiving that he was labouring in vain, himself got angry, and said to the witness with a bitter smile (*or. obl.*), 'Go away, my friend; for I find that you are a very clever person.' But Ionides, not less gently than before, answered as he was going, 'I would say the same of you, if I had not sworn to speak the truth.'

1. had to defend his cause.   2. get rid of the conjunction.

31. *Discomfiture of the Maories.*

The brigadier then sent a despatch to the commander-in-chief *informing*[1] him that on hearing of this the enemy beat a retreat, abandoning the *pah.*[2] That they might have been entirely destroyed had not our men been worn out with continuous fighting and the hard day's work. That some mounted men sent late in the night had come up with their *rear-guard,*[3] and after killing a large number and taking many prisoners had driven the rest to take refuge among the tribes. That on the next day the *sub-chief*[4] he had mentioned *in a previous despatch*[5] had called a meeting and said that he had undertaken the struggle, not for his own interests but to win liberty for all; and that as they had to bow to *the decrees of*[6] fortune he was ready to offer himself for either *purpose,*[7] whether they desired him to appease the English by his death, or to be given up to them alive. That some of the chief men had been sent to him to discuss the matter, and that he had ordered them to give up their arms and produce all the *ringleaders.*[8]

1. not present participle.   2. castra.   3. novissimum agmen.   4. regulus.
5. supra.   6. omit these words; they are a mere amplification.
7. res; *res* can mean almost anything.   8. seditionis auctor.

32. *Canine Fidelity.*

There are many instances of the fidelity shown by dogs to their masters. I *rather think*[1] every one must have heard the story told of the dog *found*[2] one. day by *Louis*,[3] King of France, guarding the body of a murdered man. It had been sitting for three days by the body, unfed, and refusing to leave it. The king, touched with pity, ordered the corpse to be buried and the dog to be taken away and kindly treated. A few days after the king took it into his head to review his army. The troops marched past the king *in single file.*[4] The dog happened to be by, and seeing his master's assassins, flew at them furiously, and barked at them. On being arrested by the king's command, and questioned, they confessed their crime and were executed. There are also other stories of dogs appearing as informers and avengers in the case of crimes that had long remained undetected.

1. nescio an. 2. use the active instead of passive. 3. Ludovicus.
4. render this by the distributive numeral.

33. *Generous Confidence.*

Alexander the Great *was foolish enough*[1] to bathe in the river Cydnus, a very cold stream, and was taken violently ill. Now there was in the army one Philip, *the most faithful*[2] and skilful of all the king's medical attendants. He undertook to alleviate the violence of the disease with his remedies. This promise pleased no one but the king ; for his friends feared that Philip was bribed and would destroy him by means of poison. At the same time a messenger brought a letter from Parmenio, one of the generals, advising him not to trust his life to Philip, and asserting that he was ready to betray and kill his master. The king *was in a difficulty ;*[3] he did not know whether he ought to trust the doctor or not. In came the latter with a cup. The king drank it off and also requested Philip to read the letter. Philip was furious, and begged the king not to believe his enemies. The king's illness abated after three days and he was enabled to appear before his troops. Then the generals regretted that they had falsely accused Philip, and *one and*[4] all begged him to forgive them.

1. temere. 2. express this by an adjectival clause, which must contain the superlatives. 3. haerere. 4. omit.

34. *Lycurgus' Honesty.*

There once lived *in the city of Sparta*[1] a man whose name was Lycurgus. He was the son of Eunomus, the brother of Polydectes, the Spartan king. On the death of the latter his wife promised to *obtain*[2] the kingdom for him and kill her son if he would only marry her. Lycurgus seemed to *consent*,[3] but saved the child's life, and *relinquishing*[4] the supreme power ruled the state in his stead. When Charilaus, for so was the child named, was *grown to manhood*,[5] he set out *on a foreign tour*,[6] to free himself from all suspicion of *aiming at being king*.[7] He was, moreover, desirous of bringing back with him anything likely to be of use to the state that he might meet with on his travels.

> 1. at Sparta (*locative*) in the city; there being no locative case to city, we cannot put it in apposition to Sparta. 2. conciliare. 3. annuere. 4. se abdicare; do not use the present participle, as it is clear he could not rule while in the act of relinquishing the supreme power. 5. adolescere. 6. abroad. 7. regnum affectare.

35. *Lycurgus as Legislator.*

He returned after an absence of some years, and brought home with him a *draft*[1] of a code of laws and *a system of domestic government*[2] *compiled*[3] from the usages of different nations he had visited. His first care was to distribute the public lands among the citizens. Moreover, after forbidding the citizens the use of gold and silver, *deeming*[4] them the cause of all quarrels and crimes, he made an iron coinage, *to prevent*[5] wealth from giving any one an opportunity of living luxuriously. Besides this he commanded the citizens to dine in public and use coarse food. To prevent these laws from *becoming obsolete*[6] at any time, he pretended that he wished to go to consult the oracle of Delphi, and *bound*[7] the citizens by an oath not to change any of his laws until *his return*.[8] Then he went to the island of Crete, and spent the remainder of his life there. He also gave orders that his bones should be thrown into the sea, lest, if they were brought back to Sparta, the people should consider themselves freed from the *obligation*[9] of their oath.

> 1. forma. 2. civilis disciplina. 3. colligere. 4. use a deponent participle where you can instead of a present participle active. 5. lest. 6. interire. 7. adigere. 8. he should have returned. 9. relligio.

36. *Caesar marches against Ariovistus.*

At the same time that this message was brought to Caesar, ambassadors came from the Aedui and the Treveri : the Aedui, to complain that the Harudes who had just been imported into Gaul were ravaging their territory, and saying that they had been unable even by giving hostages *to purchase a renewal of*[1] the peace *with*[2] Ariovistus ; the Treveri, announcing that ten cantons of the Suabians had settled on the banks of the Rhine and were attempting to cross the river. Caesar was strongly moved by this news, and thought that he must make haste lest, if a new band of Suabians should *join*[3] the old forces of Ariovistus, *resistance*[4] might become less easy. So having got together provisions as quickly as he could, he hastened by *forced* marches to overtake Ariovistus. When he had gone three days' march, news was brought to him that Ariovistus with all his troops was on his way to besiege Besançon, the chief town of the Sequani, and had already accomplished a three days' march from his own territory. Caesar felt that he must *take every caution*[5] to prevent this happening.

1. redimere.   2. 'with' here is a sign of the genitive.   3. join themselves with.   4. use an impersonal verb.   5. translate this by a single verb.

37. *The Devotion of Codrus.*

During the reign of Codrus war *broke out*[1] between the Dorians and Athenians. *In answer to his appeal*[2] to the oracle he was told that *the side*[3] whose leader fell in the war would be victorious. On receiving this answer Codrus put on a shepherd's dress and entered the enemies' camp, carrying some faggots on his shoulders. He was there slain by a soldier whom he provoked by wounding him with his billhook. When they understood the meaning of the oracle the Dorians fled, and so the Athenians proved victorious through the courage of their leader *in offering*[4] himself to destruction. We not unfrequently read in ancient writers of leaders who dared such risks, *of course,*[5] with the view of exciting their men, and this shows us *the lengths to which superstition went.*[6] Who has not heard the story of Decius devoting himself to death at a critical moment to save his country?

1. exoriri.   2. to him consulting.   3. those.   4. offering.   5. scilicet.   6. how great was the power of superstition.

38. *Contempt of Pain.*

Alexander the Great, King of Macedon, *was attended*[1] while sacrificing by the youthful nobility. One of the lads, while standing near the altar with a censer, once let a live coal fall on his hand. Though the bystanders perceived the smell of his roasting flesh he bore his agony in silence. He was unwilling to delay the sacrifice by shaking the censer, or by uttering words of ill omen, to make it void. The king, who could see what was the matter, continued the sacrifice *beyond its customary limits,*[2] as he wished to test the boy's endurance. However, he never stirred *an inch*[3] and remained motionless to the end. If we consider this well we shall feel no surprise that the Macedonians routed the Persians with such ease, when even a boy of that nation could show such a singular example of fortitude.

1. praesto esse. 2. longer than was usual. 3. transversum digitum.

39. *Doing a Thing on Principle.*

Some people are so obstinate that they refuse to believe any one, even if he speak the truth. A certain citizen of London, being ill and not knowing the reason of his sickness, sent for his medical man, who on his arrival questioned him about the illness. 'What did you eat yesterday?' said he. The other replied, 'Twelve *muffins.*'[1] The doctor remarked with a laugh, '*No wonder*[2] your stomach *is out of order,*[3] after eating so many, for if you had eaten twenty you would have died.' The *patient*[4] however strenuously denied this, and at once went out *intending to buy*[5] twenty muffins ; and on returning home he toasted and ate them. Then he went up to the top of the house and *throwing*[6] himself down headlong was killed. By this act he showed that any one could eat twenty muffins without dying in consequence.

1. placenta. 2. nimirum. 3. laborare. 4. aegrotus. 5. future participle. 6. do not translate this by the present participle, as it is clear that he was not killed while throwing himself down.

40. *The Return of Theseus.*

But when they drew near to the coast of Attica, they were so joyful that they forgot *to set up*[1] their white sail, by which they should have *given knowledge*[2] of their health and safety unto Aegeus. He seeing the black sail afar off, being out of all hope ever more to see his son again, *took*[3] such a grief at his heart, that he threw himself headlong from the top of a cliff, and killed himself. So soon as Theseus was arrived at the port named Phalerum, *he performed*[4] the sacrifices which he had vowed to the gods *at his departure;*[5] and sent a herald of his before unto the city, to carry news of his safe arrival. The herald found many of the citizens mourning the death of King Aegeus. Many others received him with great joy, and would have crowned him also with a garland of flowers, because he had brought so good tidings, that the children of the city were returned in safety. The herald was content to take the garland, and returned forthwith to the sea, where Theseus made his sacrifices. Perceiving they were not yet done, he refused to enter into the temple, and stayed without *for fear of*[6] troubling the sacrifices. Afterwards, all ceremonies finished, he went in and told the news of his father's death.

1. pandere.   2. significare.   3. concipere.   4. facere.   5. departing.
6. lest he, etc.

41. *The Austrian Rule.*

Then the old man told them, weeping, of the awful punishment of his sons, and exclaimed (*or. obl.*) : 'What *is to be*[1] the end of these woes? The *lower orders*[2] are perishing—so are the upper classes. Our chief men, accused of treachery, are slain by the Austrians *without a hearing.*[3] Hear the story from those who have escaped from *the very presence of death.*[4] I, after losing my brothers and relations by death or exile, have had my boys brutally murdered but yesterday. My grief prevents me from telling the tale.' The fugitives are brought forward and tell their story (*or. obl.*) : 'Several noble Venetians have been put to death because they were said to have held communication with the exiles : we escaped from the slaughter. Verily the foreign yoke is loathsome, nor can it be borne any longer. Does any one wish to wait for the end of the woes that we and this old man have recounted? *To arms!*[5] Recall the exiles ! implore the assistance of the French ! Free from slavery our Italy that has been oppressed so many years !'

1. remember that questions in the first or third persons require an inf. in oratio obliqua.   2. plebes.   3. indicta caussa.   4. death itself.
5. let them seize their arms.

42. *The Treachery of Sextus.*

The only Latin town that defied Tarquin's power was Gabii; *and*[1] Sextus, the king's youngest son, promised to win this place also for his father. So he fled from Rome and presented himself at Gabii ; and there he made complaints of his father's tyranny and prayed for protection. The Gabians believed him, and took him into their city, and they trusted him, so that in time he was made commander of their army. Now his father suffered him to conquer in *many*[2] small battles, and the Gabians trusted him more and more. Then he sent privately to his father and asked him what he should do to make the Gabians submit. Then King Tarquin gave no answer to the messenger, but, as he walked up and down his garden, he kept cutting off the heads of the tallest poppies with his staff. At last the messenger was tired, and went back to Sextus and told him what had passed. But Sextus understood what his father meant, and he began to accuse falsely all the chief men, and some of them he put to death and some he banished. So at last the city of Gabii was *left defenceless*,[3] and Sextus delivered it up to his father.

1. this passage is full of the word ‘and,’ get rid of it in the Latin.
2. aliquot. 3. praesidio nudatus.

43. *Alexander murders Clitus.*

When Clitus was *on the point of*[1] departing for his *satrapy*,[2] Alexander invited several of his friends to a banquet that they might *say farewell*[3] to their comrade. Amongst them were many flatterers, who praised the exploits of Alexander excessively. Clitus, however, who was in the habit *of giving full expression to his thoughts*,[4] was so far from approving of their *undue*[5] praise of Alexander, as to say that he thought the achievements of Philip more worthy of admiration. He reminded Alexander of his former services, and stretching forth his hand exclaimed, ‘It was this hand, Alexander, that saved your life at the battle *of the Granicus.*’[6] The king was so angry at these words that he rushed at Clitus to kill him, and though his friends held him back at first, he afterwards got loose, and meeting Clitus, ran him through with a spear. But he was sorry for what he had done the next moment, and remained for three days subdued by grief, and *refusing*[7] even to taste food.

1. in eo ut. 2. provincia. 3. iubere valere. 4. of saying freely what he thought. 5. excessive. 6. near (*ad*) the river Granicus. 7. avoid the use of the present participle.

44. *Filial Love.*

When Octavianus was at Samos after the battle of Actium, *he ordered*[1] the prisoners to be summoned *for trial.*[2] Among others there was brought before him an old man, named Metellus, oppressed with age and infirmities, and so much *disfigured*[3] by a long beard and ragged clothes, that his son, who *happened*[4] to be one of the judges, could scarcely recognise him. When, however, he at length recollected the old man’s features, *he was so far from being*[5] ashamed to own his father, that he ran to embrace him, and wept over him bitterly. Then returning towards the tribunal, ‘Cæsar,’ says he, ‘my father has been your enemy, and I your officer; he deserves to be punished, and

I to be rewarded. *The favour* [6] I desire of you is, either to save him *on my account,*[7] or to order me to be executed with him.' The rest of the judges were melted by so affecting a scene. Octavianus himself relented, and granted Metellus his life and liberty.

   1. let this be dependent, making 'was brought' the principal verb.
     2. in ius. 3. deformatus. 4. forte. 5. tantum abfuit ut.
         6. this. 7. propter me.

45. *The Murder of Servius Tullius.*

When all was ready Lucius went suddenly to the forum with a band of armed men, and seated himself on the king's throne before the doors of the *senate-house,*[1] where he was wont to judge the people. And *they ran*[2] to the king, and told him that Lucius was sitting on his throne. Upon this the old man went in haste to the forum, and when he saw Lucius he asked him wherefore he had dared to sit on the king's seat. And Lucius answered that it was his father's throne, and that he had more right in it than Servius. Then he seized the old man *and*[3] threw him down the steps to the ground; and he called the senators together as if he were already king. Servius meanwhile arose and began to make his way to his house, but he was overtaken and slain by some *emissaries*[4] of Lucius', who left him *in*[5] his blood in the middle of the street.

   1. curia. 2. impersonal. 3. get rid of 'and' by making the preceding verb a participle passive in agreement with 'the old man.' 4. express this by an adjectival clause. 5. covered with.

46. *A cowardly Traveller.*

One day a couple of travellers fell among some highwaymen in ambush. One of them took to his heels as quick as he could, but the other held his ground and defended himself stoutly. After a protracted struggle, the highwaymen were put to flight. Up came the cowardly traveller, and drawing his sword exclaimed, ' Where are the rogues gone ? *I'll let them see*[1] the kind of people they have attacked !' While talking like this, he was addressed by him who had stood his ground, and who now upbraided his cowardice, saying, 'I wish you had given me this help when I was struggling ! Helped by so distinguished a warrior I should have not only easily routed the highwaymen, but also killed them.' *Then with a change from banter to indignation,*[2] he continued, 'Now you may put up your sword: no more of your boasting in my presence ! Deceive those, *say I,*[3] who do not know what a poltroon you are. I know your cowardice, and that you are not one to be trusted in time of peril.'

    1. they shall feel. 2. then his bantering being changed to indignation. 3. inquam.

47. *An awkward Contretemps.*

One day[1] a youth and a maiden agreed to meet in a place where
was a beautiful lake. Now the youth was so eager to see the maiden
that he reached the lake much before the time; and as he had to
wait long, and the sun was hot, he resolved to *bathe:*[2] so having taken
off his clothes, he ordered his dog, which he had brought with him,
to guard them, and then jumped into the lake. At last, having
enjoyed the water enough, and *thinking*[3] the maiden would soon
arrive, he came out and tried to recover his clothes. But the dog, *not
recognising*[4] him *without his clothes,*[5] did not allow him to approach;
and while he was doubting what to do, he saw the maiden afar off.

> 1. forte. 2. lavari. 3. always, if you can, use a deponent parti-
> ciple. 4. avoid the present participle by saying, 'who did
> not recognise.' 5. naked.

48. *Caligula.*

Tiberius *was succeeded*[1] by Caius Caesar, also called Caligula from
the military boot which he used to wear in the camp of Germanicus
his father in childhood, when just entering on his twenty-fourth
year. At the outset, great as were the popular rejoicings, no less was
the hope that he would resemble his father, who is said to have possessed every advantage of mind and body. And indeed, as at first
even the worst princes are often good, he kept giving many signs of a
disposition *at once well controlled and highly cultivated.*[2] But shortly,
just as if he wished *to free himself from his human nature,*[3] he outdid
the very wild beasts in cruelty. He put numbers of all ranks to
death. Among others fell Macro, the commandant of the *imperial
guard,*[4] *to whose good offices he owed his elevation to the throne.*[5] After
squandering the vast riches amassed by Tiberius, he devoted himself
to *proscribing and plundering*[6] the citizens. Among other tokens of
his barbarity the following saying of his has been handed down to
posterity, 'Would that the Roman people had but one head, that I
might strike it off!' He also gave orders that he should be worshipped all over the world, and that temples should be erected in his
honour. After he had indulged in every kind of enormity for several
years, and filled Rome with bloodshed and mourning, some of the
citizens, who could no longer endure such a monster, entered into a
conspiracy against him. They at length *got*[7] a favourable opportunity,
and Caligula was slain by Cassius Chaerea, a military tribune. We
cannot refrain from wondering how such a father could have had
such a son.

> 1. remember that *succedo* takes a dative, and therefore cannot be
> used personally in the passive. 2. cum moderatus tum civilis.
> 3. to put off *(exuere)* man. 4. praetoriani. 5. by whose help
> he had been made emperor. 6. substantives. 7. nancisci.

49. *A miserable End.*

Milo of Crotona, the strongest man of his age, lost his life in a miserable way. When past middle age, after retiring from the wrestling school, where he had won so many victories, he was one day travelling without companions through a woody district in Italy. Seeing an oak close to the road *with*[1] wide crevices in its trunk, he desired to see if any of his former strength was left. He inserted his fingers into the crevices and tried to split *and*[2] tear asunder the oak. He succeeded in tearing it *down the middle*[3] and then relaxed his efforts, imagining he had done what he wanted. When the strain was taken off, the separated parts *closed*[4] again. With his hands thus fettered and held by the tree, Milo died of starvation and thirst. His friends, who had long looked for him, subsequently found his remains much disfigured by wild beasts and birds. Does it not seem an extraordinary thing that an athlete so long invincible, and who had faced greater dangers so often, should have perished in an accident of this sort?

1. express this by an adjectival clause. 2. get rid of the 'and.' How will you do so? 3. express this simply by an adjective. 4. coire.

50. *The Soldier and the Elephant.*

I must not fail to relate the valour of a veteran of the fifth legion. When an elephant on the left wing, wounded and maddened with pain, had assailed an unarmed camp follower, and after trampling him under foot, and *kneeling*[1] on him *with all his weight*,[2] with erect and *brandished*[3] trunk, and trumpeting loudly, was crushing *the life out of him*,[4] this soldier could not refrain from opposing himself in arms to the brute. When the elephant saw him coming at him with *levelled*[5] spear, abandoning the dead body, he threw his trunk round the soldier, and lifted him *into the air*[6] armed as he was. The soldier seeing *that prompt measures must be used*[7] in such an extremity, slashed away with all his might at the trunk which was wrapped round him. The elephant, forced by the agony he was enduring, threw down the soldier, and with shrill trumpetings turned and fled to the rest of the brutes.

1. genu inniti. 2. pondere suo. 3. vibrare. 4. and killing. 5. infestus. 6. in sublime. 7. constanter agi (*impersonal*).

51. *Perfidy punished.*

Brutus, the Roman general, having conquered the Palæenses, ordered them *on pain of death* [1] to bring him all their gold and silver, and promised rewards *to such* [2] as should discover any hidden treasures. Upon this a slave belonging to a rich citizen *informed against* [3] his master, and discovered to a centurion the place where he had buried his wealth. The citizen was immediately seized, and brought, together with the treacherous informer, before Brutus. The mother of the accused followed them, declaring, with tears in her eyes, that she had hidden the treasure *without her son's knowledge,* [4] and that consequently she alone ought to be punished. The slave maintained that his master, *and not* [5] the mother, had transgressed the edict. Brutus heard both parties with great patience, and being convinced that the accusation of the slave was chiefly *founded on* [6] the hatred he bore to his master, he commended the tenderness and generosity of the mother, restored the whole sum to the son, and ordered the slave *to be crucified.* [7]

1. having threatened death.   2. to those.   3. deferro.   4. abl. abs.
5. 'and not' must not be translated as usual by *neque*, as the stress falls on the single word 'mother,' not on the sentence.
6. arose from.   7. in crucem affigi.

52. *Garibaldi.*

After he had repulsed the French troops for a whole month from Rome, Garibaldi seeing all further *resistance* [1] to be impossible, escaped from that city, but being attacked by an Austrian fleet, of his thirteen vessels eight were sunk. This *last* [2] trial overcame the spirit of Annita. She was already dying, when her husband, in vain hope of saving her life, landed on the enemies' coast. Here she died, and in the midst of the thickets of an Indian forest was buried by her husband's own hand. No one knows where she lies. Let none try to *scan* [3] what he felt, as weary, but not broken, he returned to Genoa with his and her sons. Again from here he wandered, and for a short time gained a livelihood by hard labour in the *United States,* [4] till, having collected a little money, he was able to buy the island of Caprera, whence he started some years *ago* [5] to recover the kingdom of Naples for the King of Italy.

1. translate by the impersonal verb.   2. novissimus.   3. temptare.
4. civitates foederatae.   5. abhinc.

53. *Nero's Crimes.*

Claudius was succeeded by Domitius Nero at the age of seventeen, who at the outset, *that is to say,*[1] as long as he obeyed the advice of his tutor Seneca, behaved himself in such a way that he might have been held among the best emperors. Later on, spoiled by vice and flattery, he *turned out*[2] more like a monster than a human being; not even did the most cruel beasts show *such*[3] ferocity *as*[3] Nero practised. First he carried off Britannicus by poison. Next he *deprived*[4] his mother, Agrippina, of all her honours, *drove*[4] her from the city, and *ordered*[4] her to be put to death. The senate approved of this murder, *to complete*[5] the iniquity of the time. He also condemned the poet Lucan to death; he did not even spare *his old master*[6] the philosopher Seneca. He killed his wife, Poppaea, with a kick. He was not ashamed of *appearing on the stage,*[7] and living with actors and pantomimists. He also treated the Christians with barbarity, and many of them were condemned on a false *charge*[8] of setting fire to the city.

1. scilicet. 2. exsistere. 3. tantus—quantus. 4. avoid translating all of these by finite verbs. 5. lest anything should be wanting to. 6. who had formerly instructed him. 7. in scenam prodire. 8. crimen.

54. *Nero's End.*

Rejoicing as he did[1] in every known vice, he never ceased looking for fresh ones. At last he was hated and despised by his people, and being deserted by every one, he took to flight. He lay hid for a considerable time, but at last, hearing the voices of his pursuers, and fearing that he would be taken, he turned his dagger against himself. Revolt had broken out among the troops, and Galba, their general, was marching on Rome *at the head of*[2] an army. After the death of Nero he was hailed emperor by his troops, with whom he was a great favourite. Thus perished the last emperor of the Julian *family,*[3] which had so long enjoyed the sovereign power at Rome. From that time commenced the *election*[4] of emperors by the soldiers. Those who took into consideration *the laws that regulate the life of man*[5] had little difficulty in foreseeing what would be the result, when citizens were looked upon as slaves, when religion was set at nought, and when everything, in a word, was made to depend on violence and intrigue.

1. as (*ut*) he rejoiced, so (*ita*), etc. 2. with. 3. not *familia*. 4. use a verb to get rid of the abstract noun. 5. fas gentium.

55. *The Romans encouraged by hope of Plunder.*

Ascertaining[1] by his scouts that the Sabine army had started, Decius summoned a council of war and *asked*[2] why they wandered over the fields. He *advised*[2] them to attack the cities and the fortifications which were now unprotected. With the approbation of all he then led them to *the storm*[3] of the strong city of Murgantia. Such was the ardour of the troops, both in consequence of their attachment to their leader and their expectation of greater booty than they could get from forays in the open country, that they carried the city by storm within twenty-four hours. Much booty fell into their hands. To prevent this from hampering the march of the column Decius assembled the troops and addressed them thus (*or. obl.*) : 'Will you be content with this one victory? All the cities of the Samnites and with them the booty is delivered into your hands. Sell your spoils; prevail on tradesmen *by pecuniary inducements*[4] to follow the column. We shall next march on the city of Romulea, where we shall find no greater difficulties *to be encountered*[5] and still greater booty.' After the sale of the plunder an advance was made on Romulea. Without any *engineering operations*,[6] or the use of battering-engines, this city also was taken by *escalade*,[7] and sacked.

1. not the present participle, which is only used to express a simultaneous action. 2. these verbs may be understood before the oratio obliqua. 3. express this by the gerundive. 4. by gain (*lucrum*). 5. omit. 6. opus. 7. by moving up ladders.

56. *The Expedition of the Argonauts.*

The Argonauts were some young Greeks *of noble family*[1] who sailed in the ship Argo, *commanded by*[2] Jason, to Colchis, to seek for the golden fleece. They *touched*[3] at the Troad, and Herakles, who was one of the company, saved Hesione, the daughter of the Trojan king, Laomedon, from a sea monster to which she had been abandoned. So her father promised her to him with some swift steeds as the reward of his achievement, *and*[4] Herakles left *them*[4] with him until his return. Jason, on his arrival at Colchis, *won the affections of*[5] Medea, the king's daughter, and by her aid *attained his object;*[6] after espousing her he carried her off with him to Thessaly, taking with him the golden fleece. But Herakles on his return to the Troad, demanded his reward *a was agreed*[7] from Laomedon. The latter refused to give it, so Herakles took Troy by storm, slew Laomedon, and made his son Priam king.

1. born in a very high place. 2. abl. abs. 3. appellere. 4. relative. 5. sibi conciliare. 6. voti compos fieri. 7. ex pacto.

57. *The Theban Tragedy.*

Once upon a time Jocasta, the wife of Laius, the Theban king, gave birth to a son. Now an oracle had declared that a son of Jocasta would slay his father and marry his mother. Accordingly Oedipus, for that was the child's name, was exposed on a mountain, but being found *by a traveller,*[1] was carried to Athens. After a while the child grew up, and having met his father Laius by chance, slew him *in a quarrel which arose*[2] between them. Not long afterwards he received his mother Jocasta in marriage as a reward *for killing the Sphynx,*[3] a monster which *was in the habit of*[4] devastating the neighbourhood of Thebes, *and became by her the father of twin sons,*[5] Eteocles and Polynices. Having at length become aware of what had happened, he put out his eyes in his grief and abdicated the throne. His sons subsequently agreed that they should reign *alternately for a year.*[6] But Eteocles, at the expiration of his year, refused to give place to his brother, who retired to King Adrastus at Argos, and married his daughter. Thereupon there began a desperate war with the Thebans, for Polynices excited Adrastus and other princes against his brother. These were seven in number, *so the story goes,*[7] and were all slain in the war with the exception of Adrastus.

1. make this the subject of a new sentence. 2. abl. abs. 3. for (of) the Sphynx killed by himself. 4. imperfect. 5. and from her received (*suscipio,* the technical term, meaning 'to acknowledge') twin sons. 6. in alternate years. 7. they say.

58. *The Carthaginians in Spain.*

We have seen that the first war with Carthage came to an end because both sides were tired, and because Hamilcar wanted to get an army ready with which he might fight the Romans. He got the Carthaginians to send him to Spain, and there he taught his soldiers how to fight, for Spain was full of poor and brave men, who fought very hard before being conquered. When *on the point of*[1] setting out from Carthage he offered a great sacrifice to the gods ; and as he was offering, he called his young son Hannibal, who was only nine years old, and asked him if he would like to go with him. 'Yes,'[2] was the eager answer of the child. 'Then,' said his father, 'swear on this altar that you will never be the friend of the Roman people.' The boy willingly took the oath, and went with his father, and it is well known that he never forgot his promise. Hamilcar fought in Spain till he died, and conquered for Carthage all Spain up to the river Tagus. When he died his son-in-law Hasdrubal went on with his conquests till he was killed in 221, and Hannibal became commander-in-chief at the age of twenty-six.

1. in eo ut. 2. etiam.

59. *A desperate Struggle.*

The day after, those who had been left to guard the fortress, being informed of the misfortunes of their companions, that the greater part of their army had been destroyed in the pursuit of plunder, and that the bravest of them would be besieged, and shut up on a desert mountain, and, *if not presently relieved,*[1] would soon be taken through the want of provisions, went out in all haste, leaving very few of their men to guard the fortress. These the Etruscans, sallying out from their strong places, intercepted before they could join their companions ; and *surrounding*[2] them, they at last slew every one of them, after they had *performed*[3] many brave *actions.*[4] But long after, those also who had possessed themselves of the hill, being oppressed both with hunger and thirst, resolved to charge the enemy ; and a few engaging with many, they continued fighting from morning to night, and made so great a slaughter of the enemy, that the heaps of dead bodies, dispersed in many places, were a *hindrance*[5] to them in fighting.

1. impersonal (*subvenire*). 2. avoid the present participle, say, 'they slew every one of them surrounded.' 3. edere. 4. facinus. 5. dative of complement.

60. *Bajazet.*

At first he received the captive monarch with great courtesy, and entering in conversation with him, said, 'Now, king, tell me freely what thou wouldst have done with me had I fallen into thy power?' Bajazet, *who was*[1] of a fierce and haughty spirit, is said to have thus replied : 'Had the gods given unto me the victory, I would have enclosed thee in an iron cage and carried thee about with me *as a spectacle of derision*[2] to the world.' Tamerlane wrathfully replied, 'Then, proud man, *as*[3] thou wouldst have done to me, even *so*[3] shall I do unto thee.' A strong iron cage was made, into which the fallen emperor was thrust ; and thus exposed *like*[4] a wild beast, he was carried along in the train of his conqueror. For nearly three years the once mighty Bajazet was confined in this prison, and at last being told that he must be carried into *Tartary,*[5] despairing of then obtaining his freedom, he struck his head with such violence against the *bars*[6] of the cage as to put an end to his wretched life.

1. a man. 2. ludibrio (*dative*). 3. quod—idem. 4. ritu. 5. Massagetarum fines. 6. claustra.

E

61. *Noman and Polyphemus.*

Then he cried out with a mighty voice for his brethren the
Cyclopes, that dwelt hard by in caverns upon hills ; they hearing the
terrible shout came flocking from all parts to inquire *what ailed*[1]
Polyphemus ? and what cause he had for making such horrid
clamours in the night-time to break their sleeps ? if his fright proceeded from any mortal ? if strength or craft had given him his
death's blow ? He made answer from within that Noman had hurt
him, Noman had killed him, Noman was with him in the cave.
They replied, ' If no man has hurt thee, and no man is with thee,
then thou art alone, and the evil that afflicts thee is from the hand of
heaven, which none can resist or help.' So they left him and went
their way, thinking that some disease troubled him. He, blind and
distracted with the anguish of the pain, went groaning *up and down*[2]
in the dark, to find the doorway, and having found it, he removed
the stone, and sat in the threshold, *feeling*[3] if he could lay hold on
any man going out with the sheep, which were beginning to issue
forth to their accustomed pastures. But Ulysses, whose first artifice
in giving himself that ambiguous name, had succeeded so well with
the Cyclops, was not of a wit so gross as to be caught by that
palpable[4] device.

    1. what did he want (*sibi velle*). 2. huc illuc. 3. pertrectare.
                     4. apertus.

62. *Marius and the Assassin.*

News was brought that the old man was in hiding near at hand.
Compassion was felt by many who remembered his former prowess.
However, the magistrates and council of Minturnae *concluded*[1] that
Marius should immediately be put to death. No citizen would
undertake this office, but a Cimbrian went up to him, sword in hand,
with the intention of despatching him. The chamber in which he
lay was *somewhat gloomy,*[2] and a light, they tell you, glanced from the
eyes of Marius on the face of the assassin ; while at the same time
he heard a solemn voice saying, ' Dost thou dare to kill Marius ? '
Upon this the assassin threw down his sword and fled, crying,
' I cannot kill Marius.' Not even by a large reward could the
barbarian be induced to re-enter the chamber.

    1. placere (*impersonal*). 2. comparative degree.

63. *Marius ai Minturnae.*

The people of Minturnae were struck with astonishment ; pity and remorse ensued. *Should they put to death* [1] the preserver of Italy ? Was it not even a disgrace to them *that* [2] they did not contribute to his relief ? 'Let the exile go,' said they, 'and await his destiny in some other region ! It is time we should deprecate the anger of the gods, for having refused *the poor naked wanderer* [3] the common privileges of hospitality !' *Under the influence of* [4] this enthusiasm, they immediately conducted him to the sea-coast. Yet, in the midst of their expedition, an unforeseen delay was occasioned ; for the Sylva Maricae or Marician Grove, was held so sacred that nothing *entering it* [5] was suffered to be removed ; and to go round it would be tedious. At last an old man of the company exclaimed 'that no place, however religious, was inaccessible, if it could contribute to the safety of Marius ;' upon which he took some of the baggage in his hand, and marched *directly* [6] through the grove. His companions followed with the same alacrity ; and when Marius came to the sea-coast, he found a vessel in readiness to receive him.

1. infinitive, an indignant question. 2. *quod*, with indicative, substantival clause. 3. the wanderer (*hospes vagabundus*), a poor naked man. 4. moved by. 5. which had once (*semel*) entered it. 6. recta.

64. *The use of Athletics.*

Epaminondas, *the* [1] valiant captain of the Thebans, who as well in virtue and prowess as in learning surpassed all the noblemen of *his* [2] time, daily exercised himself in the morning with running and leaping, in the evening in wrestling, to the intent that in battle also he might, the more *strongly* [3] embracing his adversary, put him in danger ; and also that in the chase running and leaping he might either overtake his enemy, or, being pursued, if extreme need required, escape him. Similarly before him did the worthy Achilles, for whilst his ships lay at anchor, he suffered not his people to slumber in idleness, but daily exercised them and himself in running, wherein he surpassed all others ; and therefore Homer throughout all his work calleth him the swift-footed Achilles. *The great Alexander,* [4] being a child, excelled all his companions in running. Wherefore once upon a time one demanded of him if he would run in the great games of Olympia ; whereunto Alexander answered in this form, 'I would very gladly run there if I were *sure* [5] to run with kings ; for if I should contend with a private person our victories would not be equal.'

1. ille. 2. that. 3. arcte. 4. again (*quid ?*) did not Alexander, etc. 5. future participle.

65. *A stern Father.*

Before the end of the year a conspiracy was formed, in which many of the young nobility were *concerned*,[1] and among the rest the two sons of Brutus the consul. A slave of the name of Vindicius became acquainted with their designs, and *gave information*[2] to the consuls, who immediately went with a strong guard, apprehended the conspirators, and seized the letters. *As soon as it was day*[3] Brutus ascended the tribunal. The prisoners were brought before him and tried *in form.*[4] The evidence of Vindicius was heard, and the letters to Tarquin read; after which the conspirators were asked if they had anything to urge in their defence. Sighs, groans, and tears *were their only answer.*[5] The whole assembly stood with downcast looks, and no man ventured to speak. This mournful silence was at last broken with slow murmurs of *Banishment!*[6] *Banishment!* But the public good, which *predominated over*[7] the feelings of a parent, urged Brutus to pronounce on them the sentence of death.

1. conscius. 2. indicare. 3. when it grew light (*illucescere*). 4. iusto iudicio. 5. they only answered by. 6. let them go into exile (supine). 7. was stronger than.

66. *The Return to Ithaca.*

He whose life hitherto had been full of evils, now slept securely, forgetting all; his eyelids bound in such deep sleep, as only yielded to death: and when they reached the nearest Ithacan port by the next morning he was still asleep. The mariners, not willing to awake him, *landed him*[1] softly, and laid him in a cave at *the foot of*[2] an olive-tree, which made a shady recess in that narrow harbour, *haunted*[3] by almost none *but*[4] the sea-nymphs; for few ships before this Phaeacian vessel had put into that haven, by reason of the difficulty and narrowness of the entrance. Here leaving him asleep, and disposing in safe places near him the presents with which King Alcinous had dismissed him, they departed for Phaeacia; where these wretched mariners never again set foot; but just as they arrived, and thought to salute their native land, *in sight of*[5] their city's turrets, and in open view of their friends who from the harbour with shouts greeted their return, their vessel and all the mariners which were in her were turned to stone by Neptune's vindictive wrath; who *resented*[6] thus highly the contempt which those Phaeacians had shown in convoying home a man whom the god had destined to destruction.

1. nave exponere. 2. express this by an adjective, cf. *summus mons*, the top of the mountain. 3. frequentare. 4. if you except. 5. cum maxime intuentes. 6. ulcisci.

67. *The Battle of Marathon.*

The Persian army was drawn up along the plain about a mile from the sea, and their fleet was ranged behind them on the beach. The Athenians held the *rising* [1] ground above the plain, in order to *protect* [2] their flanks by the mountains on each side, and to prevent the cavalry from attacking their rear. Miltiades, anxious to join battle as soon as possible, ordered his soldiers to advance, running over the mile of ground which separated them from the foe. Both the Athenian wings *were successful*, [3] but the centre was *broken* [4] by the Persians and compelled to fly. Then Miltiades, having recalled his wings from pursuit, charged and broke the Persian centre. Thus the Athenians saved Greece from becoming a Persian *satrapy*, [5] and raised their own city to be the capital of Greece. We must not forget that the Athenians were the first to face the Persians on the battle-field. Before this the very name of Persian was enough to strike a chill into the hearts of their adversaries. Nor must we fail to recognise the devotion of the Plataeans, who alone of the Greeks sent their little force to help their allies.

1. editus.   2. tegere.   3. victory stood in the power of (*penes*).
4. perrumpere.   5. province.

68. *The Pacification of the Galekas.*

The defeated enemy on ceasing from flight immediately sent envoys to the general *to treat for* [1] peace, promising to give hostages and to do what he required of them. With these envoys came the *sub-chief*, [2] who, as I reported *previously*, [3] had been sent by the general to his people. The Galekas, when he communicated the general's demands, had seized and imprisoned him, but sent him back after the battle. While suing for peace they laid the blame of their conduct on the people and begged forgiveness, *alleging that it was unpremeditated*. [4] The general, while complaining *of their having* [5] gone to war without due cause, agreed to pardon their inconsiderate conduct, and *required them to find* [6] hostages. Part of these were given on the spot, part which had to be brought from a *considerable* [7] distance were promised within a few days. The people were ordered to return home, and the chiefs promised *to remain faithful to* [8] Queen Victoria.

1. de.   2. regulus.   3. supra.   4. propter imprudentiam.   5. quod.
6. imperare.   7. express this by a comparative.   8. officium
praestare erga.

69. *Death of Caesar.*

Pretending to salute[1] him the conspirators surround Caesar; and forthwith Cimber, *who was to give the signal*,[2] drew close to him as if intending to make some request. When Caesar refused, and tried to put the matter off to another time with *a wave of his hand*,[3] he tore his toga from his shoulders; then as he exclaimed, 'Why, this is violence!' Casca next wounded him a little below the neck. Caesar caught Casca's arm and drove his dagger through it; he then attempted to get away, but was crippled by another wound. On perceiving that he was assailed on all sides with drawn daggers, he wrapped his head in his toga, and at the same time drew down the folds to his feet, covering even the lower part of his body *that*[4] he might die with more decency. Twenty-three wounds pierced him. For a considerable while he lay exposed after death, as every one took to flight. At length three slaves put him on a litter and carried him home with his arm hanging down.

1. under pretence of saluting (*officium*). 2. who had undertaken the first part (plural). 3. gestus. 4. how do you translate 'that' when there is a comparative in the sentence?

70. *After the Murder.*

Caesar being slain in this manner, Brutus, standing in the midst of the *house*,[1] wished to speak, and to detain the other senators who were not *privy to*[2] the conspiracy, in order to tell them why they had done this deed. But they, overpowered with fear, fled in all haste out of the door, and no man followed them; for *it was agreed*[3] among them that they should kill no man but Caesar only, and should win the rest by entreaties to defend their liberty. All the conspirators *but*[4] Brutus, when they were deciding this matter, *thought it good*[5] also to kill Antonius, because he was a wicked man and one who *in nature*[6] favoured *tyranny*;[7] also because he was in great favour *with*[8] the soldiers and held high office at the time, being consul *with Caesar*.[9] But Brutus would not agree to it: first, because he said it was not honest; secondly, because he thought there was hope of change in him. So Brutus by this means saved Antonius' life, who then disguised himself and *stole away*[10] out of the city; but Brutus and his companions, having their swords bloody in their hands, went *straight*[11] to the Capitol, persuading the Romans to take their liberty again.

1. curia. 2. conscius. 3. convenit. 4. excepting (abl. abs.), *or* if you except, *or* praeter. 5. visum est. 6. pro indole sua. 7. regnum. 8. apud. 9. Caesar being his colleague. 10. furtim egredi. 11. recta (via).

71. *The Trojan War.*

The following[1] is the account given by ancient writers of the Trojan war. Paris, *one of the numerous sons of Priam,*[2] King of Troy, his vessel having been *carried*[3] to the Peloponnesus, carried off Helen, the wife of the Spartan king, the most beautiful woman of the time. Infuriated by this insult, the Greeks joined their forces and waged war on the Trojans, *led by Agamemnon,*[4] King of Mycenae, and his brother Menelaus. On Troy being invested by the Greeks, the inhabitants withstood the siege for a long time. Among the Greeks was pre-eminent the valour of Achilles. He slew Hector, the bravest of the Trojans, but himself died *of an arrow-wound inflicted by Paris.*[5] In the tenth year of the siege Troy was taken by *the following*[6] stratagem. A wooden horse filled with men was left in front of the gates, and the Greeks embarked on their vessels and retired. The horse being admitted by the unwitting Trojans into the city, the men inside came out stealthily and opened the gates. The Greeks returned, and attacking the city carried it by storm, nor did *they refrain from*[7] burning it after killing all its inhabitants.

1. in hunc modum. 2. Priam had several sons, one of whom, etc.
3. delatus. 4. abl. abs. 5. having been wounded.
6. huiusmodi. 7. sibi temperare quin.

72. *Shut the Door after you.*

Swift had a servant-maid who was so careless that she always forgot to shut the door *in spite of his repeated orders.*[1] One day she came and asked leave to go away to spend a few days with her mother, who lived *some twenty miles off.*[2] Leave was given her, but as usual she forgot to shut the door on her departure. Some hours after Swift sent his servant-man with his *dogcart*[3] *with orders to*[4] fetch the girl back as soon as possible. She had by this time reached her mother's house, but had to get into the dogcart and return to her master's house. On her arrival she went to Swift and asked what he wanted. He replied, 'I sent for you to shut the door, *which*[5] you forgot to do when you went away. You can now go back to your mother.' He never cared in the least what amount of inconvenience he inflicted on any one; there was always something bitter in his jests.

1. although he ordered this again and again. 2. a viginti fere millibus passuum. 3. vehiculum. 4. and ordered. 5. the thing which.

73. *Mardonius' Warning.*

The Athenians sent a message to Sparta, and informed that state of Alexander's arrival. Upon this the Spartans sent an embassy to Athens. After this embassy had arrived, the Archons summoned the people to a general assembly. Alexander declared that he was sent by Mardonius, *who had a commission*[1] from the great king to announce to the Greeks that he would forget former offences, reinstate them in their dominions, rebuild their houses and temples, and receive them into the number of his allies ; that they should, moreover, live entirely according to their own laws. Such was the will of the king. Alexander added, in the name of Mardonius : 'What *infatuation*[2] drives you, ye Athenians, to carry on war against a monarch whom ye can never conquer, and against whom even all *resistance*[3] is ineffectual? Ye know the army of Xerxes, and its deeds. Ye know also the force which is under my command ; should you even conquer me, another army, equal to mine, stands in readiness. Renounce, then, the thought of maintaining a conflict with the great king. Do not by your own act and deed deprive yourselves of your native land.'

1. who had been ordered.   2. dementia ; do this speech in oratio obliqua.   3. turn this by a verb.

74. *Revolt in Gaul.*

Meanwhile Sabinus, with the force that he had received from Caesar, reached the borders of the Sequani. At the head of this tribe was Viridovix, who also held the chief command of those states which had revolted, and had collected from them an army and considerable supplies. During these few days the Aulerci, having massacred their council because they refused *to support*[1] the war, closed their gates, and joined Viridovix. Besides this, a large multitude had assembled from all parts of Gaul, consisting of *bankrupts*[2] and banditti, who were drawn off from their ordinary labours in the fields by the hope of booty and the passion for war. Sabinus encamped in an advantageous position, and, though Viridovix led out his forces every day and offered battle, refused to fight, and gave the enemy such an *idea*[3] of his cowardice that they actually came up close under the ramparts.

1. to be supporters (auctor).   2. perditi homines.   3. opinio.

75. The News from Elateia.

The news that Elateia was taken possession of by Philip arrived at Athens late in the evening, and *spread universal consternation.*[1] The citizens had already left the forum for their houses, and the magistrates were at their evening meal in the Prytaneum, when the courier arrived. In an instant all the *streets*[2] were crowded with people ; *astonishment*[3] and alarm *were on every face;*[4] the forum was emptied, and the wooden *stalls*[5] of the shopkeepers burned. At break of day the people were assembled, and the Prytanes in their places, when the Archon publicly announced the sad news. Upon this the herald, according to custom, asked, with a loud voice, *who*[6] would mount the *platform.*[7] No one answered, till at last Demosthenes arose. *This*[8] consummate orator *stirred*[9] the despairing minds of his fellow-citizens to hope and courage ; he demonstrated to them that Philip had occupied Elateia only *from apprehension*[10] as to *the intentions*[11] of the Thebans ; he acknowledged that he had many *adherents*[12] in Thebes, but maintained that the greater part of the people *harboured sentiments hostile*[13] towards the king.

1. consternation seized the minds of all (*stupor, invadere*). 2. via. 3. stupor. 4. every face showed. 5. taberna. 6. numquis. 7. suggestum. 8. is, ut erat, etc. 9. erigere. 10. because he doubted. 11. express this by an indirect question. 12. fautores 13. alienis animis esse.

76. A new kind of Notepaper.

Histiaeus, the tyrant of Miletus, who had saved the life of Darius the Persian king, was subsequently kept by him at Susa, *both*[1] as an honour, *and*[1] also because *he was suspected of fomenting*[2] a rebellion. In his absence Aristagoras, one of his kinsmen, was put over the state. In order to communicate with him Histiaeus contrived a very cunning plan. He shaved the head of a slave, and then branded a letter on his smooth pate. He kept him until the hair grew, and then sent him to Aristagoras. On his arrival at Miletus, Aristagoras *had his head shaved,*[3] and read easily what Histiaeus had written. Now the letter recommended the Greek cities to rebel against Darius ; and not long after Aristagoras, after exciting the minds of the Greeks by frequent emissaries, declared war against the Persians. The result of the struggle was long doubtful. The Persians at length *wrested*[4] victory from the Greeks. It is well known that dire *atrocities were committed*[5] on the rebellious states.

1. cum—tum. 2. he seemed to be the originator (*auctor*). 3. use *curare* with the gerundive. 4. reportare. 5. saeviri (impersonal).

77. *The Declaration of the Second Punic War.*

Meanwhile the allies received no assistance from the Romans, who, on hearing of the siege, sent ambassadors to Hannibal. On their being *referred* [1] by him to *the government* [2] at home they received but little satisfaction, as the influence of *the war party* [3] was predominant in the senate. Ambassadors were again sent after the capture of Saguntum, to ask that Hannibal should be given up for his violation of the truce. As the Carthaginians kept *beating about the bush*, [4] Q. Fabius, one of the envoys, lifting up a fold of his dress, said, 'Here do I carry peace and war: *make your choice between them.*' [5] 'War,' was the rejoinder of the Carthaginians, and Fabius said, 'I give you war.' The Carthaginians said, 'We accept it,' so war broke out afresh. Peace was impossible between these powerful nations; it was decreed by fate that one should be destroyed and the other be mistress of the world. It is better for mankind that fortune favoured the Roman arms.

1. relegare. 2. qui a consiliis erant. 3. adjectival clause, 'who favoured war.' 4. tergiversari. 5. choose which you will.

78. *Caesar's Exploits.*

The following *is a tolerably complete summary* [1] of Caesar's exploits during the nine years of his command. He reduced to the form of a province the whole of Gaul, which is bounded by the Pyrenees, the Alps, the Cevennes, and by the rivers Rhine and Rhone, and *whose frontier extends a distance* [2] of 3200 miles, and imposed on it a yearly contribution of *forty millions* [3] of sesterces as tribute. He was the first Roman leader to build a bridge, assail, and *inflict heavy losses on* [4] the Germans, who live on the eastern bank of the Rhine. He also attacked the Britons, who were before his time unknown; and after defeating them, imposed on them *a contribution in* [5] money and hostages. Thrice, *and thrice only,* [6] throughout such a career of success did he meet with a reverse: in Britain, when his fleet was almost entirely destroyed by a tempest; in Gaul, when one of his legions was routed near Gergovia; and in Germany, when his lieutenants, Titurius and Aurunculeius, were cut off by treachery.

1. fere. 2. which extends in circumference (*circuitu patere*). 3. the numeral adverbs denote so many 100,000 sestertii. 4. magnis cladibus afficere. 5. omit. 6. neither oftener (*amplius*).

79. *The Laestrygonians.*

Six days and nights they drove along, and on the seventh day they put into Lamos, a port of the Laestrygonians. So spacious this harbour was that it held with ease all their fleet, which *rode*[1] at anchor, safe from any storms, all but the ship in which Ulysses was embarked. He, as if prophetic of the mischance which followed, kept still without the harbour, making fast his bark to a rock at the land's point. Making choice of two men, he sent them to the city to explore *what sort*[2] of inhabitants dwelt there. His messengers had not gone far before they met a damsel, of stature *surpassing*[3] human, who was coming *to draw water*[4] from a spring. They asked her who dwelt in that land. She made no reply, but led them in silence to her father's palace. When they entered the palace, a woman, the mother of the damsel, but far taller than she, rushed abroad and called for Antiphas. He came, and *snatching*[5] up one of the two men, *made as if he would*[6] devour him. The other fled. Antiphas raised a mighty shout, and instantly, this way and that, multitudes of gigantic people issued out at the gates, and making for the harbour, tore up huge pieces of the rocks, and flung them at the ships which lay there, all which they utterly overwhelmed and sank. Ulysses with his single bark that had never entered the harbour escaped.

1. kept itself. 2. quisnam. 3. beyond. 4. aquari. 5. make 'snatching' the object to 'devour.' 6. seemed about to.

80. *The Siege of Numantia.*

A much more serious war broke out later on. The Numantines had sheltered some of their allies who had escaped from the Romans, *and*[1] on being ordered by the proconsul Metellus to lay down their arms and surrender the suppliants, they refused *compliance*.[2] Although *no match for*[3] the Romans in numbers and resources, they offered a valiant resistance for some years. Two Roman armies were defeated with heavy loss : this disgrace was followed by a most dishonourable peace, but as the senate refused to *acknowledge*[4] it, *hostilities*[5] recommenced. At length the Numantines, being beaten in a battle by Scipio (the same who destroyed Carthage), were reduced *to such a pitch*[6] of despair as to slay each other. The city was then taken and destroyed.

1. get rid of 'and ;' think which is the most important verb : let the rest be subordinate clauses. 2. verb. 3. impar. 4. ratam habere. 5. impersonal verb. 6. eo.

81. *Brutus' Oath.*

Her father and her husband cried aloud; but Brutus drew the knife from the wound, and holding it up, spoke thus : ' By this pure blood I swear *before the gods*[1] that I will pursue L. Tarquinius the Proud and all his bloody house with fire, sword, or in whatsoever way I may, and that neither they nor any others shall hereafter be kings in Rome.' Then he gave the knife to Collatinus and Lucretius and Valerius, who marvelled much to hear such words from L. Junius the Dullard. And they took up the body of Lucretia, *and*[2] carried it into the forum, and called on the men of Collatia to rise against the tyrant. So they set a guard at the gates of the town, to prevent any news of the matter being carried to King Tarquin ; and they themselves, followed by the youth of Collatia, went to Rome. Here Brutus, who was *chief captain*[3] of the Celeres, called the people together ; and he told them what had been done, and called on them by the deed *of shame*[4] wrought by Sextus, by all that they had suffered from the tyrants, by the abominable murder of good King Servius, to assist them in taking vengeance on the Tarquins.

1. and I make ye witnesses, O gods. 2. get rid of this ' and ' by altering the previous sentence. 3. tribunus. 4. nefandus.

82. *The Dream of Atinius.*

Atinius, a plebeian, had a curious dream. *He thought that Jupiter warned*[1] him to go to the consuls and order them to repeat the great games, as they had been *improperly*[2] performed before. However he refrained from going, as he was afraid. His son was then carried off by an illness. In spite of a repetition of the warning dream, he still neglected to go. While thus delaying he was taken violently ill and *utterly prostrated*,[3] so without further loss of time *he got*[4] his friends to carry him in a litter to the consuls. They, attaching importance to his statement, celebrated the games *with increased solemnity*,[5] and the Volsci, being at that time at peace with Rome, assembled in large numbers to witness them. Seeing this, Tullius sought the consuls and informed them *in private*[6] that large numbers of his fellow-countrymen had arrived in town, and that he apprehended treachery on their part against the Romans. The consuls reported this *suspicious*[7] affair to the senate, and a decree was issued that all the Volsci should leave Rome before nightfall. The latter were highly indignant at such an insult, and went home in a state of intense exasperation and excitement.

1. Jupiter seemed to warn. 2. vitio. 3. with sudden weakness. 4. *curare* with gerundive. 5. amplior. 6. witnesses being removed. 7. *dubius*, which you must qualify by *tam*. ' This ' with adjectives requires this addition.

83. *The Mutineers' Plan.*

The leader of the mutineers also, as was afterwards ascertained, *in accordance with* [1] the desire of all his men, had determined on fighting. He had even asserted in a council held previously that the forces of the English general would be routed *before coming to a general engagement.* [2] When the majority of the council expressed their surprise at this, he remarked, ' I am aware that what I promise is scarcely credible ; but listen to the *general idea* [3] of my plan, that you may go to battle with greater confidence. I have directed our cavalry (and they have undertaken *to carry it out* [4]), on approaching the enemy, to assail the right wing of the English on their *exposed* [5] flank, and *getting in rear of* [6] their line, to rout the army while in confusion, before our people *fire a shot.* [7] Thus, without risk to our regiments, and almost without a wound, we shall finish the war. Moreover, it will not be difficult, *owing to* [8] our superiority in cavalry.'

1. by. 2. before the lines came together (*concurrere*). 3. ratio.
4. to do it. 5. apertus. 6. having surrounded.
7. cast a dart. 8. since we, etc.

84. *The Uses of Relaxation.*

Amasis, King of Egypt, is said to have transacted public business only in the morning, and to have given up the remaining portion of the day to amusements and feasting. Some of his friends ventured to blame these *habits* [1] of life, and they admonished the king *in some such words as these:* [2] ' *Your actions,* [3] most mighty prince, are surely unworthy of so splendid a situation, when you exhibit to your subjects such a spectacle as this. Kings. if they wish to be revered by their people, must show themselves always engaged in *grave cares of state,* [4] and not deal with anything more trifling *before the eyes of* [5] the common people. For thus the royal state preserves its due honour, when in all his sayings and doings the king seems wiser and better than any one else. But now on account of your sports and banquets you will be *held* [6] of less account.' The king, however, said in answer, that archers, while they are using their bows, bend them ; but when they lay them aside, relax them, lest by always straining them they should break them, or at least render them useless. And so he said that he acted thus on purpose ; for his mind, like a bow, needed rest at times, and after being stretched by serious business, had to be relaxed by amusements.

1. ratio. 2. with almost these words. 3. turn this by a verb.
4. graves et civiles curae. 5. preposition. 6. aestimare.

85. *The End of Hannibal.*

T. Quinctius Flaminius came as ambassador to *the court of*[1] King Prusias. Immediately on his arrival soldiers were sent to guard Hannibal's abode. Hannibal had always foreseen such an end to his life, for he was aware of the hatred the Romans bore him, and had no confidence in the king's *honour.*[2] He had consequently, in order to have always means of flight, prepared seven ways out of his house, and some of them secret ones, *to prevent*[3] their being beset by guards. The soldiers, however, surrounded the house so completely that no one could escape from it. Hannibal, when he was told that the king's soldiers were in the vestibule, endeavoured to escape by his most secret door, but found it also beset by soldiers. *Observing*[4] every place to be closed by the arrangement of the sentinels, he asked for the poison, which he had prepared long before *and*[5] kept for such an extremity. 'Let us free,' he remarked, 'the Roman people from their long-continued anxiety, since they think it *a tedious thing*[6] to wait for the death of an old man.'

> 1. omit. 2. fides. 3. lest. 4. avoid the use of the present participle here; it does not denote a simultaneous action. 5. you can get rid of 'and' by making 'prepared' a participle in agreement with 'which.' 6. longum.

86. *Lysander and Cyrus.*

A vigorous line of action was determined on.[1] Cyrus at once offered 500 talents, and affirmed that if more were needed he was prepared even to coin into money the very throne *of gold and silver*[2] on which he sat. In a banquet which ensued, Cyrus *drank to the health of*[3] Lysander, and desired him to name any wish which he could gratify. *Far from asking*[4] any favour for himself, Lysander immediately requested an *addition*[5] of an obolus to the daily pay of the seamen. Cyrus was *surprised at so disinterested a demand,*[6] and conceived from that day *a high degree of*[7] respect and confidence for the Spartan commander. Lysander on his return to Ephesus *employed himself in*[8] refitting his fleet, and in organizing *clubs*[9] in the Spartan interests in the cities of Asia.

> 1. it seemed good that it should be acted (gerundive) vigorously. 2. adjectival clause. 3. propinare. 4. so much was wanting (*tantum abesse*) that he should ask. 5. translate by a verb. 6. wondering that he asked nothing for himself. 7. great. 8. totus incumbere in. 9. societas.

87. *Robbing the Gods.*

A certain freebooter, Dionysius by name, entered the temple of the Olympian Jove and tore from the statue of the god a golden mantle of great weight, with which it had been attired by Gelo the despotic ruler of Syracuse. He then told one of his followers to wrap a woollen cloak round the statue, *remarking*[1] with a laugh, 'the golden mantle is too heavy in summer and too cold in winter, but the mantle with which we now present Jove is *suitable for wear*[2] at all seasons.' Not long afterwards he was sailing to Syracuse after plundering the temple of the goddess Proserpine. As they were favoured by fair weather, he *took occasion to remark*[3] to his companions, 'Don't you observe, my friends, how propitious the immortal gods are to us, whom men call sacrilegious, because, forsooth, we rob temples?' *Also*[4] when at Epidaurus he ordered his men to remove the golden beard from the statue of Aesculapius, remarking that the god did not require a beard, since his father Apollo was beardless.

> 1. make this the principal verb. 2. idoneus. 3. simplify.
> 4. he also (*idem*).

88. *The Death of Epaminondas.*

Epaminondas, the commander-in-chief of the Boeotians at Mantinea, while pressing *too boldly*[1] on the enemy *in the thick of the fight*,[2] being recognised by the Lacedaemonians, was attacked by them with all their forces, because they thought that the safety of their country *depended*[3] on his destruction alone, nor did they retire before seeing him fall, pierced with a javelin *thrown from a distance*,[4] after he had slain many of his opponents. His fall delayed the advance of the Boeotians for a while, yet they did not leave the field before routing their adversaries. But Epaminondas *perceiving*[5] that his wound was mortal, and, moreover, that if he drew the iron which remained in the wound, broken off from the shaft, he would at once die, he kept it in till he was told that the Boeotians were victorious. On hearing this he remarked, 'I have lived long enough; for I die unconquered. Then drawing out the steel he straightway breathed his last.

> 1. comparative. 2. acie instructa. 3. situs. 4. eminus.
> 5. avoid using the present participle.

89. *A generous Foe.*

After this, in the consulship of Fabricius, an unknown person came to his camp with a letter from the king's physician, who promised to kill Pyrrhus by poison, and so end the war, if they gave him a sufficiently large reward for so great a benefit. Fabricius hated the man's wickedness ; and wrote to the king without delay, to warn him concerning the plot, adding that he did this not on account of goodwill, but lest the death of Pyrrhus should bring disgrace upon the Romans, and they should seem to have made an end of the war by treachery, when they could not by valour. Pyrrhus, having read the letter, punished the physician ; and to show his *gratitude*[1] to the Romans, gave back the prisoners without ransom, and sent Cineas again to *treat*[2] concerning peace. The Romans, however, would not hear of peace till he should have laid down his arms, drawn his forces out of Italy, and returned to Epirus in the same ships in which he came. The story goes that not long afterwards Pyrrhus fell by a woman's hand while storming a city in Greece.

1. gratus animus.   2. agere.

90. *A well-deserved Escape.*

The tribune, however, summoned his men and addressed them *as follows:*[1] 'Fellow-soldiers, let us go thither whence return is impossible. Let us die, and by our death deliver our hemmed-in legions from the blockade.' Then all set out without hope of escape, but inflamed with desire for glory and eagerness to save the army. The enemy, wondering at the approach of this little band, are at first uncertain whither they desire to go ; but on seeing them direct their march *to seize*[2] the rock, the Carthaginian leader sends against them *the elite*[3] of his cavalry and infantry. The Romans, though surrounded, resist stoutly. At length, after a long and *doubtful struggle*,[4] numbers *carry the day.*[5] Meanwhile the consul, during the fight, withdraws to an elevated and safe position. The gods granted the tribune a *fate*[6] worthy of his valour. For it came to pass, that although he received repeated wounds, none were mortal. He was found among the dead, pierced with many wounds, but still breathing, and *recovered,*[7] and often afterwards *did good service*[8] to the state by his bravery.

1. his verbis.   2. occupare.   3. strenuissimi.   4. anceps proelium.
5. superare.   6. fortuna.   7. convalescere.   8. prodesse.

91. *A Specimen of Greek Physical Science.*

Herodotus ingeniously, though absurdly, inquires into the reasons why the Nile inundates Egypt in summer rather than in winter. He says that many writers have been of opinion that this is the result of the melting of the snow in Ethiopia, and the consequent increase of the volume of the river, but that they *talk nonsense,*[1] because Ethiopia is a hotter country than even Egypt, and *how could there be*[2] any snow there? Wherefore *he says*[3] that he thinks that the Nile is rather dried up in winter than swollen in summer, and that this takes place as follows. The winter storms *blow*[4] the sun away into the south, where the fountains of the Nile are. *Arrived here,*[5] he attracts to himself an immense quantity of water, so the Nile at once begins to decrease. These waters he *next*[6] pours out over the northern countries of Europe, and out of them, *after their dispersal*[7] by means of the winds, arise rains and showers, which increase all rivers in these parts (*or. recta*). Thus it is, says he, that in winter the Nile swells less than in summer; whereas all other rivers increase in winter and diminish in summer.

1. nihil afferre. 2. what is the proper mood for continuous reported questions? 3. omit: verbs of saying can often be understood from the principal verb. 4. drive by blowing. 5. whither when he has arrived. 6. continuo. 7. when dispersed.

92. *Timon and Alkibiades.*

Once when Alkibiades had made a very good speech in the assembly, and a crowd of people *attended*[1] him home *to do*[2] him honour, Timon the *misanthrope*[3] did not pass him by or avoid him as he did others, but met him, and taking him by the hand said, 'Go on, my son, and *increase in credit*[4] with the people; you will one day bring them calamities enough.' Some that were present laughed at the saying, and said that Timon would *be falsified*[5] by the event. Some reviled him and bade him *mind his own business,*[6] for that he knew nothing of such matters. Others, however, never forgot what they had heard, and remembered what a shock the words had given them when first they heard him. So various was the judgment made of him even by his *contemporaries.*[7]

1. deducere. 2. for the sake of. 3. although hating mankind. 4. macte virtute esse. 5. be convicted (*arguo*) of falsehood. 6. sua negotia agere. 7. aequalis.

F

93. *The Black Prince and his Royal Captive.*

That evening the Prince of Wales gave a supper in his *pavilion* [1]
to the King of France. The food *served* [2] had all been taken from the
French, as the English had nothing. The French king, with his
son and his principal barons, *was seated* [3] at the chief table, and was
waited upon by the Prince himself, who *showed* [4] every mark of
humility. He would not sit down at the table, though pressed to do
so, but said that he was not worthy of so great an honour ; nor did
it become him to seat himself at the table of so great a king or of
so valiant [5] a man as he had shown himself by his actions that day.
He did *his utmost* [6] to cheer the king, saying, 'Dear sir, do not *make
a poor meal* [7] because the Almighty God has not gratified your wishes
in the event of this day. *Be assured* [8] that my father will show you
every honour and friendship in his power, and will arrange your
ransom so reasonably that you henceforward always remain friends.
In my opinion, you have *cause* [9] to be glad that the success of this
battle did not turn out *as* [10] you desired ; for you have this day
acquired such high renown for prowess, that you have surpassed all
the best knights on your side. I do not say this, dear sir, to flatter
you ; for all on your side who saw the deeds of both parties agree
that this is your due, and award you the prize and garland for it.'

1. tentorium. 2. apponere. 3. discumbere. 4. used. 5. of such
tried courage. 6. as much as he could. 7. neglect food.
8. compertum habere. 9. cur. 10. perinde ac.

94. *A Change of Condition.*

It is well known that Protagoras in his earlier days *was a porter.*
One day he was carrying a bundle of firewood secured with a cord to
the city of Abdera. Democritus, *his fellow-townsman,* [2] met him and
noticed how neatly the firewood was tied up. He asked the youth
to rest a while. The other complied with his request ; and the
philosopher inquired who had arranged the firewood. 'I did,' said
Protagoras. 'Undo your bundle,' said Democritus, 'and when it is
undone, do it up again.' When Protagoras had done so, Democritus,
lost in wonder at the cleverness of an ignorant man, exclaimed,
'Follow me, my friend : there are *probably* [3] other things also which you
can do, *such is* [4] your cleverness.' Then Protagoras threw away the
firewood and accompanied the philosopher. *He obtained a thorough
insight into* [5] philosophy, and became a philosopher himself, nor was
there any one to be compared with him *as far as philosophy went.* [6]

1. carried burdens for hire. 2. adjectival clause. 3. nescio an.
4. pro. 5. having been thoroughly taught. 6. as regards
(*quod attinet ad*) philosophy.

95. *The Samnite Wars.*

Next ensued war with the Samnites, in which the gallantry of P. Decius, a military tribune, was conspicuous ; for when the Roman army was hemmed in in a defile, with a handful of soldiers he *struck terror into*[1] the foe and relieved the army from the blockade. He was subsequently consul with Manlius Torquatus in the Latin war. Once when his men *were hard pressed*[2] in the fight, Decius devoted himself and his enemies to the *infernal deities.*[3] He then charged the enemy alone, fell pierced with their darts, and gave victory to his men, as the enemy were utterly terrified. Subsequently the consul Postumius, when fighting against the Samnites, was led into an ambush by Pontius, the enemy's leader. As the Romans could not escape they were compelled *to surrender.*[4] Peace was granted *on condition*[5] that all should pass beneath the yoke. The war was afterwards brought to an end by Q. Fabius, who completely routed the enemy with heavy loss. The Romans fought splendidly on that day ; the soldiery did not *disappoint*[6] their leader, nor did the leader disappoint his men. It is well known that 20,000 of the enemy were slain.

1. terrified. 2. laborare. 3. dii manes. 4. in deditionem venire. 5. on that (*is*) condition. 6. desum.

96. *The Exploring Party.*

On went the single ship till it came to the island of Aeaea, where Circe *the*[1] dreadful daughter of the Sun dwelt. Here a dispute arose among Ulysses' men, which of them should go ashore and explore the country ; for there was a necessity that some should go to procure water and provisions, both of which were beginning to fail them : but their courage failed them when they called to mind *the shocking fate*[2] of their fellows whom the Laestrygonians had eaten, and those whom the foul Cyclops Polyphemus had crushed between his jaws, which moved them so tenderly in the recollection that they wept. But tears never yet supplied any man's wants : this Ulysses knew full well, and dividing his men (all that were left) *into two companies,*[3] at the head of one of which was himself, and at the head of the other Eurylochus, a man of tried courage, he cast lots which of them should go up into the country ; and *the lot fell*[4] upon Eurylochus and his company, two-and-twenty in number ; who took their leave, with tears, of Ulysses and his men that stayed, for they surely thought never to see these their companions again, but that on every coast where they should come they should find nothing but savages and cannibals.[5]

1. illa. 2. turn this by an indirect question. 3. bifariam. 4. it fell by lot, *obtigit sortito* (adverb). 5. anthropophagus.

97. *Two faithful Slaves.*

When the Romans besieged Grumentum in Lucania, and the city was reduced *to the last extremity*,[1] two slaves escaped into the camp of the besiegers. The place was soon afterwards taken by storm, and plundered. The two slaves then ran to the house of their mistress, whom they seized with *a kind of*[2] violence, and carried off. *When they were asked*[3] who she was, they answered she was their mistress, and a most cruel mistress; upon whom they were going *to take revenge*[4] for all the barbarous treatment they had suffered from her. In this way they compelled her to quit the city, and conveyed her *to a safe retreat*,[5] where they concealed her with great care; and when the fury of the soldiers was abated, and tranquillity was restored in the city, they brought her back to her house, and obeyed her as before. She gave them their liberty, which was the greatest reward in her power to bestow; but certainly far *short of*[6] the services they had rendered her.

1. ad incitas. 2. quidam. 3. to those asking. 4. poenam sumere.
5. in tutum. 6. citra.

98. *The Lotos-Eaters.*

After that, for the space of nine days, contrary winds continued to drive them *in an opposite direction to the point to which they were bound*,[1] and the tenth day they *put in*[2] at a shore where a race of men dwell that *are sustained*[3] by the fruit of the lotos-tree. Here Ulysses sent some of his men to land for fresh water, who were met by certain of the inhabitants, that gave them some of their country food to eat; not *that*[4] they bore any illwill towards them, though in the event it proved pernicious; for, having eaten of this fruit, so pleasant it proved to their appetite, that they *in a minute*[5] quite forgot all thoughts of home or of their countrymen, but they would needs stay and live there among them, and eat of that precious food for ever; and when Ulysses sent others of his men to look for them, and to bring them back by force, they strove, and wept, and would not *leave*[6] their food for heaven itself, so much the pleasure of that enchanting fruit had *bewitched*[7] them. But Ulysses caused them to be bound hand and foot, and cast under the *hatches*,[8] and set sail with all possible speed from that baneful coast, lest others after them might taste the lotos, which had such strange qualities to make men forget their native country, and the thoughts of home.

1. in iter a proposito diversum. 2. appellere. 3. vesci. 4. quod.
5. puncto temporis. 6. change. 7. irretire. 8. fori.

99. *Re-election of a Veteran Commander.*

The same year the townsmen were informed that their neighbours had assembled auxiliary troops from a distance and were meditating an attack. This alarm, while many distinguished officers *made application for* [1] command, *made all look* [2] to the gallant veteran, who at first did not ask for the command, and afterwards, observing their *increasing eagerness,* [3] refused it. 'Why do you,' he asked, 'trouble me, who am already old and retired from active employment? My strength both of mind and body is not *what it was.* [4] There is no want of brave men to command us. Who can imagine that I am the only one worthy of command?' This modesty merely increased the eagerness of the people; and thinking to repress it by their respect to law, he ordered the ordinance which forbade *reappointment to the command* [5] within the same ten years to be read. It could scarcely be heard in consequence of the noise : the magistrates also said that it would be no hindrance, and that they would put *the repeal of the law* [6] *to the popular vote.* [7] Still persisting in his refusal, he kept on demanding, 'What is the use of passing laws if they are violated by those who passed them? The laws are now ruled themselves instead of ruling.' The people notwithstanding *went to the vote,* [8] and the old man was unanimously named commander-in-chief. Freed from apprehension, as they were led by such a chief, they proceeded to declare war.

1. petere. 2. omnes convertere. 3. inclinata studia. 4. the same. 5. a commander to be reappointed (*refici*). 6. uti lex abrogaretur. 7. to the people. 8. suffragia inire.

100. *The Boy King.*

One of these boy *subjects,* [1] the son of a nobleman, called Artembaris, *happening to disobey* [2] some of the royal commands, Cyrus ordered him to be seized by his guards, and soundly flogged. The lad, as soon as he was set free, ran home to his father, and complained bitterly of the treatment he had *received.* [3] The father repaired to Astyages, and showing him the bruised shoulders of his son, '*Is it thus,* [4] O King!' said he, '*that* [4] we are treated by the son of thy bondsman and slave?' Astyages sent for the herdsman, and his supposed son ; and addressing the latter, sternly said, 'How darest thou, being the son of such a father as this, treat in so vile a manner the son of one of my court?' 'Sire,' answered Cyrus, *with firmness,* [5] 'I have done nothing unto him but what was fit. The country lads (of whom he was one) chose me for their king in *play,* [6] because I seemed the most worthy of that dignity; but when all the rest obeyed my commands, this boy alone regarded not what I said. For this was he punished; and if on this account I have merited to suffer any punishment, I am here ready to suffer it.'

1. express this by an adjectival clause. 2. when he had by chance disobeyed. 3. because he had been so insultingly (*contume-liose*) injured. 4. siccine. 5. constanter. 6. use the present participle.

101. *Ulysses and the Shade of Achilles.*

While they held this sad conference, the *soul*[1] of great Achilles joined them. 'What desperate adventure has brought Ulysses to these regions,' said Achilles, 'to see the end of dead men and their foolish shades?' Ulysses answered him that he had come to consult Tiresias respecting his voyage home. 'But thou, O son of Thetis,' said he, 'why dost thou *disparage*[2] the state of the dead? *seeing that as,*[3] when alive, thou didst surpass all men in glory, thou must needs retain thy pre-eminence here below; so great Achilles triumphs over death.' But Achilles made reply that he had much rather be a peasant-slave upon the earth than reign over all the dead. So much did the inactivity and slothful condition of that state displease *his restless spirit.*[4] Only he inquired of Ulysses if his father Peleus were living, and how his son Neoptolemus conducted himself. Of Peleus Ulysses could tell him nothing; but of Neoptolemus he thus bore witness (*or. obl.*): 'From Scyros I convoyed your son by sea to the Greeks, where I can speak of him, for I knew him. He was chief in council and in the field. Only myself and aged Nestor could *compare*[5] with him in giving advice. In battle I cannot speak his praise, unless I could count all that fell by his sword.'

1. anima. 2. vitio vertere. 3. for as. 4. of such (*qui*) restless spirit was he. 5. be compared.

102. *Wouvermans.*

This poor painter was *a great master*[1] of his art, and specially excelled in painting horses. Finding that people did not know how great were his merits, and being very much *involved*[2] in debt, he was compelled to sell what he painted for very low prices. One day he was talking about his misery to a friend who was one of the few who had *recognised*[3] his genius. His friend determined to assist him, and *lent*[4] him some money, advising him at the same time to demand larger prices. Soon matters turned out well for him. Everybody so much *admired the artist*[5] who painted such expensive pictures that he soon became rich, and after paying his debts was able to reward his kind friend. This is one of many stories which illustrate the saying, that the more you value yourself, the more you will be valued by others.

1. peritus. 2. obstrictus. 3. agnoscere. 4. commodare.
5. admiration of the artist moved everybody.

103. *Speech is Silver, but Silence is Gold.*

A certain lawyer once lived at Marseilles. Such was his eloquence that he *got the credit of being able*[1] to persuade the judges as he wished. It happened that a highwayman, a most worthless fellow, was *on the point of*[2] being charged *with*[3] killing a traveller and appropriating his money. As it was well known that the lawyer I have mentioned had received a *retainer*[4] to speak against the robber, the friends of the latter promised to give him a large sum of money on condition that he should refrain from speaking when the accusation was brought against the criminal. *The end of it was*[5] he held his tongue. He was not, however, able to conceal the fact, for on asking another lawyer what his fee had been, and on getting his answer, he replied, ' *Why*,[6] I got more for holding my tongue!'

1. was considered to be able. 2. in eo ut. 3. *quod;* introducing virtually suboblique clause. 4. money. 5. Quid quaeris? (lit. ' what do you want to know?') 6. at.

104. *Augustus.*

After the murder of C. Julius Caesar by the conspirators civil war raged for a considerable time. At length Octavianus, who subsequently received the *title*[1] of Augustus, became the sole ruler of the state. Warned, however, by the example of Caesar he refused to be king. Being, however, made commander-in-chief, he was at the head of the army and thus enjoyed *unlimited*[2] power. Next, *on receiving the appointments*[3] of censor and chief of the senate, he *was the dispenser of*[4] civil law. When the office of tribune was conferred on him he proved most acceptable to the *lower orders.*[5] Not long after he was elected consul and *wielded*[6] true consular power within the city. *To cut my story short*,[7] he discharged in person all the various magistracies, and thus became king *all but in name.*[8]

1. agnomen. 2. infinitus. 3. being made. 4. administered. 5. plebs.
6. used. 7. not (*ne*) to say more. 8. tantum non.

105. *The Close of the Carlist War.*

When news was brought to Madrid that the rebellion was crushed, although by choosing Martinez Campos, the ablest of all the generals, as their leader, they had done everything that human wisdom could suggest, yet as the struggle had been so long and doubtful, and so many reverses had been sustained, their joy being, *as it were*,[1] unforeseen, was without bounds, and before the authorities had given any orders, the churches were filled with the Spanish ladies giving thanks to heaven. Four days were set apart for *national thanksgiving*,[2] a greater number than had ever been decreed in any other war. The arrival of General Campos, as people of all ranks thronged to meet him, was more *generally attended*[3] than that of any previous commander; and his triumphant entry considerably exceeded any customary manner of doing honour to *such*[4] an occasion. Satisfaction was general *at the prospect of Spain*[5] at length *obtaining rest*[6] *after the fatigues*[7] of so protracted a war.

1. velut.   2. supplicatio.   3. celebratus.   4. ille.   5. because it seemed, etc.   6. *acquiescere;* these verbs having no supine stem, how will you contrive to make a future infinitive?   7. wearied.

106. *Caesar at Munda.*

After all these things were ended, he was chosen consul *the fourth time*,[1] and went into Spain to make war with the sons of Pompey, who were yet but very young, but had notwithstanding *raised*[2] a great army, and showed *that they had manhood and courage worthy to command it*,[3] insomuch as they *put*[4] Caesar himself in great danger of his life. *The greatest battle that was fought*[5] between them in all this war was by the city of Munda. For then Caesar, seeing his men sorely distressed, ran into the press among his men that fought and cried out unto them, 'What, are ye not ashamed to be beaten and taken prisoners, yielding yourselves *with your own hands*[6] to these young boys?' And so with all the force that he could *make*,[7] having *with much ado*[8] put his enemies to flight, he slew above thirty thousand of them in the field, and lost of his own men a thousand of *the best*[9] he had. After the battle he told his friends that he had often before fought for victory, but that this last time now he had fought for the safety of his own life. This was the last war that Caesar made. But the triumph he *made*[10] for the same did more offend the Romans than anything that ever he had done before; because he had not overcome captains that were strangers, but had destroyed the sons of the noblest man of Rome whom fortune had overthrown.

1. quartum.   2. conscribere.   3. that they were worthy to (*qui*) command it on account of their manly courage.   4. adducere.   5. impersonal.   6. ultro.   7. omit.   8. scarcely.   9. put the superlative in the adjectival clause.   10. agere.

107. *Dean Swift and his Servant.*

One day Swift, wishing to go out, asked for his boots. The servant brought them. '*Hallo! why*[1] are they not cleaned?' asked the Dean. ' Why, *sir*,[2] as you are going *to dirty*[3] them at once, I did not think it *worth while*[4] to clean them,' replied the man. When Swift was *just*[5] going out, the servant came and asked him for the key of the *larder*.[6] 'What for?' asked Swift. ' To get my breakfast, sir,' was the answer. ' Why, you will be hungry again in a couple of hours,' said his master, 'and it is not worth while to eat just now.' This was a smart answer enough. So was the following. When a friend who had given orders not to admit him came to return his visit, Swift called out, ' I am not at home.' ' Not at home!' exclaimed the other. ' You are an impudent fellow,' was the rejoinder ; ' don't you believe what I say? Why, I believed your servant when she said you were out!'

1. why, pray (*tandem*). 2. dominus. 3. caeno oblinere. 4. operae pretium, *or simply*, operae. 5. in eo esset ut. 6. cella.

108. *The Battle of Naseby.*

The boiling and ungovernable ardour of Prince Rupert persuaded an engagement. The main body of the Royalists was commanded by the king himself, who *displayed*[1] all the conduct of a prudent general and all the valour of a stout soldier. The battle was chiefly lost through a mistake of Prince Rupert, who, having routed the enemy's left wing, was so inconsiderate as to lose time in attacking the *artillery*[2] of the enemy, which had been left with a good guard of infantry. Meanwhile the Royalists were hard pressed by the valour and conduct of Fairfax and Cromwell, and when Rupert rejoined the king he found the infantry totally discomfited. Charles exhorted the cavalry not to despair, and cried aloud to them, ' One charge more, and we recover the day.' But the disadvantages under which they laboured *were too evident, and*[3] they could by no means be induced to renew the combat. Charles was obliged to quit the field and leave the victory to the enemy. All the king's artillery and munitions of war fell into their hands, and his infantry, after suffering heavily, was totally dispersed, so that scarcely any victory could be more complete. Among the other spoils were seized the king's private effects, and his letters to the queen, which the Parliament afterwards caused to be published and distributed.

1. praestare. 2. tormenta. 3. adeo non fallere ut.

109. *Faithful in Death.*

A *Duke of Savoy*,[1] who *made some pretensions to*[2] the city of Geneva, sought to gain it by surprise : he scaled the walls in the night ; but the *enterprise*[3] was not as prosperous as he wished. When it was known that a great number of the besiegers had mounted the walls, the citizens ran to arms, and repulsed their enemies, who were too weak to resist them. Those who fell into their hands *were led to*[4] an ignominious death. Among the prisoners was an officer who had particularly distinguished himself for his valour. The news of his misfortune being carried to his wife, she flew to the place where her husband was to perish, and demanded to embrace him for the last time. They refused her this favour ; and the officer was hung *without her being permitted*[5] to approach him. She nevertheless followed the body of her husband to the place where it was exposed, and remained without taking any nourishment till death, which she waited for with impatience, came *at last*,[6] and closed her eyes *while she was stretched*[7] over the dead body of her husband.

1. Dux Sabaudiae. 2. affectare. 3. res. 4. were visited with (*afficere*). 5. neither was she permitted. 6. sero demum. 7. (of her) stretched.

110. *Mardonius burns Athens.*

The Athenians, abandoned by Sparta, on whose *faithful alliance*[1] they had relied, were now compelled a second time to flee from their native land. Scarcely had the fugitives reached the island of Salamis, when the Persians marched into Attica. Mardonius once more offered the Athenians peace on *the*[2] terms before brought by Alexander ; but when this high-spirited people, now bereft of all assistance, again rejected the proposal, *the remaining*[3] edifices, temples, and *country-seats*[4] were laid waste, *and the few houses at Athens, which after the last destruction had been rebuilt*,[5] were demolished and burned : the Athenians saw from the island of Salamis *the effects of*[6] this childish revenge. They sent a new embassy to Sparta, with the threat, that as, without the help of the confederates, they were too weak for resistance, they *were disposed*[7] to make peace with the Persians. They might then show the Peloponnesians that their entrenchments on the isthmus would be but an indifferent protection, *when*[8] the landing of the Persians on the unguarded coasts of the Peloponnesus should be supported by the fleet of Athens.

1. fides. 2. those (*is*). 3. adjectival clause. 4. villa. 5. and the houses, if any had been rebuilt. 6. turn by an indirect question. 7. in animo habere. 8. if.

III. *A wily Impostor.*

The *following*[1] story, which is related about Louis XI., King of France, shows how great is the force of superstition. This king used to employ a certain Galeottus, as physician and *astrologer*,[2] to foretell future events; to whom within five months he is said to have given such large sums of money that his purse was quite *exhausted*.[3] And yet this astrologer *used*[4] his master very *roughly:*[4] few would have *given*[5] to their servants such *outrageous language*[5] as this impostor *gave*[5] the king. But Louis did not dare to forbid him his presence or to dismiss him, as he had done many of his *ministers*.[6] For one day, when in his anger he threatened him with punishment, the wily man replied : ‘ I know well that some time or other you will expel me from court, or even put me to death, as you have done to other courtiers. But take this warning, that you will not live eight days after you have dismissed or slain me.’ These words prevented the king from carrying out his purpose ; nay, they so terrified him, that ever after he did nothing but flatter and bribe Galeottus, *which was doubtless a mortification to a prince*[7] whom throughout all his life so many brave and good men had obeyed.

1. huiusmodi.   2. mathematicus.   3. deficere.   4. contumelia afficere.
    5. convicia ingerere.   6. qui a consiliis erant.   7. which
        doubtless a prince bore ill (*aegre*).

II2. *Angles or Angels.*

It happened that Gregory, who under the title of the Great afterwards occupied the papal chair, had observed in the market-place of Rome three Saxon youths *exposed for sale*,[1] whom the Roman merchants *in their trading voyages*[2] to Britain had bought of their *mercenary*[3] parents. Struck with the beauty of their fair complexions and blooming countenances, Gregory asked to what country they belonged; and being told they were Angles, he replied that they ought more properly to be denominated Angels. Inquiring further concerning the name of their province, he was informed that it was Deira, a district of Northumbria. ‘ Deira,’ replied he, ‘ that is good. *They are called*[4] to *the mercy of God*[5] from His anger. But what is the name of the king of that province?’ He was told that it was Aella. ‘ Alleluia,’ cried he, ‘ we must endeavour that the praises of God be sung in their country.’

1. venumdare.   2. while they go for the purpose of trading.   3. for
    gain; make ‘ parents ’ the subject, and change the verb.
      4. make the verb active.   5. God, pitying them.

While Caesar was thus engaged, he was anxious to know what was being done elsewhere. A message was brought to him from Titurius, whom he had left to command the troops at the bridge : ' The Belgians have changed their plan, and have come down to the river. I fear they will cross it at a *ford*[1] and thus attack us in the rear.' Caesar immediately despatched his horse and light troops to prevent their carrying out this design. These *squadrons*,[2] crossing the river by the bridge, reached the ford before the Belgians had passed it, and attacked them with their missiles while they were still *struggling*[3] in the middle of the stream. Part of them who had already gained the opposite side *were surrounded and cut in pieces by the cavalry*.[4] The Belgians were forced to retreat to their former encampment, where they heard that Divitiacus had collected the Aeduan forces and had entered their confines and was now wasting their homes with sword and fire. They therefore determined to abandon their *attempt*[5] and to return each to defend his own land.

1. vadum. 2. turma. 3. impeditus. 4. the cavalry cut in pieces while surrounded. 5. inceptum.

114. *Pontius encourages the Samnites to fight.*

In the year 433 B.C. C. Pontius was generalissimo of the Samnites. He, when the envoys, who had been sent *to make restitution*,[1] returned *without obtaining*[2] peace, said before the assembly that any anger the gods might have felt towards them for the breach of the treaty had been atoned for. What more could have been done to appease the gods and soften man's wrath than what they had themselves done ? The enemies' property which had been taken as booty, and which seemed to be their own according to the laws of war, had been restored ; the originators of the war had been surrendered ; and their goods, to prevent any guilt remaining among them *by contact with them*,[3] had been carried to Rome. Was anything else owing to the Romans, to the treaty, or to the gods, the arbiters of treaties ? *If he in his weakness had no appeal to*[4] human laws *in his contest*[5] with the stronger, he appealed to the gods, who avenge haughtiness when unbearable, and implored them to *make*[5] the anger of those who remained unsatisfied after the restitution of their property and the addition of that of others *recoil on their own heads*.[6] Those who could not avoid war were justified in having recourse to war, and arms were lawful to those whose only hope was in arms. Their previous wars

had been waged against the gods rather than men ; *the impending
one*[7] would be waged under the leadership of the gods themselves.

  1. res dedere.   2. express this by the abl. abs.   3. ex contagione.
  4. if nothing was left to him in his weakness (adjective).   5. omit.
  6. turn (*vertere*) on them.   7. adjectival clause.

115. *King Agrippa.*

Agrippa, having been condemned by the Emperor Tiberius *on the
charge of*[1] having spoken insolently of him, was placed in chains
before the palace gate. Oppressed with the *terrific*[2] heat of the sun,
he felt that he should die of thirst unless he could get some water.
Seeing Thaumastus a slave pass by with a pitcher of water, he
entreated him to give him leave to drink. The slave kindly gave
him the pitcher ; and having allayed his thirst, 'Be sure,' he said,
'Thaumastus, that one day I shall be released from chains, and I
shall not forget thy benevolence.' When Tiberius died, Agrippa was
not only set free from prison by Caligula, but also soon after was
chosen *to occupy the throne of*[3] Judea. Having obtained this honour,
he was not so base[4] as to forget Thaumastus ; *but he sent*[5] for him and
told him that he would now pay the price for the water which he
had drunk when a captive. So he appointed him *steward*[6] of the
royal house.

  1. *quod;* virtually sublique; *i.e.* not 'because he had spoken,' but
'because (they said) he had spoken.'   2. nimius.   3. to (*qui*) be
put over.   4. tantum abfuit ut turpiter.   5. also depending on
tantum abfuit ut, repeating *ut.*   6. villicus.

116. *The Death of Demosthenes.*

Demosthenes contrived at least to escape the insults of the tyrannical conqueror. Archias at first endeavoured to entice him from his
sanctuary by the blandest promises. But Demosthenes, forewarned,
it is said, by a dream, fixing his eyes intently on him, exclaimed,
'*Your acting*,[1] Archias, never touched me formerly, nor do your
promises now.' And when Archias began to employ threats, 'Good,'
said Demosthenes, 'now you speak as from the Macedonian tripod ;
before you were only playing a part. But wait a while, and let me
write my last directions to my family.' So taking his writing materials, he put the reed into his mouth, and bit it for some time, as was
his custom *when composing:*[2] after which he covered his head with
his garment and reclined against a pillar. The soldiers, imagining
this to be a mere trick, began to laugh, but Demosthenes suddenly
fell dead. The reed had been poisoned.

  1. when you were acting (*partes agere*).   2. *inter* with gerund.

117. *A wise Dog.*

At Verona a rascal of a servant, who afterwards stole my jewels, got a friend of his to inveigle my dog away, with *a companion* [1] of course, and having locked him up, persuaded me to offer a reward *instead of leaving* [2] the affair in the hands of the *police*, [3] as they advised me to do. *Of course* [4] almost before the *bills* [5] *were issued* [6] the dog was brought back by my servant's friend. I gave the *poor fellow* [7] a good scolding for leaving his loving mistress. He seemed much hurt by what I said and barked loudly as if *to protest.* [8] The next day on my ordering the servant, whom I did not suspect, to take him out for a walk, he refused to go, and got under a chair growling angrily. On my desiring the servant to fetch a chain, as he was endeavouring to fasten it in his collar, the dog suddenly bit the man's thumb till the blood ran down : he had never attempted anything of that kind before, as he liked him.

1. amica.   2. and not to learn.   3. quaesitor urbanus.   4. ut fit.
5. libellus.   6. dispergere.   7. misellus.   8. crimen defendere.

118. *The Bishop and the Rustic.*

The other day a bishop was desirous to reach London as soon as he could, and starting by himself, left orders that his carriage should follow and pick him up. By some mishap the coachman drove by the wrong road, and the bishop soon was aware that unless he could find some other horse to take him home again he would be seriously inconvenienced. *Under these circumstances* [1] he addressed himself to a rustic whom he found halting at an inn by the wayside, and begged him to take him into his cart and help him on his journey. The man granted his request, but said that he must first go and drink something before starting. He goes in, returns, and says that he will no longer do what he has promised. 'What?' says the bishop, 'why will you not *stand by* [2] your agreement?' 'I would,' says he, 'and willingly ; but my wife in there says you may be one of those *inspector chaps* [3] who go about and try to cheat people of their money.' The bishop offered to pay the tax, but the more eager he was the less willing was the man to take him, lest he might find out *to his cost* [4] that he had driven himself and *his captor* [5] to the nearest gaol.

1. since these things (*quae*) had themselves then.   2. praestare.
3. aediliculus.   4. impenso suo.   5. adjectival clause.

119. *The Fall of the Roman Republic.*

Octavianus did not return to Rome till the 29th year before the birth of Christ, when he *celebrated*[1] a threefold triumph *over*[2] the Pannonians, the Dalmatians, and the Egyptians. The doors of the temple of Janus were closed for the third time. The exhausted provinces of the empire were all for repose, and acquiesced in the sole exercise of authority by Octavianus, who after receiving many gifts and honours, had the title of Emperor *conferred*[3] on him by the senate for life. Thus perished the republic, which had been *tending*[4] nearly a century to this end. As men went *from bad*[5] to worse the dissoluteness of their lives made the further existence of the republic impossible. Nor did the citizens fully comprehend *the significance*[6] of the change, as the sovereign power had *arbitrarily*[7] been intrusted to one or more persons at different times in consequence of various conspiracies.

    1. agere.   2. de.   3. change the subject, so as to make this verb active.   4. vergere.   5. omit.   6. turn by an indirect question.   7. ex arbitrio.

120. *The Oxen of the Sun.*

So great was his terror lest, through his own fault or that of his men, any violence should be offered to the holy oxen, that even then, tired as they were with the perils and fatigues of the day past, and though night was fast coming on, he compelled them to re-embark immediately, and make *the best of their way*[1] from that dangerous station ; but his men *with one voice*[2] *opposed*[3] it ; so much did the temptation of a little ease and refreshment prevail over the sagest counsels. They expostulated, that the nerves of Ulysses seemed *to be made*[4] of steel, and his limbs not liable to lassitude like other men's ; that *waking or sleeping*[5] seemed *indifferent*[6] to him ; but that they were men, not gods, and felt the common desire for food and sleep. That in the night-time all the winds most destructive to ships are generated. That the best sacrifice to the sea was in the morning. With such *sailor-like*[7] arguments, which the majority have always ready *to justify disobedience*[8] to their betters, they forced Ulysses to yield to their demand, and against his will to take up his night-quarters on shore. But he first *exacted from them*[9] an oath that they would neither maim nor kill any of the cattle which they saw grazing, but would be content with such food as Circe had stowed their vessel with when they parted from Aeea.

    1. as quickly as possible (*quam celerrime*).   2. all.   3. adversari.   4. constare.   5. whether he was awake or asleep.   6. parum interesse.   7. nautarum in modum.   8. to excuse themselves when they disobey.   9. bound (*adigere*).

121. *How Caesar won the Confidence of his Men.*

In forming his estimate of a soldier Caesar was guided neither by character nor rank, but merely by prowess;[1] *his treatment*[2] *of his men was alike strict and indulgent.*[3] He was strict, not everywhere and always, but only when in presence of the enemy; then he was so vigorous an *enforcer*[4] of discipline as neither to announce the times of march or battle, but kept his men ready and *on the watch for*[5] every movement, and led them whithersoever he chose; a thing which he often did for no reason, especially in bad weather and on feast days. He was so fond of them too that once, on hearing of a reverse experienced by his men, he *allowed*[6] his hair and beard *to grow,*[7] and did not cut them till he had avenged it. Thus he made them both deeply attached to himself and wonderfully resolute.

1. Caesar neither judged a soldier by character nor rank, but merely by prowess. 2. he treated. 3. with like (*par*) severity and indulgence. 4. exactor. 5. intentus. 6. submittere.

122. *The Franco-German War.*

In 1870 the Spaniards, who had deposed their queen, Isabel II., made choice of a relation of the King of Prussia as their king. There had long been bitter *jealousy*[1] between *France*[2] and Prussia, and, though the prince refused the offer of Spain, the French showed such an overbearing spirit that a war broke out. The real desire of France was to obtain the much-coveted frontier of the Rhine, and the emperor heated their armies with boastful proclamations which were but the prelude to direful defeats. At Sedan the emperor was forced to surrender himself as a prisoner, and the tidings no sooner arrived at Paris than the whole of the people turned their wrath on him and his family. His wife, the Empress Eugenie, had to flee, a republic was declared, and the city prepared to *stand*[3] a siege. The Germans advanced, and put down all resistance in other parts of France. Great part of the army had been made prisoners, and there was little steadiness left among those who now took up arms. Paris, which was blockaded, after suffering much from famine, surrendered in February 1871; and peace was purchased in a treaty, by which great part of Alsace and Lorraine, and the city of Metz, were given back to Germany.

1. simultas. 2. the French. 3. tolerare.

123. *Earl Tostig and the Pope.*

So he and Earl Tostig turned about to go home again. But when they had got a little way from Rome, they were attacked by robbers, who stripped them of all that they had. So they went again to the Pope, and Earl Tostig spoke out like a stout Englishman. 'He wondered,' he said, ' that [1] the Pope should be so fierce to people who came from a long way off, when nobody *minded at all* [2] about him close under the walls of Rome. Here they all were robbed of everything they had, and he was not at all sure *that* [3] the Pope might not *have had something to do with* [4] the robbery. If the Pope did not cause everything that had been taken away *to be made good* [5] to them, as soon as he got back to England, he, Earl Tostig, would tell the king and the whole English people how they had been treated, and he would take care that not a penny of English money was paid to the Pope *any more.*' [6]

1. why.   2. ne parvi quidem facere.   3. whether (*an*).   4. conscius esse.   5. praestare salvus.   6. in posterum.

124. *Defeat of the French Fleet.*

The French, relying on the superior sailing qualities of their ships and the skill of their officers, continued to avoid our men and would not await their onset, and as long as they *could avoid coming to close quarters,* [1] extended their line and tried to *outflank* [2] ours, if possible, or to attack one of our vessels at a time with two of their own. Our captains, whose men were less trained and whose pilots were less skilled, as they had been suddenly *pressed* [3] from merchant vessels, and did not even know the names of the ropes, were also greatly hindered by the slow rate of sailing and clumsiness of their ships. So, provided only they had a chance of fighting hand to hand, they boldly exposed their vessels one by one to a couple of the enemy, and *grappling* [4] with them, and so holding both of them, they fought *on both sides* [5] and boarded their opponents, and killing a large number of their crews, sunk part of them, took several, crew and all, and drove the rest into port.

1. use an open space.   2. circumvenire.   3. productus.   4. manum ferream inicere.   5. diversus.

125. *Theseus and the Minotaur.*

About this time Minos was king in Crete. His son Androgeos was slain *by Aegeus,* [1] the King of the Athenians. So Minos waged war on the Athenians, who at the same time were *suffering* [2] from a famine. When they consulted the oracle they were told that they would have no end to their trouble before they made satisfaction *at Minos' discretion* [3] for the death of his son. Minos ordered them to send *seven youths at a time* [4] yearly, with the same number of maidens, to be de-

G

voured by the Minotaur, a beast partly *resembling* [5] a bull and partly
a human being, which lived in a labyrinth. Theseus set out with
the chosen youths, and by the help of Ariadne, the king's daughter,
who had fallen in love with him,[6] slew the Minotaur and escaped from
the labyrinth unhurt. So the Athenians were freed from the tribute.

> 1. make this the subject. 2. laborare. 3. ex Minois arbitrio.
> 4. what numeral must you use? 5. in appearance.
> 6. who had been seized with love for him.

126. *Fidelity not to be bought.*

In admirable terms [1] does Philip in one of his letters blame his son
Alexander *for trying to win* [2] the goodwill of the Macedonians by
profuseness. 'What induced you,' said he, ' to suppose that men
you had bribed would remain faithful to you? *Is it really your purpose to get* [3] the Macedonians to hope you will be, not their king, but
a mere abettor and purveyor [4] of money?' Well *does he use the words* [5]
'abettor' and 'purveyor' as being *unfit* [6] for a king; still better does he
term profuseness bribery. For he who receives bribes becomes more
worthless, and more and more ready to expect them. This was his
advice to his son, but let us consider it addressed to us all.

> 1. praeclare. 2. virtually suboblique, *i.e.* because he said that
> he tried to win. 3. an tu id agis ut. 4. minister et
> praebitor. 5. omit. 6. sordidus.

127. *Scipio.*

Publius Cornelius Scipio had by a deed of singular daring saved
the life of his father when wounded in a battle against Hannibal.
This *dutiful conduct* [1] won [2] him the goodwill of the people when a
candidate for the aedileship on a subsequent occasion. At this time
he showed signs of a haughtiness and *indifference* [3] which distinguished
his whole life. When he was opposed by the tribunes of the people
as being younger than was legally admissible,[4] he haughtily replied, ' If
it is the universal wish to make me aedile, I am old enough.' After
the death of Scipio's father and uncle, C. Nero was sent *to take* [5] their
place *with the rank* [6] of propraetor. Shortly afterwards the senate
resolved to reinforce the army in Spain and send a proconsul. When
the assembly was convened *for the election* [7] of a proconsul *not a single
one* [8] of the more experienced leaders dared to undertake so perilous a
command. Scipio at length, who was only twenty-four at the time,
declared his intention of *offering himself as a candidate*,[9] and was
unanimously chosen as proconsul of Spain.

> 1. pietas. 2. conciliare. 3. incuria. 4. since he was of a younger
> age than was allowed by law. 5. in. 6. omit. 7. gerundive.
> 8. express the emphasis by the place in the sentence where you
> put *nemo*. 9. petere.

128. *Before the Battle of Cannae.*

At daybreak on the next morning, the red ensign, which was the well-known signal for battle, was seen *flying*[1] over Varro's head-quarters; and he issued orders, it being his day of command, for the main army to cross the river, and form in order of battle on the right bank. Hannibal, it seems, thought that the ground on either bank suited him equally; and he too forded the stream at two separate points, and drew out his army opposite to the enemy. The strong town of Canusium was scarcely three miles off in his rear; he had left his camp *on the other side of*[2] the river; if he were defeated, escape seemed hopeless. But when he saw the wide open plain around him, and looked at his numerous and *irresistible*[3] cavalry, and knew that his infantry, *however*[4] inferior in numbers, were far better and older soldiers than the great mass of their opponents, he felt that defeat was impossible.

1. propositus. 2. citra. 3. adjectival clause. 4. ut—ita.

129. *Caesar's Reasons for crossing the Rhine.*

When the war with the Germans was over, Caesar decided for many reasons that he must cross the Rhine. The *weightiest*[1] reason was that he saw that the Germans were so easily induced to come into Gaul, and so wished that they should be afraid for their own safety, seeing that an army of the Roman people was able and ready to pass the Rhine. *There was the further reason*[2] that the cavalry division of the Usipetes, which, as I said in a previous chapter, had crossed the Meuse to plunder and to forage, had, when their friends had fled, withdrawn beyond the Rhine to the territory of the Sugam-bri and joined them. When Caesar sent envoys to them to require them to surrender the men who had attacked him and invaded Gaul, they replied that the Rhine was the boundary of the Roman rule; if he did not think it *fair*[3] that they should cross into Gaul *without his consent,*[4] why should he claim that anything beyond the Rhine should *belong*[5] to his rule or *jurisdiction?*[6]

1. iustus. 2. there was also added (*accedere*, impersonal). 3. aequus.
4. he being unwilling. 5. be of. 6. potestas.

130. *Customs of the Egyptians.*

The Egyptians differ much from other men. They *smear them-selves*[1] with mud when they mourn for their dead, nor do they think it right to burn or bury them, but *embalm*[2] them and place them in *catacombs.*[3] They *knead*[4] mud with their hands and dough with their feet. The women *see to*[5] *public affairs*[6] and business, the men to needlework and the household; the former carry burdens on their shoulders, the latter on their heads. When their parents are in want, the former are obliged to maintain them, while it is *optional*[7] for the latter. They worship the images of many animals, and the animals themselves still more; but *different*[8] peoples worship *different*[8] animals. To such an extent is this carried that it is a capital offence to kill some creatures even by accident, and in case of their death by disease or mishap, it is *usual*[9] to bury and lament them. Apis is worshipped by all, a black ox, marked with certain spots, and differing in its tail and tongue from other oxen. It is rarely born, and the day *of its birth*[10] is a day of *high*[11] festival for the people.

1. smeared: not principal verb. 2. medicare. 3. penetrale. 4. subigere. 5. curare. 6. forum. 7. liber. 8. others—others. 9. sollemnis. 10. adjectival clause. 11. maxime.

131. *Aristides.*

Aristides, when leaving Athens, raised his hands to heaven and besought the gods that the Athenians might never *have occasion*[1] to remember him. Three years later, when Xerxes was marching on Attica by forced marches through Thessaly and Boeotia, the Athenians annulled this decree, and by public proclamation recalled all exiles; in this they were principally influenced by apprehension concerning Aristides, fearing, namely, that if he joined the foe he would bribe and win over to the side of the foreigners many of the citizens. They certainly little knew the man, since he before his recall from exile had roused the Greeks by his appeals to defend their liberty; and also, after Themistocles had been intrusted with the chief command, assisted him both by deeds and advice, and *on public grounds*[2] thought it no scorn to raise to the highest pinnacle of glory a man who was in private his most bitter enemy.

1. be compelled. 2. for the sake of the republic.

132. *An Incident of the Indian Mutiny.*

Havelock approved of his advice, and though he was *disappointed*[1] in his *expectation*[2] of reinforcements, feeling that the one *resource*[3] for the general safety consisted in rapid action, set out by *forced*[4] marches to relieve the beleaguered garrison. On the march he was informed by deserters of what was going on in Lucknow, and of *the critical state of affairs.*[5] Thereupon he *induced*[6] a private of *a native cavalry regiment*[7] by great rewards to carry a letter to Sir Robert Inglis. He sent the letter written in Greek characters in order that, if it was intercepted, our plans might not become known to the enemy. If he was unable to get up to the fortifications he advised him to throw a stick with the letter tied to it inside the *lines.*[8] In this letter he wrote that he had set out with his troops and would speedily be there, and encouraged them to keep up their *old*[9] resolution. The native being frightened threw the stick *according to his instructions.*[10] It *unfortunately*[11] stuck in a wall, and was unnoticed by our men for two days, but on the third day it caught the eye of one of the soldiers, and was pulled out and taken to the general.

    1. deicere. 2. opinio. 3. auxilium. 4. great. 5. in what danger things were. 6. persuaded. 7. Indica turma. 8. munitio. 9. pristinus. 10. as it had been ordered. 11. casu.

133. *Death of Philip of Macedon.*

On the day *after the nuptials of his daughter,*[1] King Philip was leading a procession, clothed in white robes and crowned with a chaplet. His body-guard followed him *at some distance,*[2] in order that the person of the sovereign might be seen by all his subjects. While they were thus proceeding through the city, a youth suddenly rushed out of the crowd, and drawing a long sword which he had concealed under his clothes, plunged it in Philip's side, who fell dead upon the spot. The assassin was pursued by some of the royal guard, and having stumbled in his flight was despatched before he could reach the place where horses had been provided for his escape. Thus fell Philip, in the twenty-fourth year of his reign and forty-seventh of his age. When we consider *his achievements,*[3] and how, partly by *policy,*[4] partly by arms, he raised his country to be mistress of Greece, we must acknowledge him to have been an extraordinary man. *In ambitious designs*[5] he equalled his son Alexander, but he was prevented by a premature death from carrying them out; nor would Alexander himself have been able to perform his great achievements had not his father handed down to him the necessary means and instruments for their completion.

    1. after his daughter (had been) married. 2. longius. 3. what he achieved. 4. consilio. 5. in the boldness of his designs.

134. *Harsh Treatment of Debtors at Rome.*

The plebeians began to *mutter*[1] that though fighting abroad in defence of liberty and the empire, they were while at home captured and oppressed[2] by the citizens, and that the liberty of the people was more *assured*[2] in war than in peace, and among the enemy than among their fellow-citizens; and this *ill-feeling growing apace*[3] of itself was set in a flame by the unutterable woe of a single individual. An old man rushed into the forum with all the signs of his misery *about him*:[4] his clothes were filthy, his body was paler and leaner than that of a dead man, and his long beard and hair *gave an additional look of wildness*[5] to his face. In spite of his *piteous guise,*[6] men began to recognise him and say that he had been an officer, and while commiserating him to mention publicly other particulars of honourable services of his in war. In reply to their questions as to the cause of his wretched state, he said that while serving during the war with the Sabines, in consequence of the hostile incursions, he had not only lost his crops, but also had his house burned, all his goods carried off, and his cattle driven away; taxation had been decreed in his *season of difficulty,*[7] and he had *got into debt;*[8] that the debt *swelled*[9] by interest had stripped him first of his ancestral landed property, then of his other resources, and at last like a plague had reached his person; that his creditor had dragged him off, not into slavery, but to a *prison and place of torture.*[10] Then he proceeded to show his back scarred with recent marks of the lash.

1. fremere.   2. .safe.   3. gliscere.   4. omit.   5. ad hoc efferare.
6. tanta deformitas.   7. iniquum tempus.   8. aes alienum facere.   9. cumulare.   10. ergastulum et carnificina.

135. *Caesar's Refusal of the Crown.*

Antonius, who was one of the Luperci, abandoning the ancient *regulations*[1] for that *procession,*[2] ran to Caesar's tribunal carrying in his right hand a laurel wreath intertwined with the diadem, of old the sign and token of kingly power. When he got there he ordered his companions in the procession to raise him up, and thus placed the laurel on his head, signifying that he was worthy to reign. Caesar, however, *turned aside*[3] as if unwilling to receive it. Seeing this the people showed their delight by their applause. When Antonius offered it a second time, Caesar again refused it, and there ensued a long struggle. As often as Antonius offered it, a few of his followers signified their approval; as often as Caesar refused it, *the applause*[4] became general. It was certainly a strange thing that they who were ready to endure everything that a conquered people has to put up with by order of their kings, should loathe the name of king as if *inimical*[5] to liberty.

1. consuetudo.   2. cursus.   3. voltum avertere.   4. use a verb impersonally.   5. exitialis.

136. *Different Interpretations of Dreams.*

A runner who intended to go to the Olympic games imagined while asleep that he was being driven in a four-horse car. Next day he paid a visit to the *diviner*.[1] *His explanation was*,[2] 'You will be successful, for this is betokened by the swiftness and might of the steeds.' The same man went afterwards to Antiphon. He, however, replied, 'You must of necessity be defeated. Don't you see that four ran before you?' Another runner told an intrepreter that during sleep he had seemed to have become an eagle. Quoth the other, 'You are successful, for than yon bird none can fly swifter.' Antiphon, however, said to him, 'Don't you see that you are defeated? for the bird *you mention*,[3] *though*[4] pursuing and driving other birds before it, ever comes last itself?

1. coniector. 2. verb. 3. iste. 4. participle.

137. *Outwitting the Ladies.*

Once upon a time the senators of a certain city were deliberating on a matter of paramount importance. The *discussion*[1] was adjourned till the next day, *stringent injunctions being given*[2] to keep it a secret. A senator's wife kept pestering him to find out *the subject of the debate*.[3] He told her that it had been ordered to keep it a secret. The lady's curiosity, *as usual*,[4] was inflamed, and her inquiries became more pressing. The senator, who saw *his only chance of rest was to satisfy*[5] her curiosity somehow or other, informed her that the debate was as to whether it were better for the state that each man should have two wives, or that each woman should have two husbands. Hearing this she rushed out of doors and laid the matter before the rest of the women. On the morrow they assembled in crowds before the senate-house and *protested against such an enormity*.[6] The senators were at a loss to know what they meant. Then the husband who had humbugged his wife advanced to the middle of the house and explained the occurrence amid universal merriment. When the ladies perceived this they retired to their homes in dudgeon at being laughed at. *The result of it was that*[7] they entirely gave up questioning their husbands as to the subject of the debates.

1. res. 2. cavere. 3. what had been done in the senate. 4. ut fit.
5. that rest would not be given him unless he had satisfied.
6. begged that nothing of the sort (*talis*) should be done. 7. why (should I say) more? they, etc.

138. *Unruffled Equanimity.*

A certain philosopher had a slave, a worthless and unmanageable fellow, who, however, had a smattering of philosophy, as he had often heard his master *lecturing.*[1] He committed *some*[2] fault *or other,*[2] and his master ordered him to be whipped. The punishment was being inflicted, and thinking it unadvisable to bear it in silence he exclaimed, ' What harm have I done, *pray?*[3] this does not become you. *A real philosopher*[4] is never angry. I with my own ears have heard you express yourself admirably on this topic. Your present conduct does not even suit even your learning, not to say yourself.' In reply to these and many other remonstrances of the same kind, the philosopher blandly remarked, ' *I angry with you?*[5] Do you gather from my face or my voice or my words that I am angry with a slave?' Then turning to the inflicter of the punishment he observed, ' *Be good enough to*[6] go on with your business while I and my servant discuss this admirable theme.' *The upshot was that*[7] the servant showed no subsequent desire for argument with his master.

Throughout this piece set yourself to prune the English down to its absolute meaning ; the language used is very exuberant.

1. disserere. 2. nescio quid. 3. tandem. 4. a philosopher, if he is a real philosopher. 5. question. 6. quin. 7. quid multa? *or,* quid quaeris?

139. *Philip's Treaty with Carthage.*

The great struggle now going on between Rome and Carthage attracted the attention of the whole *civilized*[1] world. It was evident that Greece, distracted by intestine quarrels, must soon be swallowed up by whichever of those great states might prove successful ; and of the two, the ambition of the Romans, who had already gained a footing on the eastern shores of the Adriatic, was by far the most formidable to Greece. After the conclusion of the peace with the Aetolians, Philip prepared a large fleet, which he employed to watch the movements of the Romans, and in the following year he concluded a treaty with Hannibal, which among *other clauses*[2] provided *that*[3] the Romans should *not*[3] be allowed to retain their conquests on the eastern side of the Adriatic.

1. humanior. 2. other things. 3. remember that *ut non* is only used in consecutive clauses.

140. *'We meet again at Philippi.'*

Brutus was *on the point of*[1] transporting his army from Abydos to the opposite continent; and the night before he lay in his tent awake, as was his custom, and *in deep thought*[2] about what might be the event of the war; for it was natural for him to watch great part of the night, and no general ever required so little sleep. With all his senses *about him*,[3] he heard a voice at the door of his tent, and looking towards the light, he saw a terrible appearance in human form. At first he was struck with astonishment; but when he saw that it neither did nor spoke anything to him, but stood in silence by his bed, *he asked*[4] it 'Who it was?' The spectre answered, 'I am thy evil genius, Brutus; thou shalt see me at Philippi.' Brutus answered boldly, 'I'll meet thee there,' and the spectre immediately vanished.

> 1. in eo ut. 2. make this the principal verb of your period.
> 3. in possession of (*compos*). 4. begin a fresh period.

141. *The Firmness of Pericles in Difficulties.*

Oppressed at once by war and pestilence, their lands desolated, their homes filled with mourning, it is not surprising that the Athenians were seized with rage and despair, or that they *vented their anger*[1] on Pericles, whom they deemed the author of their misfortunes. But that statesman still *adhered to*[2] his plans with unshaken firmness. Though the Lacedaemonians were in Attica, though the plague was *raging*[3] in the city, he was *vigorously pushing*[4] his schemes of offensive operations. A foreign expedition might *not only*[5] divert the popular mind, *but*[5] would prove beneficial by relieving the crowded city of part of its population. Accordingly a fleet was fitted out, of which Pericles took the command *in person*,[6] and which committed devastations upon various parts of the Peloponnesian coast.

> 1. stomachum erumpere. 2. used the same. 3. crudescere.
> 4. totus incumbere in. 5. cum—tum. 6. himself.

142. *A Faithful Friend.*

There is a remarkable instance transmitted to us of the affection borne to Edwin by his servants. Cuichelme, King of Wessex, was his enemy; but finding himself unable to maintain open war against so gallant and powerful a prince, he determined to use treachery against him, and he employed one Eumer for that criminal purpose.

The assassin having obtained admittance *by pretending*[1] to deliver
a message from Cuichelme, drew his dagger and rushed upon the
king. Lilla, an officer of his army, seeing his master's danger, and
having no other means of defence, interposed with his own body
between the king and Eumer's dagger, which was pushed with such
violence, that after piercing Lilla, it even wounded Edwin; but
before the assassin could renew his blow he was despatched by the
king's *attendants*.[2]

1. under the pretence. 2. satelles.

143. *Lysander's Ability.*

Lysander was the third of the remarkable men whom Sparta produced during the war. In ability, energy, and success he may be
compared with Brasidas and Gylippus, though immeasurably
inferior to the former *in*[1] every *moral quality*.[2] He was born of
poor parents, and was by descent one of those Lacedaemonians who
could never enjoy the *full rights*[3] of Spartan citizenship. His
ambition was boundless, and he was wholly unscrupulous about the
means which he employed to gratify it. In pursuit of his objects
he hesitated at neither deceit, nor perjury, nor cruelty, and he is
reported to have laid it down as one of his maxims in life, to avail
himself of the fox's skin where the lion's failed.

1. as regards. 2. indoles moresque. 3. ius et privilegium.

144. *The Gracchi.*

At this time Tiberius Gracchus, a tribune of the people, *proposed*[1] an
agrarian law *to prevent*[2] any one from holding more than 500 acres
of public ground. This was highly disapproved of by the wealthy,
and so *a strong opposition was offered*[3] to Gracchus. *He stood as a
candidate for*[4] the tribunate for the ensuing year. The patrician
order was highly indignant, and he was put to death in the Capitol,
whither he *had fled for sanctuary*.[5] Ten years later his brother
Caius made an effort to follow up the same *policy*.[6] His desire was
to diminish the power of the patricians and to put himself at the
head of the people. Confusion ensued; *people came running together*[7]
from all quarters. Caius was slain by the Consul Opimius, and
with him perished Fulvius Flaccus.

1. ferre. 2. lest. 3. impersonal. 4. ambire *or* petere. Make this
   a dependent clause, and let the principal verb of the period
   be 'he was put to death.' 5. se recipere. 6. consilium.
   7. impersonal.

145. *A City taken by Storm by the Turks.*

In a moment the armed defenders are hurled from the wall, the gates flung open. In rush the foe, some in column, some scrambling up the forsaken walls : they fill the whole city, and everywhere fighting is going on. Unwonted and unheard-of *atrocities are committed*[1] on the inhabitants. At length after immense slaughter the struggle *abated in fury*,[2] and the general gave orders that quarter should be given to *non-combatants*.[3] An end was put to the massacre, and the non-combatants began to surrender. The soldiers flung themselves on the spoil by their leader's permission. As plunder was being removed considerably greater in quantity, and consisting of more valuable articles, than he had *hoped or expected*,[4] Mustapha is said to have prayed with upraised hands that if his own good fortune and that of his men seemed excessive to God and man, that it might be vouchsafed to him to lessen that jealousy with as little harm as possible to himself and the state. They say that while turning round in the midst of his prayer he stumbled and fell. This omen was considered by those who *interpret*[5] matters by results to have had reference to Mustapha's own fate, who not long afterwards suffered the punishment of the bowstring by the Sultan's command. The reason of this is wrapped in obscurity.

1. saeviri in (impersonal). 2. senescere. 3. inermis.
4. translate by substantives. 5. coniectare.

146. *Lysander's Liberality.*

His loss was long felt[1] by the Athenians, in time of peace as well as of war. *He had*[2] numerous farms and gardens in different places, yet such was his generosity that he never placed in any of them a watchman to guard the fruit, for fear that any one might be prevented from enjoying anything he might have a fancy for. He was always followed by *footmen*[3] provided with coin, that he might be able to give at once, if any one asked his help, lest by putting off *his charity*[4] he should seem to refuse it. Often, if he happened to meet any one who was ill clothed, he gave him his own coat. Such preparations were daily made for his dinner as to enable him to invite any people he might meet who were *without invitations to go elsewhere*:[5] he never allowed a day to pass without doing this. His protection, aid, and *purse*[6] *were at the disposal of all.*[7] He enriched many men. He buried at his own expense many indigent persons who had died without leaving *means to pay for their obsequies.*[8] This being his character, no wonder his life was a happy one and his death *regarded as untimely.*[9]

1. he was long missed. 2. is this the principal idea? if not, do not make it the principal verb. 3. pedissequus. 4. omit. 5. invocatus. 6. res familiaris. 7. were wanting to no one. 8. whence they should be buried. 9. acerbus.

147. *Caesar's Veterans.*

The bravery of Caesar's troops [1] is attested *by the fact that* [2] having on one occasion experienced a reverse near Dyrrhachium, they asked of their own accord to be punished, so that their general thought them worthy rather of consolation than of punishment. In their remaining engagements they achieved easy victories over vast forces of the enemy, being themselves frequently vastly inferior in numbers. *Why,* [3] one cohort of the sixth legion that was intrusted with the defence of a fort resisted four of Pompeius' legions for some hours, nearly every man being pierced with the countless darts of the enemy, of which no less than one hundred and thirty thousand were found within the lines! Nor can we wonder at it, *if we consider* [4] the heroic actions of individual soldiers—Cassius Scaeva the centurion, or C. Acilius the private, for instance, *not to mention* [5] others. Scaeva, after losing an eye, with his thigh and shoulder shot through, and one hundred and twenty holes in his shield, kept his post as guardian of the gate of a fort intrusted to him. Acilius in a naval engagement *off* [6] Marseilles, after having his right hand, which he had laid on an enemy's ship, cut off, imitating that famous example set by Cynaegirus *as told in Grecian history,* [7] sprang on board the vessel, driving before him all his opponents with the *boss* of his shield.

1. turn this by an indirect question.   2. substantival clause introduced by *quod*.   3. denique.   4. if any one considers.   5. ne referam.   6. ad.   7. apud Graecos.   8. umbo.

148. *Victory restrained by Humanity.*

Our leader had begun to hope that as he had cut off the enemy from their supplies, he would be able to finish the business without fighting and loss to his troops. Why, thought he, should he, even in a victory, lose any of his men? Why should he allow soldiers who had deserved so well of him to be wounded? Why, in fine, should he tempt fortune, especially as it was a general's duty to effect as much by *strategy* [1] as by main force? He also felt pity for his fellow-citizens, who he saw *would have to be* [2] slain, and preferred to effect his purpose without injury to them. This resolve of their leader did not meet with general approval. The men began to assert openly that, as so good a chance of victory was being let pass, they would not fight when he wanted them to do so. The general adhered to his decision, and retired a little way from the place to lessen the alarm of the foe, whose leaders, taking advantage of the opportunity afforded them, retired to their camp. He then, after occupying the heights and cutting off all access to the river, *erected a fortified camp* [3] as near as he could to that of the enemy.

1. consilium.   2. express this by the gerundive.   3. castra communire.

149. *Alkibiades' Wooing.*

It is said that Alkibiades *gave a box on the car*[1] to Hipponikus, the father of Kallias, whose birth and wealth made him a man of great repute. And this he did unprovoked by any quarrel between them, but *only*[2] because in a frolic he had agreed with his companions to do it. People were justly offended at this insolence when it *became known*[3] through the city; but early the next morning Alkibiades went to Hipponikus' house, and knocking at the door went in to him, took off all his garments, and presenting his naked body to him, desired him to scourge and chastise him as he pleased. Hereupon the old man forgot all his resentment, and not only pardoned him, but afterwards gave him his daughter in marriage. She *became*[4] a virtuous and dutiful wife, but at last seeing that her husband could never be persuaded to use her as she deserved, she went to the archon *to claim a divorce.*[5] Alkibiades, however, was so ashamed of this that he came in, caught her up, and carried her home again, no one daring to oppose him.

1. colaphum infringere.   2. non nisi.   3. percrebrescere.   4. make this an adverbial clause.   5. divortium impetrare.

150. *A Cockney Sportsman taken in.*

Mr. Sempronius Green, a London merchant, paid a visit to a village in Kent for pleasure, as he said, and not on business. He repeatedly said that he wished to buy a country place, to which he might invite his friends, and where he might amuse himself without *interruption.*[1] When this got about, one Fox, a banker, said that he had a country house, but not *for sale;*[2] however Mr. Green might make use of it, if he pleased, as if it were his own. At the same time he invited *the unfortunate man*[3] to dinner next day. The invitation was accepted. Fox then got hold of some anglers and begged them to fish next day in the river close to the house. Mr. Green came to dinner *punctual to the minute.*[4] A sumptuous repast had been prepared by Fox. Numerous anglers turned up, and made presents of fish to Fox. Mr. Green's cupidity was excited, for he was a keen fisherman, and he implored Fox to sell his villa. Fox at first expressed his unwillingness. *To cut a long story short,*[5] Mr. Green *got his way.*[6] He bought the villa *at Fox's own price.*[7] Next day he invited his friends. As they continued to fish all day without result, he asked his next neighbour why *they were so unsuccessful.*[8] The other replied, 'No one ever fishes here: there are no fish. So I was wondering what *was up*[9] yesterday.' Mr. Green was frantic. But what could he do?

1. interpellator: concrete for abstract.   2. venalis.   3. homo.   4. tempori.   5. quid multa?   6. impetrare.   7. for as much as Fox wished.   8. why they could not catch fish.   9. had happened.

151. *Caesar caught Napping.*

In attacking the Nervii with eight legions Caesar was hurried into
a battle before he knew where he was. He had[1] everything to do
himself all at the same time—to *unfurl*[2] the standard, to give the
signal, to get back the soldiers from their work, to call back some
who had gone for *stuff to make a rampart*,[3] to address the men, and
finally to give the word. He told them to remember their old
valour. The enemy was so close upon them and so ready for fighting
that they could scarcely put on their helmets and take their shields
out of their cases. So great was the confusion that the soldiers
could not reach their own ranks, but had to fight as they stood.
Added to all this[4] there were thick *artificial*[5] hedges, constructed by
the enemy, which prevented them from seeing where they were
going. When Caesar saw how matters *were going*[6] he seized a shield
from a common soldier and rushed into the fight. All this he has
narrated himself with the same clearness which he used when he sent
word to the senate, 'Veni, vidi, vici.'

1. express this by the gerundive. 2. proponere. 3. agger. 4. huc
accedere. 5. omit, as it is implied in 'constructed.'
6. had themselves.

152. *A Dilemma.*

Two individuals who were *at sea*,[1] one being the owner of the
ship and the other of the cargo, caught sight of a shipwrecked sailor
swimming and holding out his hands to them : moved with pity,
they *steered*[2] towards him, and took him on board. A short while
after they too were assailed by a storm of such violence that the
owner of the vessel, who was also the pilot, got into a boat, and from
thence directed the course of the vessel, as best he might, by a rope
which was made fast to the stern and to which the boat was attached;
while *the owner*[3] of the cargo *fell on*[4] his sword on the spot. The
aforesaid[5] shipwrecked sailor flew to the helm and assisted the vessel
to the best of his ability.[6] When the sea had gone down and the
wind abated the vessel got into port. The man who had fallen on
his sword, being but slightly wounded, was easily cured. Then each
of the three asserted the vessel and cargo to be his.

1. in alto. 2. navim applicare. 3. adjectival clause. 4. incumbere.
5. ille. 6. as far as (*quoad*) he could.

153. *The Keltic Invasion of Greece.*

Some years after the death of Alexander, Macedonia was invaded by the Kelts. A second invasion of the same barbarians compelled the Greeks to raise a force for their defence, which was intrusted to the command of the Athenian Callippus. On this occasion the Kelts, attracted by the report of treasures, which were now *perhaps*[1] little more than an empty name, penetrated as far southwards as Delphi, with the view of plundering the temple. The god, it is said, vindicated his sanctuary on this occasion in the same *supernatural manner*[2] as when it was attacked by the Persians : it is *at all events*[3] certain that the Kelts were repulsed with great loss, including that of their leader Brennus. Nevertheless some of their tribes succeeded in establishing themselves near the Danube ; others settled on the sea-coast of Thrace ; whilst a third portion passed over into Asia, and gave their name to the country called Galatia.

1. nescio an. 2. divinitus. 3. ceterum.

154. *Unbelief in Greece and the Teaching of Socrates.*

The desperate struggles between the nobles and the people, which were caused by the war in so many cities, made men *disregard*[1] everything except the interests of the *party*[2] to which they belonged. In their hatred against the opposite faction in the state, men lost their care for the state itself. *The interest*[3] of the party was put in the place of law, custom, and piety. This, together with other causes, tended to break down the belief of educated Greeks in their old religion, and *their old distinctions*[4] between right and wrong. The war spread violence all over Greece. Men acted as if mere force gave a right to everything, and some even taught that this was so. *In this bad time*[5] a man arose at Athens named Socrates, who had such thoughts of truth and goodness as *no*[6] Greek had ever had before him. He taught that it was better to suffer wrong than do wrong ; and that the gods wished men to honour them, not by beliefs and observances, but by doing good. His way of teaching was by asking questions, until he made people see how little they knew. The Athenians *misunderstood*[7] him ; he was accused of corrupting youth, and condemned to death.

1. parvi facere. 2. partes. 3. adjectival clause. 4. what was of old between (*intercedere*). 5. his tam foedis temporibus.
    6. nemo. 7. in malam partem accipere.

155. *Cleon's Abuse of the Generals.*

Meanwhile news came that the Spartans were still undefeated, and that *matters looked as if*[1] the siege would have to be abandoned. These tidings were very distasteful to the Athenians, who had looked on Sphacteria *as their certain prey.*[2] They began to regret having let slip the favourable opportunity for making a peace, and *to vent their displeasure*[3] upon Cleon, the *director*[4] of their conduct on that occasion. But Cleon *put on a face of brass.*[5] He abused the Strategi. His political *opponent,*[6] Nicias, was then one of these officers, a man of quiet disposition and moderate abilities, but thoroughly honest and incorruptible. Him Cleon now singled out for his vituperation, and pointing at him with his finger, exclaimed, 'It would be easy enough to take the island if our generals were men. If I were general I would do it at once.'

1. not much was wanting but that.   2. all but (*tantum non*) taken.
3. impersonal.   4. auctor.   5. perfricta fronte.   6. adjectival clause.

156. *Cleon caught in his own Trap.*

This burst of the tanner[1] made the assembly laugh. He was saluted with cries of '*Why don't*[2] you go, then?' and Nicias, thinking *probably*[3] to catch his opponent in his own trap, *seconded*[4] the voice of the assembly by offering to place at his disposal whatever force he might deem necessary for the enterprise. Cleon at first endeavoured to avoid the dangerous honour thus thrust upon him. But the more he drew back, the louder were the assembly in calling upon him to accept the office ; and as Nicias seriously repeated his proposition, he *adopted with a good grace*[5] what there was no longer any possibility of evading, and he asserted that he would take Sphacteria within twenty days, and either kill all the Lacedaemonians upon it or bring them prisoners to Athens.

1. when the tanner had exclaimed this.   2. quin (with indicative).
3. nescio an.   4. assentiri.   5. boni consulere.

157. *Fortune favours Cleon.*

Never did general set out upon an enterprise under circumstances more singular ; but, what was still more extraordinary, fortune enabled him *to make good*[1] his promise. In fact, as we *have seen,*[2] Demosthenes had already resolved on attacking the island, and when Cleon arrived at Pylus, he found everything prepared for the assault.

Accident favoured the enterprise. A fire kindled by some Athenian sailors who had *landed*[3] for the purpose of cooking their dinner, caught and destroyed the woods with which the island was *overgrown,*[4] and thus deprived the Lacedaemonians of one of their principal defences. Nevertheless, such was the awe inspired by the reputation of the Spartan arms, that Demosthenes considered it necessary to land *about*[5] 10,000 men *of different descriptions,*[6] although the Lacedaemonian force consisted of only about 420 men.

1. praestare. 2. have shown above. 3. descendere. 4. obsitus. 5. ad. 6. variae armaturae.

158. *Defeat of the Besieged.*

But this small force for a long while kept their assailants at bay; till some Messenians, stealing round by the sea-shore, over crags and cliffs which the Lacedaemonians had deemed impracticable, suddenly appeared on the high ground which overhung their rear. They now began to give way, and *would soon*[1] have been all slain; but Cleon and Demosthenes, being anxious to carry them prisoners to Athens, sent a herald to summon them to surrender. The latter, in token of *compliance,*[2] dropped their shields, and waved their hands above their heads.

1. not much was wanting but that, etc. 2. obsequium.

159. *Cleon completely successful.*

They requested, however, permission to communicate with their countrymen on the mainland; who after *two or three*[1] communications, sent them a final message 'to take counsel for themselves, but to do nothing disgraceful.' The survivors then surrendered. They were 292 in number, 120 of whom were native Spartans *belonging to the first families.*[2] By this surrender the *prestige*[3] of the Spartan armies was in a great degree destroyed. The Spartans were not indeed deemed invincible; but their previous feats, especially at Thermopylae, had inspired the notion that they would rather die than yield; an opinion which could now no longer be held. Cleon had thus performed his promise. On the day after the victory he and Demosthenes started with the prisoners for Athens, where they arrived within twenty days from the time of Cleon's departure.

1. again and again. 2. born in a very high place. 3. existimatio.

H

160. *The Homeric Poems.*

Of the Homeric poems the Iliad and the Odyssey were the most distinguished and have alone come down to us. *The subject of the Iliad was*[1] the exploits of Achilles and of the other Grecian heroes before Ilium or Troy : that of the Odyssey was the adventures and wanderings of Odusseus or Ulysses after the capture of Troy when on his way back to his native island. Throughout the flourishing period of Greek literature these unrivalled works were universally regarded as the *productions*[2] of a simple mind; but there was very little agreement respecting the place of the poet's birth, the details of his life, or the time in which he lived. Seven cities laid claim to Homer's birth, and most of them had legends to tell respecting his *romantic*[3] parentage, his alleged blindness, and his life of an *itinerant*[4] bard acquainted with poverty and sorrow.

1. in the Iliad are related. 2. oriundus. 3. fabulosus. 4. vagabundus.

161. *Socrates on Ruling.*

Socrates likewise observed that a sceptre in the hand could not make a king ; neither were they rulers *in whose favour*[1] the lot, or the voice of the people, *had decided,*[1] or who, by force or fraud, had secured *their election*[2] unless they understood the art of governing. And although he would readily allow it not less *the province*[3] of the prince to command than of the subjects to obey, yet he would afterwards demonstrate that *the most skilful*[4] pilot would always steer the ship; the master, no less than the mariners, submitting to his direction. The owner of the farm left the management of it, he said, to the servant, whom he thought better acquainted than himself with agriculture ; the sick man sought the advice of the physician; and *he who engaged in bodily exercises,*[5] the instructions of those who had most experience. And whatever there may be, continued Socrates, requiring either skill or industry to perform it, when the man is able, he doeth it himself ; *but if not,*[6] he *hath recourse,*[7] if prudent, to the assistance of others ; since in the *management*[8] of the distaff even a woman may be his instructor ; neither will he content himself with what he can have *at hand,*[9] but inquireth out with care for any one who can *best*[10] serve him.

1. who were favoured by. 2. most votes. 3. omit. 4. each most skilful. 5. gymnasticus. 6. sin minus. 7. decurrere. 8. verb. 9. praesto. 10. potissimum.

162. *The Vikings.*

Led by the younger sons of royal houses, the Vikings swarmed in all the harbours and rivers of the surrounding countries. Their course was marked by fire and bloodshed. Buildings sacred and profane were burned to the ground; and great numbers of people were murdered or dragged away into slavery. The terrified inhabitants fled at their approach, and beheld in them the judgments of God foretold in the prophets. Their *national flag* [1] was the figure of a black raven, woven on a blood-red ground, from whose movements the Northmen augured victory or defeat. When it fluttered its wings, they believed that Odin gave them a sign of victory; but if the wings hung down, they imagined that the god would not prosper their arms. Their swords were longer and heavier than those of the Anglo-Saxons, and their battle-axes are mentioned as formidable weapons. As years went on, such of these fierce warriors as had settled on the sea-board of Britain amalgamated with the inhabitants, and aided to form that English race, which springing from so many different predatory ancestors, has preserved the characteristics of each, and *welded* [2] them into the sword which guards its own liberty instead of seeking to enslave its neighbours.

1. insigne gentis.   2. *conflare;* introduce the metaphor by, *ut ita dicam* (so to speak).

163. *Defeat of the Caledonians.*

Ascertaining this, the enemy quickly changed his plan and made a nocturnal attack in force on the 9th legion as being the weakest, and having killed the sentinels while asleep, or in confusion, broke their way in. The fight was already raging in the camp itself, when Agricola, whose scouts had accurately informed him of the enemy's route, following on their track, ordered the most active of his cavalry and infantry to attack them in the rear while fighting, and soon ordered all to raise a shout; their standards glitter in the grey dawn; the Caledonians are panic-struck at the twofold difficulty, and the courage of the Romans returns; assured of safety, they fight for glory, and even make a sortie; a desperate struggle took place in the narrow entrances of the gates until the enemy was defeated. Both armies fought desperately; the one, to appear to have rendered assistance, the other, not to have stood in need of it; and unless the marshes and woods had covered the flight of the foe, the victory thus won *would have finished the war.*[1]

1. debellare.

164. *Osman Pasha at Plevna.*

After the crossing of the Danube by the Russians, Osman Pasha, the commander-in-chief of the Turkish armies, who held Plevna with a strong force, resolved to fortify it strongly and assemble a force sufficient to stand a siege, with the intention of delaying the Russian advance on Constantinople. Acting on this resolve the town, *naturally*[1] strong, was admirably fortified by the Turkish *engineer officers*.[2] The Russians endeavoured to take the town by storm, but were easily repulsed, as the attempt was made with insufficient forces. The Russians were reinforced, but as the Turks were successful in several subsequent engagements, the Russian general gave up all hope of carrying the works by storm, and resolved to blockade the town until want of supplies should compel the Turks to surrender. After several months the garrison, being utterly without provisions, endeavoured to cut their way through the Russians, but being repulsed, Osman was compelled to surrender with the whole of his army.

1. natura. 2. praefecti fabrum.

165. *A double entendre.*

That was a very humorous remark[1] of Hannibal the Carthaginian when an exile at the court of King Antiochus. *It*[2] ran as follows. Antiochus was showing him on *parade*[3] a large force which he had prepared with the view of waging war on the Romans, and was *manœuvring*[4] his troops all ablaze with gold and silver standards. He made to march pass scythed chariots and elephants with *howdahs*,[5] and cavalry with glittering bridles, saddle-cloths, gorgets, and horse-trappings. The king, *swelling with pride*[6] at the sight of so great and splendid an army, turned his eyes on Hannibal and remarked, 'Do you think this will do for the Romans?' Then Hannibal, *with a covert sneer*[7] at the cowardice of his expensively equipped soldiers, replied, 'I certainly think they will do for the Romans though they are very greedy.' Nothing that he could have said could have been *neater*[8] or more satirical. The king's *question*[9] *bore on*[10] the numbers of his men, Hannibal's answer was an allusion to the spoil they would afford.

1. facetissime cavillari. 2. that joke (*cavillatio*). 3. campus.
4. convertere. 5. turris. 6. gloriabundus. 7. eludere.
8. lepide. 9. use a verb. 10. was concerning.

166. *Mary Queen of Scots surrenders to Elizabeth.*

Meanwhile Mary had engaged, by her *charms and caresses*,[1] a young gentleman, George Douglas, to assist her in escaping. He conveyed her *in disguise*[2] into a small boat, and himself rowed her ashore. She hastened to Hamilton, where *her adherents*[3] had already assembled ; and in a few days an army of 6000 men was ranged under her standard. The regent also made haste to assemble forces ; and notwithstanding that his army was inferior in number to that of the Queen of Scots, he took the field against her. A battle was fought near Glasgow on the 13th of May, which was entirely decisive in favour of the regent, and was followed by a total dispersion of the queen's party. That unhappy princess fled southwards from the field of battle with great precipitation, and at last embraced the resolution of taking shelter in England. She embarked on board a fishing vessel, and landed the same day at Workington, about thirty miles from Carlisle ; whence she immediately despatched a messenger to London, notifying her arrival, desiring leave to visit Elizabeth, and craving her *protection*,[4] in consequence of former professions of friendship made by that princess.

1. formae illecebris. 2. having changed her dress. 3. sui. 4. fides.

167. *The Use of a Real Friend.*

The best way to represent *to the life*[1] the manifold uses of friendship *is*[2] to think and see how many things there are which a man cannot do of himself, and then it will appear that it was a sparing *speech*[3] of the ancients to say 'that a friend is another himself,' for a friend is far more than himself. *Men*[4] have their time, and die many times in the desire of something which they principally take to heart—*the bestowing*[5] of a child, the finishing of a work, or the like. If a man has a true friend, he may rest almost secure that the care of these things will continue after him ; so that a man has, as it were, two lives in his desire. A man has a body, is confined to a place, but where friendship is, there all offices of life are, as it were, granted to him and his *deputy*,[6] for he may exercise them by his friend. How many things are there which a man cannot with any grace or comeliness say or do himself? A man can *scarcely*[7] allege his own merits, much less extol them ; a man cannot sometimes brook to supplicate or beg, and a number of the like ; but all these things are graceful in a friend's mouth, which are blustering in a man's own.

1. ad vivum. 2. the English present must often be rendered by a Latin future. 3. replace the noun by a verb. 4. quisque. 5. collocare. 6. vicarius. 7. nisi fronte perfricta.

168. *The Athenian Expedition to Sicily.*

The power of the Athenians was now on the wane. The event destined to produce that catastrophe—the *intervention* [1] of the Athenians in the affairs of Sicily—was already in progress. A quarrel had broken out between Egesta and Selinus, both which cities were seated near the western extremity of Sicily; and Selinus, having obtained the aid of Syracuse, was pressing very hard on the Egestaeans. The latter appealed to the interests of the Athenians rather than to *their sympathies.* [2] They represented how great a blow it would be to Athens if the Dorians became predominant in Sicily, and joined the Peloponnesian confederacy; and they undertook, if the Athenians would send an armament to their assistance, to provide the necessary funds for the prosecution of the war. Their most powerful advocate was Alkibiades, *whose ambitious views are said* [3] to have extended even to the conquest of Carthage. The quieter and more prudent Nicias and his party *threw their weight into the opposite scale.* [4] But the Athenian assembly, dazzled by the idea of so splendid an enterprise, decided on despatching a large fleet under Nicias, Alkibiades, and Lamachus, with the design of assisting Egesta, and of establishing the influence of Athens throughout Sicily, by whatever means might be found practicable.

1. do not use a substantive. 2. their love for them. 3. who, such was his ambition, is said, etc. 4. translate the meaning, not the metaphor.

169. *The Mutilation of the Hermae.*

At every door in Athens, at the *corners of streets,* [1] in the market-place, before temples, gymnasia, and other public places, stood Hermae, or statues of the god Hermes, consisting of a *bust* [2] of that deity surmounting a quadrangular pillar of marble about the height of the human figure. When the Athenians rose one morning towards the end of May 415 B.C., it was found that all these figures had been mutilated during the night, and reduced by unknown hands to a shapeless mass. The act inspired *political* [3] as well as *religious* [4] alarm. It seemed to indicate a *widespread* [5] conspiracy, for so sudden and general a mutilation *must have been* [6] the work of many hands.

1. compitum. 2. imago. 3. civilis. 4. adjectival clause.
5. percrebrescere. 6. there was no doubt but that, etc.

170. *Alkibiades is suspected.*

The sacrilege might only be a preliminary attempt[1] of some powerful citizen to seize the despotism, *and suspicion pointed its finger at Alkibiades.*[2] Active measures were taken and large rewards offered for the discovery of the perpetrators. A public board was appointed to examine witnesses, which did not, indeed, succeed in eliciting any facts bearing on the actual subject of inquiry, but which obtained evidence respecting similar acts of impiety committed at previous times *in drunken frolics.*[3] In these Alkibiades himself was implicated; and though the fleet *was on the very eve*[4] of departure, a citizen rose in the assembly and accused Alkibiades *of having profaned*[5] the Eleusinian mysteries by giving a representation of them in a private house, producing in evidence the testimony of a slave.

1. it seemed likely that, beginning with sacrilege (*a sacrilego facinore orsum*), etc. 2. and this suspicion brought it about that Alkibiades should be pointed at (*digito monstrari*). 3. per vinolentiam. 4. was all but (*tantum non*). 5. virtually suboblique.

171. *The Battle of Syracuse.*

At last the Syracusan fleet weighed anchor and left the harbour. A considerable portion was detached to guard the barrier at the mouth of the harbour. Hither the first and most impetuous attack of the Athenians was directed, who sought to break through the narrow opening which had been left for the passage of merchant vessels. Their onset was repulsed, and the battle then became general. The shouts of the combatants and the crash of the iron *heads*[1] of the vessels as they were driven together, resounded over the water, and were answered on shore by the cheers or wailings of the spectators as their friends were victorious or vanquished. For a long time the battle was maintained with heroic courage and *dubious result.*[2] The Athenians were at length defeated and began to fly. As the Athenian vessels neared the shore the crews leaped out and made for the camp with all speed, while the boldest of the land army rushed forward to prevent the ships from being seized by the enemy. However·they lost about fifty ships and with them all hope of victory or retreat.

1. rostra. 2. ancipiti Marte.

172. *The End of the Athenian Expeditionary Force.*

The Athenians still numbered 40,000 men; and as all chance of escape by sea was now hopeless it was resolved to retreat by land to some friendly city, and there defend themselves against the Syracusans. As the soldiers turned to quit that fatal encampment, *the sense* [1] of their own woes was for a moment *suspended* [2] by the sight of their unburied comrades, who *seemed* [3] to *reproach* [4] them with the neglect of a sacred duty; but still more by the wailings and entreaties of the wounded who clung around their knees, and implored not to be abandoned to certain destruction. *Amid this scene of woe,* [5] the courage and conduct of Nicias were admirable. Though suffering from an incurable complaint he was everywhere seen encouraging his troops to resist to the end. Having formed the army into *a hollow square,* [6] with the baggage in the middle, he endeavoured to march to the territory of the Sicels, but being surrounded by the enemy, he was forced to *surrender.* [7] The prisoners were sent to the *quarries;* [8] Nicias himself was condemned to death.

1. change the subject. 2. reprimere. 3. scilicet. 4. obicere. 5. in his tam foedis calamitatibus. 6. orbis. 7. in deditionem venire. 8. lautumiae.

173. *Columbus' Account of his Exploits.*

After a while the sovereigns commanded Columbus to recount his exploits. Then he stood *forth,* [1] with a mind, as always, calm and stedfast, but with words sometimes *somewhat high,* [2] as in such great glory. He praised the several islands which he had visited, the temperateness of the sky, the soil of the earth suitable for any increase whatsoever; at the same time he exhibited fruits and even flowers grown there. As to gold, he confessed that no great quantity had as yet been found, but the natives, he said, *with consistent voice* [3] affirmed that great abundance of this metal could be found in the higher places. That the race of men were simple in mind, and not imbued with false religion, so that they would most willingly receive the precepts of Christian faith. Hearing this, the queen was strongly moved; the rest, less perfect in mind, indulged their own hope, according as each desired either wealth or dominion, or some greater and holier things. When the speech of Columbus was finished, the king and queen, with their courtiers, *fell on their knees* [4] and gave thanks that so great a thing had been accomplished under their auspices; then, as if for some great victory gained by arms, *hymns* [5] were sung by the altar of the royal *chapel.* [6]

1. in medium. 2. comparative. 3. consensu. 4. with bent (*summissus*) knee. 5. divine songs. 6. aedicula.

174. *Cortes and his Rivals.*

Cortes, receiving his commission with the warmest *expressions of respect* [1] and gratitude to the governor, immediately erected his standard before his own house, appeared *in a military dress*,[2] and assumed all the ensigns of his new dignity. His utmost influence and activity were exerted in persuading many of his friends to engage in the service, and urging forward the preparations of the voyage. All his own funds, together with whatever he could raise *by mortgaging* [3] his lands and Indians, were expended in purchasing military stores and provisions, or in supplying the wants of such of his officers as were unable to equip themselves *in a manner suited to* [4] their rank. Inoffensive and even laudable as their conduct was, *his disappointed competitors* [5] were malicious enough *to give it a turn to his disadvantage*.[6] They represented him as aiming already with little disguise at establishing an independent authority over his troops, and endeavouring to secure their respect and love by his ostentation and interested liberality. *They reminded* [7] Velasquez of his former *dissensions* [8] with the man in whom he now reposed so much confidence, and foretold that Cortes would be more apt to avail himself of the power which the governor was inconsiderately putting in his hands to avenge past injuries than to requite recent obligations.

1. professing his sense of respect (*significationem observantiae*). 2. paludatus. 3. pignori opponere. 4. pro. 5. those who were put after him. 6. in peius vertere. 7. do not put in a principal verb; turn it by a request: ' let Velasquez consider.' 8. simultas.

175. *An Unfortunate Mistake.*

There was one of Caesar's friends, called Cinna, who had a marvellously strange and terrible dream the night before. *He dreamed that Caesar* [1] bade him to supper, and that he refused, and would not go : then that Caesar took him by the hand, and led him against his will. Now Cinna hearing at that time that they burned Caesar's body in the market-place, notwithstanding that he feared his dream, and *had an ague on him* [2] besides, he went into the market-place to *honour* [3] his funeral. When he came thither, one of the common people asked him what his name was ? He was straight called by his name. The first man told it to another, and that other unto another, so that it ran at once through them all that he was one of those who murdered Caesar (for indeed one of the traitors to Caesar was also called Cinna); wherefore, taking him for Cinna the murderer, they fell upon him with such fury that they soon despatched him in the market-place. This stir and fury made Brutus and Cassius more afraid than all that was past, and therefore within a few days after they departed from Rome.

1. for (acting as a link to the previous sentence) Caesar seemed. 2. febri aegrotare. 3. celebrare.

176. *German Habits.*

It is well known that no German people dwell in cities, and that they cannot even endure adjoining houses. They live separate and scattered, attracted either by springs, woods, or plains. The villages they build do not, *as with us,*[1] consist of houses attached to and connected with each other. Each man surrounds his home with an open space, either as a *security*[2] against risk from fire, or in consequence of ignorance of *architecture.*[3] They do not even use mortar or tiles, but merely *rough-hewn*[4] wood for all purposes. They plaster some parts with earth, so refined and glistening as to counterfeit paintings and coloured outlines. They are also in the habit of digging subterranean cavities, and covering them with a thick layer of manure, as a shelter in winter and a storehouse for their crops, mitigating the excessive cold by *the use of*[5] such places. On the approach of an enemy he can only ravage the open fields. The hidden stores are either unknown, or escape notice *by the very fact*[6] of their having to be sought.

1. in nostrum morem. 2. remedium. 3. use a verb. 4. informis
5. omit. 6. eo ipso quod.

177. *The Crimean War.*

After ordering the *generals of division*[1] to disembark their men as quickly as possible, Lord Raglan landed in person. *No enemy was in sight.*[2] Lord Raglan riding on *too far*[3] with a few attendants *was within an ace of being*[4] captured or killed, as some Cossacks made a rush at him from an ambush. Not long afterwards he defeated the Russians in a pitched battle on the river Alma. The enemy were so panic-stricken that they passed by their camp in utter rout and fell back on Sebastopol. Numbers were killed and wounded, and much booty fell into the hands of our troops. Sebastopol was then invested and siege-works begun. At times the garrison took the opportunity to assail our outposts, and *skirmishes*[5] were of frequent occurrence. Time wore on, *the scale of hope being equally balanced,*[6] as the besieged, having stores previously collected, were better provisioned than the allies. Two desperate battles were fought, resulting in the defeat of the Russians, who retired into the city. Sebastopol was at last taken by the allies, and its fortifications were burned and destroyed.

1. legati. 2. make this a dependent clause. 3. comparative. 4 minimum abfuit ut. 5. proelia parva. 6. neutro inclinata spe.

178. *The Effect of Cortes' Machinations.*

As soon as this was known, the *disappointed*[1] adventurers exclaimed and threatened ; the *emissaries*[2] of Cortes, mingling with them, inflamed their rage ; the ferment became general ; the whole camp was almost in open mutiny ; all demanding with eagerness to see their commander. Cortes was not slow in appearing ; when, with one voice, officers and soldiers *expressed*[3] their astonishment and disappointment at the orders which they had received. It was unworthy, they cried, of the Castilian courage to be daunted at the first aspect of danger, and infamous to fly before any enemy appeared. For their parts, they were determined not to relinquish an enterprise that had hitherto been successful, and which tended so visibly to advance the glory and interest of their country. Happy under his command, they would follow him with alacrity through every danger in quest of those settlements and treasures which he had so long held out to their view ; but if he chose rather to return to Cuba, and tamely give up all his hopes of distinction and opulence to an envious rival, they would instantly choose another general to conduct them in that path of glory which he had not *spirit*[4] to enter.

1. spe deiectus. 2. adjectival clause. 3. everything after this in oratio obliqua. 4. animus.

179. *A Trick of Alkibiades.*

Such was the man who now opposed the application of the Lacedaemonian ambassadors. Their reception had been so favourable, that Alkibiades, alarmed at *the prospect of their success*,[1] resorted to a trick in order to defeat it. He called upon the Lacedaemonian envoys, one of whom happened to be his personal friend ; and he advised them not to tell the assembly that they were furnished with full *powers*,[2] as in that case the people would bully them *into extravagant concessions*,[3] but rather to say that they were come to discuss and report. He promised if they did so to speak in their favour, and induce the assembly to grant the restitution of Pylus, to which he himself had hitherto been the chief obstacle. The ambassadors did as they were advised, and the Athenians in their anger dismissed them forthwith.

1. their by no means doubtful success. 2. auctoritas. 3. make a dependent clause of this.

180. *The Battle of Sistova.*

The battle of Sistova *was the crowning point* [1] of the war between the Russians and Turks. After the capture of Plevna the Russians began the crossing of the Balkans. Several of the defiles had already been *occupied* [2] by the Turks, and the Russians found great difficulties in their way both from the resistance of the enemy and the deep snow with which the mountains were covered. Meanwhile the Russian commander-in-chief, having ascertained that a large force of the enemy were in retreat with the view of forming a junction with fresh levies and falling back on Constantinople, resolved to prevent them from carrying out their plan. Two of his bravest generals were intrusted with the execution of this plan. Dividing their forces into two divisions, they proceeded by forced marches against the enemy, suffering great hardships from the cold and snow. Both at length became hotly engaged with the Turks. A desperate struggle took place, but at last one of the Turkish armies was completely routed, and the general of the other perceiving that the Russians had effected a junction, and despairing of success, surrendered with his whole army.

1. debellatum est.   2. do not use *occupare*.

181. *The Spartans at Thermopylae.*

In the course of the night Leonidas knew what had happened. He saw that if he did not retreat immediately he must be surrounded and perish ; but the law of Sparta forbade the soldier to leave his post, and Leonidas had no fear of death. *He ordered* [1] the other troops to retire while there was yet time, but himself, with his 300 Spartans, remained *to die* [2] at his post. The other troops departed, but the 700 Thespians bravely resolved to stay and die with Leonidas. And now, before the Persians could descend behind him, Leonidas and his 1000 men threw themselves upon the host in front. Leonidas soon fell, but his soldiers fought on until the Persians, who had crossed the mountain, *were close at hand.* [3] Then ceasing the attack, they took up their last position on some rising ground, to defend themselves against the enemy, who now surrounded them. Here all died, fighting bravely to the last. Their heroic and voluntary death was not in vain. *At a moment when* [4] the hearts even of the braver Greeks were wavering, and men were inclined to forsake the common cause in order to save themselves, Leonidas gave a splendid example of constancy and *self-sacrifice*, [5] and showed the Greeks how a citizen ought to do his duty.

1. edicto (abl. abs.).   2. future participle.   3. subesse.
4. cum maxime,   5. unmindful of self.

182. *The Heights of El-Bodon.*

At the same time *acting on their orders*[1] a general advance of the cavalry on the left wing of the French began, and all the *chasseurs à pied*[2] *swarmed*[3] on the height above. Our cavalry failed to withstand the shock, but fell back some distance, and accordingly the French cavalry charged *with increased élan,*[4] and began to *deploy*[5] troop after troop and take us on our exposed flank. When our leader perceived this he gave the signal to the *5th Foot,*[6] which were lying concealed in the brushwood. They dashed forward at once and charged the French dragoons with such fury that none of them held their ground, but, all not only turned and fell back, but even made for the heights in *headlong*[7] flight. However, as their infantry continued to resist, the battle *raged with renewed fury.*[8] Desperate courage was shown on either side. Night at length put a stop to further fighting. In spite of the ferocity of this death-struggle, we are told that our men conversed amicably with the enemy, when watering parties from either force went down to the river.

1. as they were ordered.   2. levis armatura.   3. se profundere.
4. acrius.   5. explicare.   6. 5th legion.   7. incitatus.
8. recrudescere.

183. *A Haunted House.*

There was in a certain city a house of good size but of ill repute and *one dangerous to life.*[1] In the silence of night a sound of iron, and *on listening*[2] more closely, a rattling of chains used to be heard, at some distance at first and afterwards quite close at hand: soon an apparition used *to come into view,*[3] an old man *in a piteous state*[4] of emaciation and filth, with a long beard and rough hair; he had irons on his legs and chains on his hands, which he used to rattle. In consequence of this the apprehension of the inmates used to keep them awake through nights of gloom and terror: illness ensued, and, as the dread *intensified,*[5] death; for even by day, though the spectre was no longer visible, the recollection of it refused to leave their eyes. So the house was abandoned, and entirely given up to the ghost; but a *notice was left up*[6] in case any one ignorant of such an evil should choose to buy or hire it.

1. pestilens.   2. if you should listen.   3. apparere.   4. confectus (participle).   5. crescere.   6. proscribi (impersonal).

184. *The Ghost laid.*

A stranger came to the town and read the *notice*.[1] On hearing the
rent, he made careful inquiry, as he thought the cheapness suspicious,
and heard the whole story, *in spite of which*[2] he took the house.
When evening began to close in, he ordered a bed to be made, and
dismissed his attendants. He then sat down to write, lest his mind
being unoccupied should hear ghosts and imagine groundless alarms.
Soon the iron began to be struck, and the chains to rattle : he never
lifted his eyes. Then the sound increased and drew nearer, and *at one
moment*[3] was heard at the door, *the next*[3] inside the room. He looked
round, saw, and recognised the ghost described to him. It stood
still, and kept *beckoning*[4] to him with its finger. He in reply gave
it to understand by *a wave of*[5] his hand that it was to wait a little,
and again applied himself to his work. The ghost kept rattling its
chains over his head as he wrote. On looking up again he saw it
beckoning as before. Without any further delay he took up his
candle and followed it. The ghost moved slowly as if impeded by
its chains : when they arrived at the courtyard it suddenly vanished
and abandoned its companion, who next day went to the magistrates
and advised them to have the spot dug up. Bones were found
mingled with fetters. They were collected and received a public
funeral. The house ever after was freed of the ghost, which had
been duly *laid*.[6]

1. titulus. 2. nihilominus. 3. iam—iam. 4. innuere.
5. omit. 6. condere.

185. *Tit for Tat.*

Titus the huntsman was one day wandering in the wood with his
brother, when, hearing a noise behind a tree, he *looked up*,[1] and saw
a bear embracing the tree with its feet, as if just about to ascend.
The tree was between them, so that neither could Titus nor his
brother see the bear (except the claws), nor the bear them. Thereupon Titus silently approached, and seizing the beast by the claws
prevented him from climbing, or moving at all. But neither could
he himself let go, for he perceived that the bear would seize him, so
he bade his brother run home and fetch his bow. At last, after he
had waited a long time as though in chains, and utterly exhausted,
was about to let go, he saw his brother approaching. (*Or. obl.*)
'Why have you *been so long?*'[2] said he ; and he replied that he had
found the people at home dining, so he had stayed to dinner. 'Catch
hold of the claws,' said Titus, 'that I may kill him ; for I can manage
the bow better.' So his brother caught hold ; and then 'I too will
go home,' said Titus, 'and when I have had my dinner I will come
and kill the bear.'

1. suspicere. 2. tamdiu cessare.

186. *News of the Battle of the Boyne.*

Meanwhile *Dublin*[1] had been *in violent commotion.*[2] On the 30th of June it was known that the armies were *face to face*[3] with the river between them, and that a battle was *almost*[4] inevitable. The news that William had been wounded came that evening, and *spread*[5] so fast, and was so increased by being repeated, that couriers started bearing the glad tidings of his death to the French ships in the ports of Ireland. A thousand wild rumours wandered *to and fro*[6] among the eager crowds, all wondering what had happened : 'a fleet under the white flag had been seen ; an army commanded by a French general had landed in England ; there had been hard fighting on the Boyne, but the Irish had won the day; the Prince of Orange was a prisoner.' While the *Jacobites*[7] heard and repeated these stories, the few *Protestants*[8] who were still out of prison, fearing to be torn in pieces, shut themselves up in their *innermost chambers.*[9] But towards five in the afternoon a few runaways came straggling in with the truth.

1. Eblana. 2. vehementissime commoveri. 3. obvius. 4. modo non.
5. percrebrescere. 6. hither and thither. 7. qui a regis partibus erant. 8. Gulielmani. 9. penetralia.

187. *Assize Wit.*

One day at Chester, when a barrister was *pleading*[1] before the judge, the heat became so excessive that the judge ordered the windows to be opened. Thereupon the court was filled with the sound of a donkey's voice which began to bray stoutly in the yard. As the barrister continued notwithstanding to plead, the judge remarked, 'One at a time, *please.*'[2] This caused a laugh ; the barrister however, though he did not venture to retort openly, got a chance at last, for while the judge himself was speaking, the ass began to bray again. Then the barrister, dropping his voice, yet in such a manner as to allow the judge to *overhear*[3] him, observed, '*I must say*[4] I never heard an *echo*[5] in this court before.' The *opposing counsel,*[6] a well-known wag and inveterate joker, *catching him up,*[7] exclaimed, 'What ! not with those long ears of yours ?'

1. caussam dicere. 2. tandem. 3. exaudire. 4. equidem. 5. reper-cussus sonus. 6. adversary. 7. contra.

188. *Asia.*

In consequence of Asia having been the *birthplace*[1] of mankind, the seat of the first great empires, and the country in which the Christian religion, *not to speak of*[2] others, made its first appearance, *it has been the theatre*[3] of the most stirring events in history. There can be no doubt that the languages of Europe as well as many of its institutions *have an Asiatic origin.*[4] The ancients had but an extremely imperfect knowledge of *its geography.*[5] They were just aware of the existence of a northern ocean, and frequently mention the Hyperboraei as inhabiting its shores. Such tribes as lived to the north of the Caspian and Black Seas were known as Scythians, and certain portions which of right belong to Asia are placed by Herodotus in Europe. Only what is now called Asia Minor and forms part of the Turkish dominions was called Asia by the Romans, who divided it into Asia within and Asia without the Taurus Mountains, considering them to be *the limit of civilization.*[6] Asia Minor has become greatly impoverished and is far less thickly populated than of old, in consequence of internal wars and dissensions for so many centuries, and the oppressive rule of the Turks.

1. use a verb. 2. ne dicam. 3. simplify this idea. 4. are to be traced (*oriundus*) from Asia. 5. its boundaries and the nature of its places. 6. the boundary between civilized and uncivilized nations.

189. *The Captain and the Carpenter.*

Many years ago Frederick the Great was King of Prussia. He being very desirous of surpassing his neighbours in war, and taking their land, resolved to make his army as powerful as possible. So he ordered his captains to go into all the towns and choose *the biggest*[1] men they could find, and force them to serve under him as soldiers. A certain captain accordingly saw one day a *carpenter*[2] of wonderful stature, and went into his house, and requested him to make a large wooden chest. The man asked him to explain more accurately how large he wished it to be; and he replied (*or. obl.*), 'So large that you could lie down within it.' He returned after a few days, and found the chest ready, but when he saw it, he complained, saying that it was less than he had ordered it to be. (*Or. obl.*) 'Not at all,' replied the carpenter, ' and that I may prove to you how big it is, I will lie down inside.' With these words he placed himself, not without difficulty, in the chest, and no sooner had he done this, than the captain closed the chest and fastened it with an iron bolt, and so, calling his comrades, carried off the big man to the army. When, however, they arrived, the chest was opened and the man was found dead.

1. each biggest. 2. faber tignarius.

190. *Diocles and the Thief.*

Diocles was a philosopher who was so poor that he did not fear lest he should be robbed, and therefore was accustomed to leave his house at night open and unguarded. For he knew that thieves always find out where gold is collected before they enter a house : nor would any one be so foolish as to incur danger *of death*,[1] except for the sake of the greatest gain. One night, however, Diocles was lying on his bed, when he saw a thief come in, and go round searching everything, in the hope of finding some gold or valuable possession. The thief did not perceive that Diocles was awake, as he held his peace and lay quite still : yet the philosopher saw him clearly, since it was too dark for the other to see if his eyes were open. At last, when he had sought everywhere in vain, he began to utter terrible curses against Diocles, but in a *low*[2] voice, lest he should wake : and when Diocles heard this, he said (*or. obl.*), 'Hush, my friend ; and do not by any means be angry, for I indeed am sorry that you are unable to discover any gold : but if I who live here cannot find any in the daytime, how can *one*[3] expect that a stranger could light upon it by night ?'

1. of the head.   2. summissus.   3. ecquis.

191. *Priscus and Paullina.*

His wife Paullina resolutely declared that she would die with her husband. But the philosopher, who feared to leave a woman whom he had tenderly loved *to be mocked*[1] by the world, said (*or. obl.*), 'I have already shown how the ills of life are to be alleviated : you prefer the glory of death. Of firmness of mind each of us may have an equal share, but the greater renown will be yours.' Then with one blow they made an incision into their arms. Priscus, whose body was now aged and emaciated by a *low*[2] diet, bled very slowly : accordingly, to hasten his end, he ordered the veins of his thighs and hams to be cut asunder. Soon after, worn out by excruciating pains, lest by his sufferings he should weaken his wife's courage, or by beholding her tortures should lose his own patience, he advised her to retire into another room. Tiberius, however, who had conceived no enmity against Paullina, and desired, if possible, to prevent an *aggravation*[3] of the odium which his cruelty had aroused, ordered her death to be prevented. The freedmen therefore bound up her arms and stopped the blood : nor is it certain whether this was done *contrary to her wish*.[4] Meanwhile her husband drank some poison, but without effect : and at last was carried into a bath, where he was suffocated by the vapour.

1. as a laughing-stock.   2. parcus.   3. do not use a substantive.
4. Paullina being unwilling.

I

192. *A Choice between Evils.*

There lived at Corinth a father who had two sons, and who, as he was a foolish man, did not *carry out the advice of sensible friends*[1] about his boys, but trusted in all things to oracle-mongers and impostors of all sorts. And once an old soothsayer came to Corinth, who foretold that after no long interval of time there would be an earthquake in the city, which would destroy not the older people, but the children. At a loss what he should do, the father resolved at last to send the boys out of the way of the danger, considering that he himself was safe. So he sent them to a friend at Athens, begging him by a letter to maintain them and look after them till the earthquake *should occur.*[2] The children having arrived, at first were orderly, and did nothing else than what they were ordered, only admiring the house and the animals that were kept there. But at last they *took to mischief,*[3] injuring the things and beasts in the house. For they shaved the cat, and hung up the monkey by his tail, and *so forth.*[4] So at last the Athenian wrote to the Corinthian, saying he would rather have their earthquake than such children.

1. obey his friends giving sensible advice.   2. should have occurred ; notice the superior exactness of Latin.   3. in peius verti.
4. with many such games

193. *The Caudine Forks avenged.*

'We accept the omen,' said the consuls, 'and invoke *such*[1] fear on the heads of our enemies as may prevent them from defending even their ramparts.' Then, dividing their forces, they approached the enemies' works, and making a simultaneous attack from every side, assailed their camp. While part fill up the trenches and part tear down the rampart, *it was*[2] not their inborn valour alone, but also fury that stimulated their minds, already smarting with resentment. 'These are not the Caudine Forks,' they reminded each other, 'nor the pathless glens where our mistake *was punished*[3] by treachery : ours is the courage of Romans, which neither walls nor trenches can withstand.' They slay alike those that resist and those that are scattered, armed and unarmed, slaves and free, men and beasts of burden : nor would any *living creature*[4] have survived, had not the consul *given the signal for retreat,*[5] and driven his men with commands and menaces from the hostile camp.

1. is.   2. notice the redundant ' it.'   3. use the active verb.
4. animal.   5. receptui canere.

194. *Glorious Actions live in Story.*

Alexander the Great is said to have had many historians to tell of his exploits, yet when standing by Achilles' *barrow* [1] on *the promontory of* [2] Sigeum, he exclaimed, 'O lucky youth, *to have* [3] found a bard to sing of thy valour.' Lucky he surely was : for unless that glorious Iliad had been written, the barrow which had covered his bones would also have covered his fame. Again, did not our glorious Pompeius here, whose successes are only equalled by his valour, present *the freedom of the city* [4] before a general assembly of his soldiers to Theophanes of Mitylene, who had narrated his exploits ? Did not our own brave fellows, though mere peasants and common soldiers, stirred by an *indescribable* [5] delight in glory, ratify his action with hearty cheers as if sharers in his renown ?

1. tumulus. 2. omit. 3. who (= in that thou) hast. 4. civitas. 5. quidam.

195. *Livy's merits as a Historian.*

Livy's *style* [1] is indeed admirable : but before expressing *our judgment* [2] of him, we must determine clearly what was the end he had in view. No one who peruses his writings with attention will be of opinion that he ever intended to write an exact history. His aim was to give to his countrymen a *series of annals,* [3] easy of comprehension and pleasant to read, which, while satisfying their amour propre, should avoid relating incredible occurrences and flattering them *unduly.* [4] Nor did he ever (though he *collated* [5] carefully, *with this end in view,* [6] the writings of some ancient authors) betake himself to the fountain-head and source, nor *test* [7] the good faith of his authorities by a careful examination of the old legends.

1. there is no word for this; turn it by a verb. 2. what we think.
3. fasti. 4. nimis. 5. recensere et comparare. 6. to effect this. 7. periclitari.

196. *A Letter from a Husband to a Wife.*

ROME, *May* 14, 1879.

My dearest wife,—You say in your letter that my absence affects you *in no slight degree,* [1] and that your only solace is *the fact of your having* [2] my letters instead of me and being able to put them in my *place.* [3] I am delighted that you miss me, and delighted also you are content to put up with these consolations. I in my turn read your letters *over and over again,* [4] and often take them up as if they were fresh ones : but it makes me miss you all the more ; for who ever wrote such delightful letters as my wife does ? Yet write oftener, though the *pleasure I feel is mingled with pain.* [5] Goodbye. Your affectionate husband.

1. non mediocriter. 2. quod, etc. 3. vestigium (*i.e.* place in chair, at table, etc.). 4. express this by using the frequentative verb.
5. it delights me in such a way as to pain me.

197. *A City surprised by Treachery.*

Meanwhile Philemenus with 1000 Africans had been sent to *secure*[1] another gate by stratagem. The guards were accustomed to let him in at all hours, whenever he returned from hunting ; and now, when they heard his usual whistle, one of them went to the gate to admit him. Philemenus called to the guard from without to open the *wicket*[2] quietly, *for his friends*[3] had killed a huge wild boar, and could scarcely bear the weight any longer : the guard, accustomed to have a share in the spoil, opened the wicket; and Philemenus and three other conspirators, disguised as countrymen, stepped in, carrying the boar between them. They instantly killed the poor guard as he was admiring and *feeling*[4] the prize, and then let in about thirty Africans who were following close behind. With this force they mastered the *gate-house*[5] and towers, killed all the guards, and *hewed asunder*[6] the bars of the main gates to admit the whole *column*[7] of Africans, who marched in on this side also in regular order, and advanced towards the market-place.

> 1. occupare. 2. portula. 3. oratio obliqua. 4. manibus pertrectare.
> 5. qualify 'house' by an adjectival clause. 6. securibus discindere. 7. agmen ; remember difference between *acies*, the line of battle, and *agmen*, the column on the march.

198. *Lord Clive's Donkey.*

The *directors*,[1] on receiving news of Clive's brilliant success, instantly appointed him governor of their possessions in Bengal, *with the highest marks of gratitude and esteem.*[2] His power was now boundless, and far surpassed even that which Dupleix had attained in the south of India. Meer Jaffier regarded him with slavish awe. On one occasion the Nabob spoke with severity to a native chief of high rank, whose followers had been engaged in a brawl with some of the Company's Sepoys. 'Are you yet to learn,' he said, ' who that Colonel Clive is, and in what station God has placed him ?' The chief, who, as a famous jester and an old friend of Meer Jaffier, *could venture to take liberties*,[3] answered, ' *I affront*[4] the Colonel ! I, who never get up in the morning *without*[5] making three low bows to his jackass !'

> 1. qui a consiliis erant. 2. and expressed how grateful they were to him and how they praised him. 3. sometimes ventured on some remark (*nonnihil audere*). 4. indignant question. 5. quin.

199. *Britain and the English.*

But the threat of fresh inroads found Britain torn with civil quarrels, which made a *united*[1] resistance impossible, while its Pictish enemies strengthened themselves by a league with marauders from Ireland, Scots as they were then called, whose pirate-boats were harrying the western coast of the island, and with a yet more formidable race of pirates who had long been pillaging along the British Channel. These were the English. We do not know whether it was the pressure of other tribes, or the example of their German brethren who were now moving *in a general attack*[2] on the Empire from their forest homes, or simply the barrenness of their coast, which drove the hunters, farmers, fishermen, of the three English tribes to sea. But the daring spirit of their race already broke out in the secrecy and suddenness of their swoop, in the fierceness of their onset, in the careless glee with which they seized either sword or oar. 'Foes are they,' sang a Roman poet of the time, ' fierce beyond other foes, and *cunning as they are fierce;*[3] the sea *is their school of*[4] war, and the storm their friend; they are sea-wolves that live on the pillage of the world.'

1. with joined forces. 2. una. 3. whose cunning is a match for (*par*) their ferocity. 4. teaches them.

200. *Ambition of Napoleon the First.*

Napoleon I. was gifted with ambition as wonderful as his genius, and it was his misfortune and that of France. Sprung from *the Revolution,*[1] of which at the outset he defended the *principles,*[2] he turned aside for the advantage of himself and his family the movement of the nations which were demanding liberty. His glory, which will perhaps equal that of Alexander, would have been much greater if he had laboured for humanity *instead of pursuing*[3] his selfish views, and his name, cursed to-day by many historians, would have been loved by posterity. If he had remained faithful to law and to honour, he would not have destroyed *without warrant*[4] and by force and craft the *established*[5] government; he would not have assassinated the Duc d'Enghien ; nor would Paris have twice seen what she had not seen since the reign of an insane king, Charles VI., an army of foreigners mistress of her gates, her streets, and her palaces.

1. res novae. 2. sententia. 3. and had not pursued. 4. iniuria.
5. legitimus.

201. *Weak Points in a strong Character.*

In his private conduct[1] he was severe, morose, inexorable, banishing all the softer affections as natural enemies to justice, and as suggesting false motives of acting from favour, clemency, and compassion. In public affairs he was the same : had but one rule of policy, to adhere to what was right, without any *regard*[2] to times, circumstances, or even to *a force that could control*[3] him; for instead of managing the power of the great so as to mitigate the ill or extract any good from it, he was urging it always to acts of violence by a perpetual defiance, so that, with the best intentions in the world, he often did great harm to the republic. This was his general *behaviour*,[4] yet from some particular facts explained above, it appears that his strength of mind was not always impregnable, but *had its weak points of*[5] pride, ambition, and party zeal, which, when managed and flattered to a certain point, would sometimes betray him into meanness, contrary to his ordinary rule of right and truth. The last act of his life was agreeable to his nature and philosophy. When he could no longer be what he had been, and when the ills of life overbalanced the good, which by the principles of his sect was a just cause for dying, he put an end to his life with *a*[6] spirit and resolution which would make *one*[7] imagine that he was glad to have found an occasion of dying in his proper character. *On the whole*,[8] his life was rather admirable than amiable, fit to be praised rather than imitated.

1. domi et intus. 2. ratio. 3. those that could control (participle).
4. verb. 5. afforded certain approaches to. 6. is. 7. you.
8. ut brevi rem absolvam.

202. *A Letter.*

LONDON, *Nov. 5.*

My dear Robert,—I write a few lines before starting. I am going to spend the winter in France, and shall soon send you a *summary*[1] of my doings. I do wish you would write oftener. By the way, you will allow me to remark, I had some difficulty in deciphering your last, in consequence of your liberal use of blots. I should like to know if you got the prize, how your parents are, when your sister is to be married to the General, etc. I am ashamed *of*[2] your remissness in writing.—Sincerely yours,   M. T. C.

1. not a substantive. 2. quod.

203. *The Triumvirate.*

This was the state of things[1] when Pompeius returned in 61. It was again thought that he would bring his army into Rome, and so rule the senate. But he did not, and came back to Rome as a simple citizen. He found, however, when the first gratitude was over, he was not so powerful as he expected to be. Gradually he quarrelled about many little matters with the senate. Caesar saw this and took advantage of it. He agreed with Pompeius and Crassus that they should all three work together to get what they each wanted. In the year 59 Caesar was made consul, and as such *proposed*[2] an agrarian law which was to give lands to Pompeius' old soldiers. Then a law was *passed*[3] by the people making Caesar the Governor of Gaul for five years, and putting him at the head of a large army. Caesar had now got what he wanted: he had got the opportunity of showing himself to be a great general, and so of gaining popularity with the Roman people. He could now make himself the equal of Pompeius, and hoped soon to become a greater man than he was. Above all, he could train up an army attached to him and ready to do whatever he told it.

1. which things when they had themselves so. 2. ferre. 3. iubere.

204. *The English and Roman Constitutions.*

If there be but one body of legislators it is not better than a tyranny: if there are only two, *there will want a casting voice,*[1] and one of them must at length be swallowed up by disputes and contentions that will necessarily arise between them. Four *would have the same inconvenience*[2] as two, and a greater number would cause too much confusion. I could never read a passage in Polybius and another in Cicero *to this purpose*[3] without a secret pleasure in applying it to the English Constitution, which it suits much better than the Roman. Both these great authors *give the pre-eminence*[4] to a mixed government, consisting of three branches, the regal, the noble, and the popular. They had doubtless in their thoughts the condition of the Roman commonwealth, in which the consul represented the king, the senate the nobles, and the tribune the people. This division of the three powers of the Roman constitution was by no means so distinct and natural as it is in the English form of government.

1. there will be no one to settle (*dirimere*) the matter by his vote.
2. labour under the same inconveniences. 3. quo in genere,
4. primas (partes) deferre.

205. *Objections to the Consular Power.*

Among several objections that might be made to it[1] I think the chief are those which affect the consular power, which had only the ornaments without the force of the regal authority. Their number had not a casting voice in it, for which reason, if one did not choose to be employed abroad while the other sat at home, the public business was sometimes *at a stand*[2] while the consuls pulled *two different ways*[3] in it. Besides I do not find that the consuls had ever *a negative voice*[4] in the *passing*[5] of a law or a decree of the senate, so that indeed they were rather the chief body of the nobility, or the first ministers of state, than a distinct branch of the sovereignty, in which none can be looked upon as a part *who are not a part of the legislature.*[6] Had the consuls been invested with the regal authority to as great a degree as our monarchs, there would never have been any occasion for a dictatorship, which had in it all the power of the three orders, and ended in the subversion of the whole constitution.

1. to omit other things to which any one might fairly (*iure*) object. 2. cessare. 3. in diversa. 4. intercedere. 5. iubere. 6. unless he has a part (*interesse*) in proposing laws.

206. *Force of Circumstances.*

(*Or. obl.*) I *have good reasons*[1] for acknowledging Lord Clive's benefits in having been freed from the subsidy which I had to pay to the Mahrattas; also in that his lordship has sent back both my son and nephew, whom the Mahrattas had kept in prison though sent *as*[2] hostages. *My share*[3] in the attack was not done of my own desire or free will, but under compulsion of the people. My authority is of such a kind that the people at large have no less power over me than I over them. This, moreover, is the reason of the hostilities, namely, I was not able to withstand the influence of the Mahratta conspirators. From my own weakness you can see I am speaking the truth: I am not foolish enough to imagine that I could overcome the English with the troops under my own command.

1. ought. 2. in the place (*numero*). 3. what I did.

207. *The Hero of Haarlem.*

Many years ago there lived at Haarlem, *one*[1] of the principal towns of Holland, a boy, whose father was a *sluicer.*[2] *One afternoon,*[3] as he was running home, he was startled by the sound of rushing water, and when he *looked up at*[4] the dyke, saw that there was a little hole through which the water was flowing. He climbed up, and putting his finger into the hole, cried for help, trusting that some one would soon come to help him. For he knew that by this means only could he save his native city from being overwhelmed. But the *day was so far advanced*[5] that no one came, and he was only found next morning by a priest, who heard the groaning, and saw the boy writhing with pain, but still refusing to leave his duty. Was ever a city more proud of its citizen than the city of Haarlem of this little boy, to whom *it had been given*[6] to win the civic crown without bloodshed?

    1. in a city; Haarlem being locative, a case which of course *urbs* has not got. 2. adjectival clause: to watch the dykes. 3. forte. 4. suspicere. 5. advesperascere. 6. contingere.

208. *A knotty Point.*

Sancho, during his governorship of the island of Barataria, was so often hungry as frequently to long to be sitting at home with his wife Teresa, for he was constantly asked to give answers, and this too very often *when he was just sitting*[1] down to dinner. Once there arrived a stranger, with a long-winded and confused complaint about some bridge or other, *at one end of*[2] which was erected a gallows. Now it had been enacted that any one who wanted to cross the bridge should say *on his oath*[3] where he was going and on what business. If he told the truth he was to be let pass; if he lied he was to be hung on the spot. It appeared that many people had been let pass after telling the truth. One day there turned up a traveller, who said his business was to be hung on the aforesaid gallows. The judges were at once in a quandary, for they reasoned as follows : if we let the man go unharmed he will have told a lie, therefore he should be hung; while if we hang him we may punish him unjustly, since he speaks the truth. The matter was therefore referred to the governor. Sancho replied that he did not take upon himself the decision of such *knotty points:*[4] that however this at any rate was clear, that the man asserts on his oath that he will be hung. Now supposing the judges condemned him, they would be acting illegally, for the law forbade the execution of a man who spoke the truth ; but if they acquitted him, they should of course put him to death, as he was guilty of perjury. The judges declared that the matter could not be *put*[5] more fairly; so the governor went on to say, 'As the reasons for acquittal are the same as those for finding him guilty, my decision is that he be let go free. If I must err, I prefer to err *on the side of*[6] mercy.'

    1. cum maxime. 2. ad extremam partem. 3. iuratus. 4. nodus. 5. concipi. 6. with.

209. *One great and two lesser Rogues.*

I remember a friend telling me that, on being robbed by the practor of a vase, the work of a well-known artist, he returned home *in a state of gloom and agitation*[1] at being deprived of so handsome a piece of plate, *an heirloom*[2] from his father and ancestors, and which he was accustomed to use on festive occasions. 'I was sitting,' said he, 'gloomily in my house. In comes one of the practor's servants and tells me to bring my *embossed*[3] tankards to the practor without delay. I was greatly disturbed,' continued he; 'I had a pair of tankards. I promised to produce them, to avoid further annoyance, and bring them to the practor's house. When I got there the practor was *taking his siesta;*[4] two *hangers on*[5] of his were strolling about. When they saw me, they said, Where are the tankards? I showed them sadly; they admired them. I began to complain that I should have nothing worth anything if I was robbed of my tankards. Then, seeing my agitation, they asked me what I would give them to be allowed to keep them. *To cut a long story short,*[6] they asked me for a thousand sestertii, and I promised to give them. In the meanwhile the practor calls for me and demands the tankards. They began to tell him that they had thought and had heard that my cups were of some value: that they were in reality a *paltry bungle,*[7] unworthy of being part of his *plate.*[8] He said that he agreed with them. Thus I got away with my tankards.'

1. simplify this before translating. 2. left. 3. sigillatus. 4. quiescere. 5. parasitus. 6. not (ne) to say many things. 7. luteum negotium. 8. argentum.

210. *Extremes of Rashness are equally dangerous.*

Some were of opinion that an attempt should be made *at all hazards*[1] and the camp of the enemy taken by storm, thinking inaction most *prejudicial*[2] to the troops. Some advised a retreat to a secure spot, that by the effect of time the soldiers might return to their duty, and that, moreover, in case of a defeat they might have a safe and easy means of retreat. The general, finding fault with either plan, said that *one was as excessive in daring as the other was deficient;*[3] that one party were proposing a dishonourable flight, while the others were counselling fighting even in a disadvantageous position. 'With what hope of success,' said he, 'can we imagine a camp can be stormed which is so strongly fortified both by art and nature? Yet what advantage do we obtain if we are defeated with loss and have to relinquish our attack on the camp? Just as if it was not success that wins the affection of soldiers for their leaders, and defeat that causes them to be disliked! Moreover, what will follow a change of camp but disgraceful flight, universal despair, and the disaffection of the troops? Consequently I am neither so bold as to approve of attacking the enemy's camp without hope of success nor so cowardly as to retreat myself, and I am of opinion that we should try every plan before rashly adopting either of these plans.'

1. omnibus modis. 2. contrarius. 3. as much valour as was wanting to one, so much was excessive in the other.

211. *An appeal to the People.*

The case has been laid before you: now bethink yourselves of what has to be done. I think I should first speak of the nature of the war, next of its importance, and lastly on your *choice*[1] of a general. Well, the war is of a nature which ought to rouse and stimulate your minds to fight the matter out: the *prestige*[2] of our nation *is at stake*,[3] a prestige which you inherit in all other respects, and especially as regards military matters: the security of your allies and friends is at stake, for which your ancestors fought many a bloody war: the most reliable and extensive revenues you have depend on it, and if you lose them you will be without the elegancies of peace and the sinews of war: on it are staked the property of many a citizen, on behalf of whom it is your duty to deliberate, both for their sake and for that of the commonwealth.

1. not a substantive. 2. gloria. 3. agitur.

212. *Cortes resolves to conquer or perish.*

Though the good fortune of Cortes interfered so seasonably on this occasion, *the detection of the conspiracy*[1] filled his mind with the most disquieting apprehensions, and prompted him to execute a scheme which he had long resolved. He perceived that the spirit of disaffection still lurked among his troops; that, though hitherto checked by the uniform success of his schemes or suppressed by the hand of authority, various events might occur which would encourage and call it forth. He observed that many of his men, weary of the fatigue of service, longed to revisit their settlements in Cuba; and that, upon any appearance of extraordinary danger or any reverse of fortune, it would be impossible to restrain them from going thither. He was sensible that his forces, already too feeble, could bear no diminution, and that a very small defection of his followers would oblige him to abandon the enterprise. After ruminating often and with much . solicitude upon these particulars, *he saw no hope of success but in* [2] cutting off all possibility of retreat, and in reducing his men to the necessity of adopting the same resolution with which he himself was animated—either to conquer or perish. With this view he determined to destroy his fleet, but as he durst not venture to execute such a bold resolution by his single authority, he laboured to bring his soldiers to adopt his ideas *with respect to the propriety of this measure.*[3]

1. the detected conspiracy. 2. the matter seemed thus only to be well managed, if, etc. 3. if he could prove their propriety.

213. *Thought for others.*

Again, *suppose* [1] that though the necessities of the human race continue the same as at present, yet the mind is so enlarged and so replete with friendship and generosity that *every man* [2] has the utmost tenderness for every man, and feels no more concern for his own interest than for that of his fellow. It seems evident that the use of justice would *in this case* [3] be suspended by such an extensive benevolence, nor would the divisions and barriers of property and obligations have ever been thought of. Why should I bind another by a *deed* [4] or promise to do me any good office, when I know that he is already prompted by the strongest inclination to seek my happiness, and would of himself perform the desired service, except the hurt he thereby received be greater than the benefit accruing to me, *in which case* [5] he knows that, from my innate humanity and friendship, I should be the first to oppose myself *to his imprudent generosity.* [6] Why raise landmarks between my neighbour's field and mine, *when my heart has made no division* between our interests, but *shares* [8] all his joys and sorrows with the same vivacity and force as if originally my own ? Every man, *upon this supposition,* [9] being a second self to another, would trust all his interests to the *discretion* [10] of every man, without jealousy, partition, or distinction. And the whole human race would form only one family, where all would be in common, and would be used freely, without regard to property, but cautiously too, with as entire regard to the necessities of each individual as if our own interests were intimately concerned.

1. fac. 2. unusquisque. 3. quae si ita se habeant. 4. stipulatio. 5. quo in genere. 6. to him imprudently generous. 7. since I do not distinguish. 8. communicare cum. 9. hoc posito. 10. arbitrium.

214. *Nature is not to be blamed for our Faults.*

Men complain falsely of their nature, saying that as it is weak and shortlived it is influenced more by chance than by good qualities. On the contrary, *on reflection*[1] you cannot find anything greater or stronger, but you will find that *resolute perseverance*[2] is what nature lacks rather than ability or duration of life. Mind is what leads and commands the life of man, and it is powerful and glorious, and stands in no need of luck when it aims at reaching renown by the path of virtue, for it can neither give nor take away integrity, industry, and other praiseworthy qualities. But if, ensnared by vicious desires, it *turns*[3] to sloth and bodily gratifications, when, after it has enjoyed for a season this destructive indulgence, strength, time and talents are gone, then the weakness of nature is blamed, and the authors of these evils each transfer to *circumstances*[4] the blame which is their own. *But if*[5] mankind were inspired with *as great*[6] a regard for good things, *as*[6] is the zeal with which they seek after things foreign to them and utterly unlikely to be of use, then indeed would nature be rarely accused of weakness.

1. by reflecting. 2. industria. 3. many English verbs have no Latin equivalent in the active voice. 4. negotium. 5. quod si. 6. tantus—quantus.

215. *Spartan Brevity.*

The authors of antiquity relate many instances to prove *the objections entertained*[1] by the Lacedaemonians to oratory. *Not to be prolix,*[2] it will suffice to relate one or two of these. While the Peloponnesian war was raging, an envoy was sent by the ephors to Tissaphernes, the satrap of Lower Asia, to endeavour to persuade him to enter into an alliance with the Lacedaemonians. The envoy refrained from making a long harangue, for on hearing the eloquent speeches of the Athenian ambassadors, he drew two lines, one straight and the other curved, both of which ended in the same point, and turning to the satrap, observed, 'Take your choice.' *Again,*[3] two centuries previous to this, the inhabitants of an island in the Aegean complained of a scarcity of food and implored assistance. The ephors replied, 'The latter part of your speech is unintelligible, and the former is already *forgotten.*'[4] So the islanders sent a second envoy. On being brought into the senate-house he showed an empty sack, and said, 'This sack must be filled.' The ephor rejoined, 'It shall be filled ; don't make use of useless words.'

1. a single verb will translate this. 2. ne multa dicam. 3. quid ? 4. use the active.

216. *The Execution of Laud.*

Seven *peers* [1] alone *voted* [2] in this important question; the rest, either from fear or shame, took care to absent themselves. Laud, who had behaved during his trial with the spirit and vigour of genius, sunk not under the horrors of his execution; but though he had usually professed himself apprehensive of a violent death, he found all his fears to be dissipated before that superior courage with which he was animated. 'No one,' said he, 'can be more willing to send me out of life than I am desirous to go.' He quietly laid his head on the block, and it was severed from the body at one blow. Sincere he undoubtedly was, and *however misguided*, [3] actuated by pious motives in all his pursuits; and it is to be regretted that he had not entertained more enlarged views and embraced principles more favourable to the general happiness of society.

1. par. 2. suffragium ferre. 3. quamvis avia aberraret.

217. *Anselm of Aosta.*

No teacher has ever thrown a greater spirit of love into his toil than Anselm. 'Force your scholars to improve!' he burst out to a teacher who relied on blows and compulsion. 'Did you ever see a craftsman fashion a fair image out of a golden plate by blows alone? Does he not now gently press it and strike it with his tools, now with wise art yet more gently raise and shape it? What do your scholars turn into under this ceaseless beating?' 'They turn only brutal,' was the reply. 'You have bad luck,' was the *keen* [1] answer, '*in a training* [2] that only turns men into beasts.' The worst natures softened before this tenderness and patience. Even *the* [3] conqueror, so harsh and terrible to others, became another man, gracious and easy of speech, with Anselm.

1. lepidus. 2. since you (*qui* causal). 3. ille.

218. *Xenophon and the King's Envoy.*

Xenophon at that time was very young and never had *seen the wars* [1] before, neither had any command in the army, but only followed the war as a volunteer for the love and conversation of Proxenus his friend. He was present when Phalinus came in with a message from the great king to the Grecians, after that Cyrus was slain in *the field*, [2] and they, *a handful of men*, [3] were left to themselves in the midst of the king's territories, cut off from their country by many navigable rivers and many hundred miles. The message imported that they should deliver up their arms, and submit themselves to the king's mercy. Before this message was answered, divers of the army conferred familiarly with Phalinus; and amongst the rest, Xenophon *happened*[4] to say, 'Why, Phalinus, we have now but these two things left, our arms and our courage; and if we yield up our arms how shall we make use of our courage?' Whereupon Phalinus smiling on him, said, 'If I be not deceived, young gentleman, you are an Athenian; and I believe you study philosophy, and what you say is very *pretty*;[5] but you are much abused if you think your courage can withstand the king's power.'

    1. stipendia facere; lit. to serve. 2. acies. 3. so few. 4. forte.
                     5. lepide.

219. *How to attract different classes of Readers.*

I may class my readers under two general divisions, the *mercurial*[1] and the *saturnine*.[2] The first *are the gay part*[3] of my disciples, who require speculations of wit and humour; the others are those of a more *sober and solemn turn*,[4] who find no pleasure but in *papers of morality and sound sense*.[5] The former call everything that is serious stupid, the latter look upon everything as impertinent that is ludicrous. Were I always grave one half of my readers would fall off from me; were I always merry I should lose the other. *I make it therefore my endeavour*[6] to find out entertainments for both kinds, and by that means perhaps consult the good of both more than I should do did I always write to the particular taste of either. As they neither of them know what I proceed upon, the sprightly reader who takes up my paper in order to be diverted very often finds himself engaged unawares in a serious and profitable course of thinking; as, on the contrary, the thoughtful man, who perhaps may hope to find something more solid and full of deep reflection, is very often insensibly *betrayed into a fit of mirth*.[7] In a word, the reader sits down to my entertainments without knowing *his bill of fare*,[8] and has therefore at least the pleasure of hoping there may be a dish *to his palate*.[9]

    1. hilaris. 2. severus. 3. since they are inclined to gay things.
    4. tristius ingenium. 5. things said seriously to train moral feeling (*mores*). 6. id igitur propositum habeo. 7. cannot refrain from laughing (*risum tenere*). 8. what is placed before him.
    9. in animum.

220. *Edward's ruthlessness.*

But the murder of Comyn had changed the king's mood to a terrible pitilessness; he threatened death against all concerned in the outrage, and exposed the *Countess of Buchan*,[1] who had set the crown on Bruce's head, in a cage made *for the purpose*,[2] in one of the towers of *Berwick*.[3] At the solemn feast which celebrated his son's knighthood Edward vowed *on*[4] the swan, which formed the *chief dish*[5] at the banquet, to devote the rest of his days to exact vengeance from the murderer himself. But even *at the moment of*[6] the vow Bruce was already flying for his life to the Highlands. 'Henceforth,' he had said to his wife at their coronation, 'thou art Queen of Scotland and I King.' 'I fear,' replied Mary, 'we are only *playing at royalty*,[7] like children in their games.' The play was soon turned into *bitter earnest*.[8] A small English force sufficed to rout the disorderly levies which gathered round the new monarch, and the flight of Bruce left his followers at Edward's mercy. Noble after noble was hurried to the block. The *Earl of Athole*[9] pleaded kindred with royalty. 'His only privilege,' burst forth the king, 'shall be that of being hanged on a higher gallows than the rest.' Bruce himself had offered to capitulate to Prince Edward, but the offer only roused the old king to fury. 'Who is so bold,' he cried, 'as to treat with our traitors without our knowledge?' and rising from his sick-bed he led his army northwards to complete the conquest.

1. domina Vacomagorum.　2. for this very (thing).　3. Curia.　4. calling to witness.　5. caput.　6. cum maxime.　7. regias partes agere.　8. seria (adj.).　9. dux Vennicontium.

221. *The Senior Wrangler.*

A senior wrangler,[1] who had but very recently gained that distinction, and who in previous years had not had time to indulge *in going into society*[2] and observing *character*,[3] determined at last to lay aside his books and pay a visit to London, and see the churches, baths, palaces, theatres,—*in a word*,[4] everything he had not seen before. He stopped at the house of a friend, where he was to dine and whose hospitality he was to enjoy. Being heartily welcomed by his relations, he said that he would like nothing so much as to go that very night to a theatre and see a play. Now it happened that he and his friends, as they had indulged in a *rather elaborate*[5] dinner, as became a day worthy of being *marked*[6] with a white *stone*,[7] made their entry into the theatre rather late, *at the very moment when*[8] the Queen's son, who was recovering from a dangerous illness, was also entering. Observing this every one stood up; the *boxes*[9] re-echoed with universal applause; people began to cheer, universal cries of 'Let us rejoice at the safety of our prince!' began to be heard. But our friend, turning to his friend, with a blushing countenance and bowing with a, *so to speak*,[10] mathematical grace, said that he could have had no idea of the enthusiasm with which the people welcomed a philosopher.

1. rixator primus.　2. communis vitae societas.　3. mores.　4. denique.　5. lautior.　6. notare.　7. lapillus.　8. cum maxime.　9. cuneus.　10. ut ita dicam.

222. *Contrast between the Emperor and the Pope.*

The contrast between Charles' conduct and that of the Pope at this juncture was so obvious that it *struck*[1] even the most careless observer; *nor was the comparison which they made to the advantage of Paul.*[2] The former, a conqueror born to reign, long accustomed to the splendour which accompanies supreme power, and to those busy and interesting scenes in which an active ambition had engaged him, quitted the world at a period of life not far advanced, that he might close the *evening of his days*[3] with tranquillity, and secure some interval for sober *thought*[4] and serious *reflection.*[4] The latter, a priest who had passed the early part of his life in the shade of the schools and in *the study of the speculative sciences,*[5] who was seemingly so detached from the world that he had shut himself up for many years in the solitude *of a cloister,*[6] and who was not raised to the papal throne until he had reached the extremity of old age, discovered at once all the impetuosity of youthful ambition, and formed extensive schemes, in order to accomplish which he scrupled not to scatter the seeds of discord and to kindle the flames of war in every corner of Europe. But Paul, regardless of the opinion or censures of mankind, *held on his own course*[7] with his wonted arrogance and violence. These, *although*[8] they seemed already to have exceeded all bounds, rose to a still greater height upon the arrival of the Duke of Guise into Italy.

1. advertere. 2. and the comparison was to the disadvantage (*deterior*) of Paul. 3. his setting (*occidere*) life. 4. translate by verbs. 5. cognitio rerum. 6. omit, as it is a modern idea. 7. literally, the metaphor being the same in both languages. 8. ut—ita.

223. *Dickens visits his Father in Prison.*

My father was waiting for me in the vestibule, and we went up to his room, and we both cried very much. I remember that he told me to take warning by seeing the prison, and to observe that when a man had one hundred sesterces *to spend*[1] and spent one hundred and one, he would be wretched. I see the fire we sat before now : there were two bricks, *one*[2] on either side of the hearth, to prevent its burning too many logs. Some other *debtors*[3] *shared*[4] the room with my father, who came in *by and by,*[5] and as the dinner was now ready, I was sent up to tell another man who was imprisoned above that I was my father's son, and to ask him to *lend*[6] me a fork. I remember I thought I should not have liked *to borrow*[7] his comb ; but he lent me his fork, and I enjoyed the dinner very much.

1. of his own (*suus*) ; put this in the right place to mark the emphasis. 2. distributive numeral. 3. reus. 4. used. 5. haud ita multo post. 6. accommodare. 7. mutuum accipere.

K

224. *Queen Margaret and the Robber.*

Queen Margaret, after a *signal*[1] defeat in one of the wars between *the houses of York and Lancaster,*[2] fled with her son into a forest, where she endeavoured to conceal herself. During the darkness of the night she was beset by robbers, who, either ignorant or regardless of her *quality,*[3] despoiled her of her rings and jewels, and treated her with the utmost indignity. The partition of this rich booty raised a quarrel among them ; and while *their attention was thus engaged,*[4] she *took*[5] the opportunity of making her escape with her son into the thickest of the forest, where she wandered for some time, overspent with hunger and fatigue, and sunk with terror and affliction. *While in this*[6] wretched condition she saw a robber approach with his naked sword, and finding that she had no means of escape, she suddenly embraced the resolution of trusting entirely to his faith for protection. She advanced towards him, and presenting to him the young prince, called out to him, ' Here, my friend, I commit to your care the safety of your king's son.' The man, whose humanity and generous spirit *had been obscured but not*[7] entirely lost by his *vicious course*[8] of life, was struck by the singularity of the event, and charmed with the confidence reposed in him ; and he vowed not only to abstain from all injury against the princess, but to devote himself entirely to her safety and protection.

1. insignis.　2. Eboracenses, Lancastrienses.　3. conditio.　4. they apply themselves (totus incumbere in) to this.　5. nancisci.　6. in his tam, etc.　7. ut—ita.　8. prava ratio.

225. *A Lecture on Physical Science.*

Anaxagoras asserted that the sun was a mass of burning iron, greater than Peloponnesus (but some attribute this idea to Tantalus), and that the moon contained houses, and also hills and ravines ; and that the *primary elements*[1] of all things were similarities of parts ; for as we say that gold consists of a quantity of grains combined together, so too is the universe formed of a number of small bodies of similar parts. He further taught *that mind was the principle of motion,*[2] and that of bodies the heavy ones, such as the earth, occupied the lower situations ; and that the light ones, such as fire, *occupied*[3] the higher places ; and that the middle spaces were assigned to water and air. And thus that the sea rested on the earth, and that the moisture is continually evaporated by the sun. And he said that the stars originally moved about in irregular confusion, so that at first any star which is continually visible appeared *in the zenith,*[4] but that afterwards it acquired a certain declination. Also that the milky way was a *reflection*[5] of the light of the sun when the stars did not appear. The comets he considered to be a concourse of planets emitting rays ; and the shooting stars he thought were sparks as it were leaping from the firmament. The winds he thought were caused by the *rarefaction of the atmosphere* [6] which was produced by the sun. Thunder he said was produced by the *collision* [7] of the clouds, and lightning by the *rubbing* [7] together of the clouds.

1. primordia.   2. that motion originated from (*oriundus*) the mind.
3. obtinere   4. coeli vertex.   5. reflected.   6. rare atmosphere.
7. translate by participles.

226. *Flight of the Parliamentary Forces.*

It is certain the *consternation* [1] was very great in London and in *the two Houses* [2] from the time that they heard that the king marched from Shrewsbury with a formed army, and that he was resolved to fight as soon as he could meet with their army. However, they endeavoured to keep up confidently the ridiculous opinion among the common people, that the king did not command, but was carried about in that of the cavaliers, and was desirous to escape from them, which they hoped the Earl of Essex would give him opportunity to do. The first news they heard of the army's being engaged was from those who fled upon the first charge, who made marvellous haste from the place of dangers, and thought not themselves safe *till they were gotten out of any possible distance of being pursued.* [3] It was certain, though it was past two o'clock when the battle began, many of the soldiers and some commanders were at St. Albans, which was near thirty miles from the field, before it was dark. These men, as all runaways do *for their own excuse,* [4] reported all for lost, and the king's army to be so terrible that it could not be encountered.

1. render by an impersonal verb.   2. utraque curia.   3. before they took away the possibility of pursuit by the distance of the road.
4. excusing themselves.

227. *The Dishonesty of Charles I.*

The king is a man of great sense, of great talents, but *so full of dissimulation, and so false,* [1] that it is impossible to trust him. While he is protesting his love for peace, he is treating underhand with the Scotch Commissioners to plunge *the nation* [2] into another war. It is now *expected* [3] that you should govern and defend the realm by your own power and resolution, and not allow the people any longer to expect safety and government from an obstinate man, *you* [4] who, at the expense of your blood, have defended the state from so many perils, and will again defend it with the same courage and fidelity against all enemies whoever they may be. Teach them not, therefore, by neglecting your own and the kingdom's safety, in which their own *is involved*,[5] to think themselves betrayed, and left hereafter to the rage and malice of an irreconcileable enemy, whom you have subdued for their sake, lest *despair teach them*[6] to seek their safety by some other means than *adhering to you*,[7] who will not stick to yourselves. How destructive such a resolution will be to you all I tremble to think, and *leave*[8] you to judge.

1. express this idea by substantives ; it will gain in vividness, 2. nostrates. 3. behoves. 4. vos, vos, inquam. 5. pendere. 6. iam desperantes. 7. acting with you. 8. beg.

228. *Spectral Haircutters.*

My freedman Marcus was sleeping one night with his younger brother. *The latter*[1] fancied he saw some one sitting on the bed, who approached a *pair of scissors*[2] to his head, and even cut off the hair on his crown. When daylight came he was found with the top of his head shorn and the hair lying about. Shortly after this occurrence was *confirmed*[3] by a second resembling it. A lad was asleep. There came (so ran his story) two beings clad in white through the window, and cropped his hair as he lay ; they then disappeared by the way they came. At daybreak he also was found with his head shorn and the hair scattered around. Nothing noteworthy resulted, except perhaps *the fact of my not being*[4] accused, *as I certainly should have been*[5] had Domitian lived longer, for a *memorandum*[6] regarding me was found in his desk ; from which *the explanation may be hazarded*,[7] that as criminals are wont to let their hair grow, the shorn heads of my servants indicated the driving away of imminent peril.

1. is. 2. cultri. 3. fidem facere ; this clause will require a little turning. 4. quod non fui ; a substantival clause acting as subject to ' resulted.' 5. future participle. 6. libellus. 7. coniectari potest.

229. *Eruption of Vesuvius and Death of Pliny.*

Pliny, who was staying at Misenum, was informed by a woman, at about *one o'clock*[1] on August 21, that a cloud of unusual size and appearance was *coming into view*.[2] He mounted to a spot from which this portent could best be observed. A cloud (it was uncertain to spectators at a distance from what mountain ; it was afterwards ascertained to be Vesuvius), was rising. A pine better than any other tree *would give an idea*[3] of its general look and shape. It was now white, now quite dirty and spotted, according as it had taken up earth or ashes. This seemed to be something of importance and *worth*[4] looking at more closely. He ordered a boat to be got ready, and hastened to the place whence others fled. Already the ashes, *the*[5] nearer they approached, grew hotter and thicker; already pumice stones also began to fall, black and *calcined*[6] and cracked with fire. After a short hesitation as to whether he should make his way back, he remarked to the steersman, who urged *the propriety of his doing so*,[7] 'Fortune helps the bold: make for *the villa of Pomponius*.'[8] Meanwhile, in several places, broad sheets of flame were gleaming from Mount Vesuvius, and their brilliancy *was thrown into bolder relief*[9] by the darkness of night. Then Pliny disembarked, went to bed, and enjoyed some real repose. Subsequently flames, and a sulphurous smell *which foretold their approach*,[10] put the others to flight and awakened him. Leaning on a couple of slaves, he rose, but at once fell back *choked*.[11] When daylight was restored, his body was found, *without any disfigurement*:[12] its *look*[13] betokened sleep rather than death.

1. the Romans counted from sunrise, say six o'clock. 2. apparere. 3. will have expressed. 4. express by gerundive. 5. quo. 6. ambustus. 7. that he should do so. 8. Pomponianum. 9. excitare. 10. praenuntius. 11. with breath choked (*obstringere*). 12. integer. 13. habitus.

230. *French and German Tactics.*

The French style of fighting was to dash forward with great *élan*,[1] and *carry*[2] the position, without paying strict attention to their *dressing*,[3] and fight *in scattered knots and parties*.[4] If hard pressed they thought it no disgrace to retreat and abandon the position, having got accustomed to this style of fighting from their experience in Africa ; it often happens that soldiers are greatly influenced by the habits of the country in which they *have long been quartered*.[5] The Germans, on the other hand, had been of opinion that they should keep to their *formation*,[6] remain by the colours, and not abandon, except for very strong reasons, a position which they had taken. Yet it did not *escape the notice of*[7] the German leader that, in consequence of the altered *conditions*[8] of fighting, they also should adopt the activity of the French, for that otherwise they would be exterminated by the enemy's *fire*[9] through fighting in *close order*.[10] Consequently they so trained their men, that combining the enemy's activity with their own steadiness, they proved victorious in almost every engagement.

1. impetus. 2. capere. 3. order. 4. rari dispersique. 5. inveterascere. 6. order. 7. fallere. 8. ratio. 9. darts. 10. conferta acies.

231. *An Instance of Self-sufficiency.*

An experienced commander had been invited by a friend to hear a celebrated professor *give a lecture.*[1] He accepted the invitation, and *the story goes on to say*[2] that the long-winded worthy spoke for several hours about the duties of a general, and military matters in general. The remainder *of the audience,*[3] who were highly gratified, asked the general for his opinion of the professor. He is said to have replied *bluntly enough,*[4] that he had often seen mad old men, but none madder than yon professor. *He was right,*[5] I think. *What greater instance*[6] of self-sufficiency or *empty windiness*[7] could there be than that a man who had never set eyes on an enemy or a camp, who had never been intrusted with the most insignificant public business, should *lay down the law*[8] on military matters to a general who had fought in so many wars?

1. disserere. 2. simplify this. 3. express this by an adjectival clause. 4. libere. 5. neque iniuria. 6. what could be, etc. 7. loquacius (adjective). 8. praecepta dare.

232. *The Contemplation of Death.*

There is a sort of delight which is alternately mixed with terror and sorrow in the *contemplation*[1] of death. The soul *has its curiosity more than ordinarily awakened*[2] when it turns its thoughts upon the conduct of those who have behaved themselves with an equal, a resigned, a cheerful, a generous or heroic temper in that extremity. We are affected with these respective manners of behaviour as we secretly believe the part of the dying person imitable by ourselves, or such as we imagine ourselves more particularly capable of. Men of exalted minds *march*[3] before us like princes, and are to the ordinary race of mankind rather subjects for admiration than example. *However,*[4] there are no ideas which strike more forcibly upon one's imaginations, than those which are raised from reflections upon the exits of great and excellent men. Innocent men who have suffered as criminals, though they were benefactors to human society, seem to be persons of the highest distinction among the vastly greater number of the human race, the dead. When the iniquity of the times brought Socrates to his execution, *how great and wonderful*[5] it is to behold him, unsupported by anything but the testimony of his own conscience, and conjectures of the hereafter, receive the poison with an air of warmth and good humour, and, as if going on an agreeable journey, bespeak some deity to make it fortunate.

1. not a substantive. 2. praeter solitum curiose introspicit. 3. incedere. 4. quanquam. 5. who is there but wonders at.

233. *An Earthquake.*

An earthquake had continued for many days; but on that night it was so *intensified*[1] that everything seemed not to be shaken but overthrown. We sat down on a *level*[2] which separated at a slight interval the buildings from the sea. It was now the first hour of daylight, and as yet day seemed doubtful and *so to speak*[3] languid. Already all the surrounding buildings were shattered. Though we were in an open space, yet, as it was quite narrow, there was a great and *well-founded*[4] apprehension of destruction. Then *at last*[5] we saw fit to leave the town. We went out and stopped : there we underwent many *extraordinary vicissitudes*[6] and great alarms. For the carriages which we had ordered to be brought out rolled *backwards*[7] though on perfectly level ground, and would not remain still even when the wheels were *propped*[8] up by stones. Moreover, we saw the sea ebb, and as it were, being driven back by the earthquake. The shore had certainly *widened*,[9] and *stranded*[10] many fish on the dry sand. On the other side a terrible black cloud was *yawning*[11] into long *rifts*[12] of flame.

1. invalescere.   2. area.   3. quasi.   4. certus.   5. demum.   6. wonderful things.   7. in contrarias partes.   8. fulcire.   9. procedere. 10. detinere.   11. dehiscere.   12. figura.

234. *The Flight from the Eruption*

Not long after, *the said*[1] cloud began to descend to earth and cover the sea. It had enveloped and concealed Capri, and had put *the promontory*[2] of Misenum out of sight. Then my mother began to implore, exhort, and command me to fly as I best could, saying that I could do so as I was young, while she, encumbered as she was by her age and weight, would die gladly if she had been the cause of my death. My reply was, that I did not choose to be saved unless *it were*[3] with her. Then, grasping her hand, I compelled her to *quicken her pace*.[4] She complies with difficulty, and blames herself *for*[5] delaying me. Already ashes were falling, but sparsely as yet. I looked back; thick darkness loomed on us from behind, following us like a torrent *bursting over*[6] the land. 'Let us turn aside,' said I, 'while we can see, *to avoid*[7] being crushed in the darkness by the crowds that accompany us.' We had hardly sat down when darkness came upon us, not *that*[8] of a moonless or overcast night, but such as there is in an enclosed place when lights are extinguished.

1. ille.   2. what projects (*procurrere*).   3. redundant   4. quod with subj. virtually suboblique; *i.e.* not 'because,' but 'because she said she delayed me.'   5. addere gradum.   6. infusus.   7. lest 8. qualis.

235. *Darkness and Consternation.*

You might hear women shrieking, children wailing, and men shouting. Some were calling for their parents, others for their children, others for their wives or husbands, and recognising them by their voices. Many were raising their hands to heaven: still more asserted that there were no longer any gods, and that this was the last night for the universe, a night destined to last for ever. There were not wanting people to increase the actual danger by false alarms. For a short time *there was a break in the darkness,*[1] which seemed to us to herald the approach of fire rather than daylight. Yet the flames stopped *at a considerable distance;*[2] darkness returned, and with it a dense fall of ashes. We had from time to time to rise and shake them off, otherwise we should have been covered or even crushed by them. At last the darkness went off as it were in smoke and fog; daylight soon reappeared in reality, the sun also shone, but with a lurid gleam *as in time of eclipse.*[3] Still greatly alarmed, we saw everything in a changed condition, and covered with a deep layer of ashes as if it were snow.

    1. relucescere.   2. comparative.   3. as (*qualis*) is usual when it
                 is eclipsed (*deficere*).

236. *How would Alexander have fared against Rome?*

It is an interesting question,[1] what would have been the result to Rome if Alexander had to be met. *The most important factors*[2] in war seem to be the number and bravery of the troops, the talent of the commanders, and fortune, *that plays so great a part*[3] in all human affairs, and especially in war. *A consideration*[4] of these points, one by one, and as a whole, easily shows the invincibility of the Roman empire. Firstly, *beginning*[5] by comparing commanders, I have no intention of denying that Alexander was a great captain; but his renown is enhanced *by the fact that*[6] he stands alone, that he died while still young, *while his success was still in the ascendant,*[7] and without experiencing a reverse of fortune. Not to mention other renowned kings and leaders, noteworthy examples of *failure which is incidental to mankind,*[8] what but length of days exposed Cyrus to a change of fortune? This too, but lately, was the case with Pompeius the Great. *The idea of*[9] Manlius Torquatus, or Valerius Corvus, both distinguished soldiers before they were generals, or the Decii, who devoted themselves to death and rushed on the foe, or Papirius Cursor, so renowned for bodily strength as well as courage, *yielding*[9] to Alexander, had they met him in battle!

    1. quaerere libet.   2. to be most powerful.   3. potens.   4. to one
       considering.   5. ut ordiar.   6. quod.   7. in incremento rerum.
       8. casus humani.   9. cessisset videlicet: repeat the verb for effect
       with each name.

237. *The Nature of God.*

If you ask me what or what kind of being God is, I shall *follow the example*[1] of Simonides, who when asked this very question by the tyrant Hiero, asked one day for consideration. When he was asked the same question next day, he asked for two. On his repeatedly doubling the number of days, and Hiero in amazement inquiring why he did so, he replied, ' Because *the longer*[2] I reflect, *the more*[2] difficult does the question appear.' But I fancy that Simonides, for he was not merely a *tuneful*[3] poet, but is said in all other respects to have been learned and wise, since many *fine and subtle points suggested themselves*[4] to him, despaired entirely of the truth, through doubt as to which point was most true.

> 1. auctore uti.   2. quanto—tanto.   3. suavis.   4. acuta atque subtilia venire in mentem.

238. *A Remonstrance.*

He then began his discourse to them in the following manner. *He could not, he said, but*[1] wonder *what motives either of expectation or disgust*[2] had led them into this revolt, that men usually rebelled against their country and their leaders either because they were dissatisfied with the conduct of those who *held the supreme power,*[3] or were displeased with the conduct of affairs: or lastly, perhaps, because they were ambitious of some greater fortune, and *had filled their minds with aspiring hopes.*[4] ' *Tell me then,*'[5] continued he, ' to which of all these causes is your revolt to be ascribed ?   Is it with me that you are offended because the payment of your stipend has been so long delayed ?   The fault, however, is not mine; for during the whole time of my command your stipend has always been fully paid.   If it be Rome then that is at fault in having neglected to discharge your former arrears, was it just that you should show this resentment by taking arms against your country, and declaring yourselves the enemies of those who had bred and nourished you ?   *How much better it would have been*[6] to have made me the judge of your complaints, and to have entreated your friends to join together in obtaining for you the relief which you desired ?'

> 1. facere non posse quin.   2. what they wanted or what had so disgusted them.   3. summam rerum obtinere.   4. in laetioris fortunae spem se erigere.   5. change to oratio recta.   6. make this into a question.

239. *Avarice.*

One very common and at the same time the most *absurd*[1] ambition that ever showed itself in human nature, is that which comes upon a man with experience and old age, the season when it might be expected he should be wisest, and therefore it cannot receive any of those *lessening circumstances*[2] which do in some measure excuse the disorderly ferments of youthful blood; *I mean*[3] the passion of getting money, exclusive of the character of the *prudent*[4] father, the *affectionate*[5] father, or the *generous*[6] friend. It may be remarked, for the comfort of honest poverty, that this desire reigns most in those who have but few qualities to recommend them. This is a weed that will grow in a barren soil. Humanity, good nature, and the advantages of a *liberal education*[7] *are incompatible with*[8] avarice. It is strange to see how suddenly this abject passion kills all the noble sentiments and generous ambitions that adorn human nature; it renders the man who is overrun with it a peevish and cruel master, a severe parent, an *unsociable*[9] husband, a *distant*[10] and mistrustful friend.

1. ineptus. 2. excusatio. 3. dico. 4, 5, 6. the Latin idiom prefers substantives, as being more direct. 7. liberalium artium disciplina. 8. shrink from. 9. incommodus. 10. abstrusus.

240. *National Conceit.*

Barbarians *are tenacious*[1] of their own customs because they want knowledge and *taste*[2] to discover the *reasonableness and propriety*[3] of customs which differ from them. Nations which hold the first rank in *politeness*[4] are frequently no less tenacious out of pride. The Greeks were so *in the ancient world*,[5] and the French are the same in the modern. *Full of themselves*,[6] flattered by the imitation of their neighbours, and accustomed to consider their own modes as the standard of elegance, they scorn to disguise or to lay aside the distinguishing manners of their own nation, or *to make any allowance*[7] for what may differ from them in others. From this cause their armies have always so behaved as to render themselves intolerable to foreign nations. They have always been hated, and have frequently incurred destruction.

Include as far as 'out of pride' in your first period; 'as barbarians,' etc.

1. embrace closely. 2. elegantia. 3. how reasonable, etc. 4. humanitas. 5. among the ancient. 6. toti in se conversi. 7. aliquid ignoscere.

241. *The Destruction of Coomassie.*

Once, *and once only*,[1] did the Ashantees make a stand. They were completely routed and fled. An advance by forced marches was then made on Coomassie, the Ashantee capital. On arriving there it was decided in a council of war to burn and destroy the town, to prevent the Ashantees from forgetting their defeat and annoying our borders or those of our allies. The troops were then marched in to destroy the town. *Their entrance was not marked*[2] by any of the confusion and terror *which usually attends the capture of a city*,[3] but a gloomy silence took such complete possession of such of the inhabitants as were present, that, alarmed as they were, they could not utter a single remark. Considerable treasure was discovered in the temples and in the king's house. Sir Garnet had given orders that no violence should be offered to the inhabitants, who looked on at the conflagration in silence. The troops set fire to all buildings, public and private, and in an hour the city was utterly destroyed. Sir Garnet then, fearing the streams would prove unfordable, as the rains were imminent, and having before him the difficulties of the route, ordered a rapid return to the coast.

1. nor more frequently (*amplius*). 2. when they entered there was not, etc. 3. such as is wont to be (the token) of captured cities.

242. *A Plea for High Schools.*

Recently, when in my own *county*,[1] the son of one of our burgesses came *to pay his respects*[2] to me. I asked him if he was at school. '*Yes*,'[3] said he. 'Where?' 'In London.' 'Why not here?' His father, who was with him, having brought the lad himself, said, 'Because we have no teachers here.' 'Why not? It is greatly to the interest of you fathers (and luckily several fathers could overhear what I said) that your boys should be taught here *in preference to any other place.*[4] For where could they spend their time more pleasantly than in their native county, where could they *be looked after better*[5] than under their parents' eyes, and where cheaper than at home? What prevents you from forming a subscription and paying masters? No gift you could give would be better for your lads or more acceptable to your county. Let those who are natives of this place be educated here, and from their childhood be taught to love and adhere to their native soil. Would also that you could secure the services of such excellent masters that neighbouring towns might *look to this place for education,*[6] and just as your sons now go to other places, strangers might collect to this spot.'

1. patria. 2. salutare. 3. etiam. 4. potissimum. 5. contineri pudicius. 6. seek study from hence.

243. *A Justification of Cicero's Tactics against Catilina.*

It will seem strange to some that Cicero, when he had certain information of Catilina's treason, instead of seizing him in the city, not only suffered but urged his escape, and forced him as it were to begin the war. But there was good reason for what he did, as he frequently intimates in his speeches; he had many enemies among the nobility, and Catilina many secret friends; and though he was perfectly informed of the whole progress and extent of the plot, yet the proofs not being ready to be laid before the public, Catilina's dissimulation still prevailed and persuaded great numbers of his innocence ; so that, if he had imprisoned and punished him at this time as he deserved, the whole faction were prepared to raise a general clamour against him, *by representing*[1] his administration as a tyranny, and *the plot as a forgery contrived to support it.*[2] *Whereas,*[3] by driving Catilina into rebellion, he made all men see the reality of their danger ; while from an exact account of his troops, he knew them to be so unequal to those of the republic, that there was no doubt of his being destroyed if he could be pushed to the necessity of declaring himself before his other projects were ripe for execution. He knew also that if Catilina was once driven out of the city and separated from his *accomplices,*[4] who were a lazy, drunken, thoughtless *crew,*[5] they would ruin themselves by their own rashness, and be easily drawn into any trap which he should lay for them. The event showed that he judged right, and by what happened afterwards both to Catilina and himself, it appeared that, *as far as human caution could reach,*[6] he acted with the utmost prudence, in regard as well to his own as the public safety.

1. tanquam. 2. (as if) he had forged (*ementiri*) the plot as a support to his power. 3. si contra. 4. conscii. 5. greges. 6. as far as (*quoad*) is given to man.

244. *The use of Foreign Travel.*

Certainly the true end of visiting foreign parts is to look into their customs and policies, and observe *in what particulars*[1] they excel or come short of our own ; to *unlearn*[2] some odd peculiarities in our manners, and *wear off*[3] such *awkward stiffnesses and affectations*[4] in our behaviour, as may possibly have been contracted from constantly associating with one nation of men, by a more free, general, and mixed *conversation.*[5] Another end of travelling which deserves to be considered is the improving our taste of the best authors of antiquity, by seeing the places where they lived and of which they wrote, to compare *the natural face*[6] of the country with the descriptions they have given us, and observe how well the picture agrees with *the original.*[7]

1. quatenus. 2. dediscere. 3. deterere. 4. rusticitas paullo inconcinnior et ineptior. 5. hominum usus. 6. ingenium. 7. exemplar.

245. *A Letter to a Brother.*

LONDON, *March* 23.

My dear Charles,—I came up to town yesterday, and shall probably come to you to-morrow. When I know for certain, I'll write you a line. *This is all in spite of*[1] my having met Mark in Kensington Gardens, who told me you were in bed *with an attack of the gout.*[2] I was of course very sorry, but nevertheless determined to come to you, with the view of paying you a visit, and also dining with you, for I suppose your cook is not afflicted with the same complaint. You can look out then for a guest with a small appetite, and one who is easily satisfied.—Believe me, your affectionate brother,

JOHN.

1. etsi.   2. ex pedibus laborare.

246. *Mary and Philip. War with France.*

That he might *work on*[1] this with greater facility and more certainty of success, he set out for England. The queen, who during her husband's absence had languished in perpetual dejection, resumed *fresh spirits*[2] on his arrival ; and without paying the least attention either to the interest or to the inclinations of her people, *entered*[3] warmly into all his *schemes.*[4] In vain did *her privy council*[5] remonstrate against the imprudence as well as the danger of involving the nation in an unnecessary war. In vain did they put her in mind of the solemn treaties of peace subsisting between England and France, which the conduct of that nation afforded her no pretext to violate. Mary, soothed by Philip's caresses or intimidated by his threats, which *his ascendant over*[6] her emboldened him at times to throw out, was deaf to everything that could be urged against his sentiments, and insisted on an immediate declaration of war against France. The council, though all Philip's address and Mary's authority were employed to gain or overawe them, after struggling long, yielded *at last,*[7] not *from conviction,*[8] but merely from deference to the will of the sovereign. War was declared against France, the only one perhaps against that kingdom into which the English ever entered with reluctance.

1. use.   2. novi animi.   3. incumbere.   4. studium.   5. qui a consiliis erant.
6. to such an extent (*eo*) had he subdued her mind.   7. sero demum.
8. convinced by arguments.

247. *Charles the Fifth's reasons for abdicating.*

Charles then rose from his seat, and *leaning on*[1] the shoulder of
the Prince of Orange, because he was unable to stand without *support*,[2] he addressed himself to the audience, and from a paper which
he held in his hand in order to assist his memory, he recounted with
dignity, but without ostentation, all the great things which he had
undertaken and performed since the beginning of his administration.
He observed, that from the seventeenth year of his age he had *dedicated*[3] all his thoughts and attention to public matters, reserving no
portion of his time for the indulgence of his ease, and very little for
the enjoyment of private pleasure ; that, either in a pacific or hostile
manner, he had visited Germany nine times, Spain six times, France
four times, Italy seven times, the Low Countries ten times, England
twice, Africa as often, and had made eleven voyages by sea ; that
while his health permitted him to discharge his duty, and the vigour
of his *constitution*[4] was equal *in any degree*[5] to the arduous office of
governing such extensive dominions, he had never shunned labour
nor repined under fatigue ; that now, when his health was broken
and his vigour exhausted by the rage of an incurable distemper, his
growing[6] infirmities admonished him to retire.

    1. inniti.   2. adminiculum.   3. impendere.   4. body.   5. ex
aliqua parte.   6. ingruere.

248. *Danaus, King of Argos.*

The Argians were so uninformed, that upon the failure of *spontaneous*[1] fountains, they often suffered for want of water, though the
ground upon which the city stood abounded with excellent springs
at a little depth.   Danaus taught them *to dig*[2] wells.   The boon was,
in a hot climate especially, of great importance.   The temper of the
Greeks was warm, *admiration and gratitude became the ruling passions
at Argos*,[3] and produced an inclination towards Danaus so violent,
that Gelanor was constrained to admit him peaceably to plead his
right to the sovereignty before an *assembly*[4] of the people held for
the purpose in the field without the city.   The dispute, however, was
so equally maintained that it became necessary to defer the decision
till the morrow.   By daybreak accordingly the people were crowding
out of the gate, when a wolf from the neighbouring mountains caught
their attention while he attacked a herd grazing near the city and
killed the bull.   This was taken as an omen declaring the divine
will ; the wolf was interpreted to signify the stranger, the bull their
native prince, and the kingdom was adjudged to Danaus.

    1. vivus.   2. deprimere.   3. to such a point (*eo*) of admiration did
the grateful minds of the Argives proceed (*gliscere*).   4. comitia.

249. *A cruel Father.*

At the sight of his father's furious and unrelenting countenance Mustapha's strength failed and his courage forsook him ; the *mutes* [1] fastened the bowstring about his neck, and in a moment put an end to his life. The dead body was *exposed* [2] before the *Sultan's tent.* [3] The soldiers gathered round it, and contemplating that mournful object with astonishment, sorrow, and indignation, were ready, if a leader had not been wanting, to have broken out into the wildest excesses of rage. After giving vent to the first expressions of their grief, they retired, each man to his tent ; and shutting themselves up, bewailed in secret the cruel fate of their favourite, nor was there one of them who tasted bread or *even* [4] water during the remainder of that day. Next morning the same solitude and silence reigned in the camp ; and the Sultan, being afraid that some dreadful storm would follow this sudden calm, in order to appease the enraged soldiers, deprived Rustan of his office and ordered him to leave the camp.

1. elinguati. 2. proicere. 3. praetorium. 4. ipse.

250. *A beautiful View.*

From the hill on which this villa stood *the spectator surveyed* [1] a wide and various prospect, rich at once in natural beauty and *historic associations.* [2] The plain at his feet was the battlefield of the Roman kings and of the *infant* [3] commonwealth ; it was strewn with the marble sepulchres of patricians and consulars, across it stretched *the long straight lines of* [4] the military ways which transported the *ensigns of conquest* [5] to Parthia and Arabia. On the right, over meadow and woodland, lucid with rivulets, he beheld the white turrets of Tibur, Aesulae, and Praeneste, strung *like a row of pearls* [6] on the bosom of the Sabine mountains ; on the left the glistening waves of Alba sunk in their green *crater,* [7] the towering *cone* [8] of the Latian Jupiter, the oaks of Aricia and the pines of Laurentum, the sea bearing sails of every nation to the strand of Ostia.

1. there lay before (*patere*) one who looked (participle). 2. memoria rerum. 3. iam nascens. 4. in long straight lines. 5. the victorious eagles. 6. gemmarum in modum. 7. lake. 8. summit.

251. *The unhappy Colony.*

After his departure everything tended fast to the wildest anarchy. Faction and discontent had often *risen* [1] so high among the old settlers that they could hardly be kept within bounds. The spirit of the new-comers was too ungovernable to bear any restraint. Several among them of better rank were such dissipated, hopeless young men as their friends were glad to send out in quest of whatever fortune might betide them in a foreign land. Of the lower order many were so profligate and desperate that their country was happy to throw them out as *nuisances in society.* [2] Such persons were little capable of *the regular subordination, the strict economy, and the persevering industry* [3] which their situation required. The Indians, observing this misconduct, and that every precaution for sustenance or safety was neglected, not only withheld the supplies of provisions which they were accustomed to furnish, but harassed them with continual hostilities. All their subsistence was derived from the stores which they had brought from England ; these were soon consumed : then the domestic animals sent out to breed in the country were devoured ; and by this inconsiderate waste they were reduced *to such extremity* [4] of famine as not only to eat the most nauseous and unwholesome roots and berries, but to feed on bodies of the Indians they slew, and even on those of their companions who sunk under the oppression of such *complicated* [5] distress. In less than six months, of five hundred persons whom their leader left in Virginia only sixty remained, and these so feeble and dejected that they could not have survived *for ten days* [6] if succour had not arrived from a quarter whence they did not expect it.

1. use a different metaphor ; take one from fire. 2. communis pestis.
3. turn these abstract ideas by verbs. 4. eo. 5. multiplex.
6. to the tenth day.

252. *Caesar contrasted with Sertorius.*

Caesar, *of all men,* [1] knew best when to trust Fortune : Sertorius never trusted her at all, nor ever *marched a step along a path* [2] he had not patiently and well explored. The best of Romans slew the one, the worst the other. The death of Caesar was that which the wise and virtuous would most deprecate for themselves and for their children; that of Sertorius what they would most desire. And since, Quinctus, we have seen the ruin of our country, and her enemies are intent on ours, let us be grateful that the last years of life have neither been useless nor inglorious, and that it is likely to close, not *under the condemnation*[3] of such citizens as Cato and Brutus, but as Lepidus and Antonius. It is with more sorrow than asperity that I reflect on Caius Caesar. Oh! had his heart been unambitious as his style, had he been as prompt to succour his country as to enslave her, how great, how incomparably great, were he! Then perhaps at this hour, O Quinctus, and in this villa, we should have enjoyed his humorous and erudite discourse; for no man ever tempered *so*[4] seasonably and so justly the materials of conversation. How *graceful*[5] was he! how unguarded! His whole character was uncovered; as we represent the bodies of heroes and of gods.

1. as no one (else); *or*, if any one else. 2. do not translate the metaphor literally. 3. abl. abs. 4. more. 5. lepidus.

253. *Contemptuous Silence.*

The first of these is a general silence, which I would not advise any one to interpret in his own *behalf.*[1] It is often *the effect of prudence*[2] in avoiding a quarrel when they see another drive so fast that there is no stopping him without being run against, and but very seldom the effect of weakness in believing suddenly. The generality of mankind are not so grossly ignorant as some overbearing spirits would persuade themselves; and if the authority of a character or a caution against danger make us suppress our opinions, yet neither of these are of force enough to suppress our thoughts of them. If a man who has endeavoured to amuse his company with improbabilities could but look into their minds, he would find that they imagine he lightly esteems of their sense when he thinks to impose upon them, and that he is less esteemed by them in his attempt in doing so. *His endeavour*[3] to glory at their expense becomes a ground of quarrel, and the scorn *of*[4] indifference with which they entertain it begins the immediate punishment; and indeed, if we should even go no further, silence, or a negligent indifference, *has a deeper way of wounding*[5] than opposition, because opposition proceeds from an anger that has a sort of generous sentiment for the adversary mingling along with it, while it shows that there is some esteem in your mind for him, in short, that you think him worth while to contend with. But silence, or negligent indifference, proceeds from anger, mixed with a scorn that *shows*[6] another he is thought by you too contemptible to be regarded.

1. partes. 2. (the token of) those who avoid (participle). 3. the very fact (*id ipsum*) that he wishes. 4. and. 5. descends deeper.
6. arguere.

254. *Study is incumbent on the Great.*

Does not every one understand how far from real nobility are those who, devoted to ease and indolence, appear born for the sole *gratification*[1] of their stomachs? For where can principle and honour exist in the most profound ignorance? Where, in such a *case*,[2] is the brightness of virtue? Where is true magnanimity? Where, in short, are the rest of those excellences without which nobility itself can by no means exist? In the old Roman republic it was considered a disgrace for patricians and famous men to be ignorant of letters. Pomponius has handed down to posterity for ever the well-known testimony of Mucius, who, on hearing one Sulpicius arguing in a negligent manner on a *point of law*,[3] said, 'It is infamous that a patrician of noble birth should be ignorant of the law.' *Every one remembers*[4] too the violent terms in which Tully reproached Verres, and L. Piso, a man of illustrious descent, with their ignorance of letters, as though they had blemished their ancestral nobility with a stain of the foulest character. But this mark of infamy we do not read of as having ever been applied to a plebeian; so that it is evident that the study of the noblest sciences is, by a peculiar right, not so much the business of those in an humble sphere as of patricians and men of exalted station.

1. use a verb. 2. man. 3. ius. 4. turn this by a question.

255. *Maximin's Youth.*

About thirty-two years before that event, the Emperor Severus, returning with his army from the East, halted in Thrace to celebrate with military games the birthday of his younger son Geta. The country-people flocked in crowds to behold their sovereign, *and*[1] a young barbarian of gigantic stature earnestly solicited, in his rude dialect, that he might be allowed to contend for the prize of wrestling. To avoid the *possible*[2] overthrow of a Roman soldier by a Thracian peasant, some of the stoutest of the followers of the camp were selected to be matched with him, sixteen of whom he successively laid on the ground. His victory was rewarded by some trifling gifts and a permission to *enlist*[3] in the troops. The next day the happy youth was distinguished above a crowd of recruits, exulting after the fashion of his country. As soon as he perceived that he had attracted the Emperor's notice, he instantly ran up to his horse and followed him on foot in a long and rapid career. 'Thracian,' said Severus with astonishment, 'art thou disposed to wrestle after thy race?' 'Most willingly, sir,' replied the youth, and *almost in a breath*[4] overthrew seven of the strongest soldiers in the army. Appointed immediately to serve in the horse-guards, who always attended on the person of the sovereign, Maximin, whose father was a Goth, and his mother of the nation of the Alani, at length reached *the imperial purple*.[5]

1. get rid of 'and.' 2. forte. 3. ascribi. 4. without delay. 5. imperium summum.

256. *Alkibiades' Intrigues.*

The Spartans were here, as they wished to be, out of the way of Tissaphernes ; and, in the hope of being able to carry on the war without Persian subsidies, they levied a tribute of thirty-two talents on the Rhodians, who found thus early that freedom from the yoke of Athens was a blessing which must be paid for. But another cause for their inaction lay in the intrigues of Alkibiades. For a man who had *made treachery his trade*[1] there could obviously be no alternative but that of pre-eminence or ruin ; and pre-eminence could be retained only by constant success. His treasons had indeed destroyed the Athenian fleet and army in Sicily, and had inflicted a terrible blow on Attica itself by the fortification of Dekeleia ; but in the waters of the Aegean things began *to wear a different aspect*.[2] It was true that he had brought about the revolt of Chios, and that this had been followed by the defection of other cities on the islands and on the Asiatic continent. But Chios had been miserably ravaged ; Lesbos had been reconquered ; and they *had to contend everywhere with the passive resistance of the people*,[3] who were sadly indifferent to the freedom held out for their acceptance by Sparta. They were still more irritated by the rising of the people in Samos and by the *airs of superiority* assumed towards them by the Persian satrap. An order to kill Alkibiades was therefore sent out to the admiral Astyochos ; but the Athenian exile was more than a match for the stupid treachery of the Spartans, and he made his way to Tissaphernes, *contrasting*[5] probably the secret assassinations of an oligarchic community with the open courts and straightforward decrees of a *vulgar demos*.[6]

1. was altogether occupied (*totus versari*) in treachery. 2. aliter se habere. 3. and the people resisted them in will (though) not by deed. 4. arroganter agere. 5. rationem secum habere. 6. contempta plebes.

257. *Intrepidity of Socrates.*

His enemies, as it is firmly believed, hired the comic poet Aristophanes to make Socrates odious and ridiculous by means of a scurrilous farce in order to *sound*[1] the common people, and, if the *attack succeeded*,[2] to venture still further. This trifle was called ' The

Clouds.' Socrates was the *chief character*,[3] and the person who acted this part took pains to counterfeit him to the very life. Socrates was accustomed never to go to the theatre, except when the plays of Euripides, in the *composition*[4] of which, as some think, he himself had a share, were acted. On the day on which this lampoon was to be performed he nevertheless went. He knew that many strangers who were present asked what this Socrates, thus jeered at in the play, was in *the original*.[5] He stepped forward in the middle of the performance, and continued standing in a place where everybody could see him, and compare him with the copy. This was *fatal*,[6] as it were, to the poet and the comedy. His best hits had no longer effect, for the look of Socrates excited such respect, and such a sort of awe at his intrepidity, that the piece *went off without applause*.[7] So the enemies of the philosopher found themselves forced to put off their purpose of attacking him to a more favourable time.

> 1. temptare.　2. res ex sententia procedere.　3. primaria persona.
> 4. condere.　5. revera.　6. fraudi.　7. frigere.

258. *Colonel Blood.*

One of them was known to have been concerned in the attempt on Ormond, and Blood was immediately concluded to be the *ringleader*.[1] When questioned, he frankly avowed the enterprise, but refused to tell his accomplices. 'The fear of death,' he said, 'should never engage him either to deny guilt or betray a friend.' All these extraordinary circumstances made him the general subject of conversation; and the King was moved by an *idle curiosity*[2] to see and speak with a person so noted for his courage and his crimes. Blood might now esteem himself secure of pardon, and he wanted not address to improve the opportunity. He told Charles that he had been engaged with others in a design to kill him with a carbine above Battersea, where his Majesty often went to bathe; that when he had taken his stand among the reeds, full of these bloody resolutions, he found his heart checked with an *awe*[3] of majesty, and he not only relented himself, but diverted his associates from their purpose; and he warned the King of the danger which might attend his execution, *saying*[4] that his associates had bound themselves by the strictest oaths to avenge the death of any of the confederacy, and that no precaution or power could secure any one from the effects of their *desperate*[5] resolutions.

> 1. auctor.　2. vana cupido.　3. relligio.　4. omit.　5. qualify the
> adjective with a demonstrative adverb.

259. *Darius' Mistake.*

There was in Darius' army a Macedonian refugee named Amyntas, one *who had some knowledge of*[1] Alexander's character. This man, when he saw Darius intended to advance against the enemy within the passes and defiles, advised him earnestly to keep where he was, in the broad and open plains, it being the advantage of a numerous army to have *field-room enough*[2] when it engages with a lesser force. Darius told him he was afraid the enemy would endeavour to run away, and so Alexander would escape out of his hands. 'That fear,' replied Amyntas, 'is needless; you may assure yourself that he will hasten to meet you, and is most likely already on his march.' But Amyntas' counsel was to no purpose, for Darius immediately broke up his camp and marched into Cilicia, at the same time that Alexander advanced into Syria to meet him; and missing one another in the night, they both turned back again. Alexander, greatly pleased with the event, made all the haste he could to fight in the defiles, and Darius to draw his army out of them and recover his former ground. For now he perceived his error in engaging himself in a country in which the sea, the mountains, and the river Pinarus running through the midst of it, would necessitate him to divide his forces, render his horse almost unserviceable, and give aid to *the weakness*[3] of the enemy.

1. not without knowledge of. 2. iustum pugnandi spatium. 3. such was their weakness.

260. *Carausius' Policy.*

During the reign of Diocletian, Carausius, a man of obscure birth and a barbarian (for now not only the army but the senate was filled with *foreigners*[1]), had *obtained*[2] the government of Boulogne. He was also intrusted with the command of a fleet stationed in that port to oppose the Saxon pirates, who then began cruelly to infest the north-west parts of Gaul and *the opposite shore of Britain.*[3] But Carausius made use of the power with which he had been intrusted, not *so much*[4] to suppress the pirates, as to aggrandize himself. He even permitted their depredations, that he might intercept them on their return and enrich himself with the retaken plunder. By such methods he acquired immense wealth, which he distributed with so politic a bounty among the seamen of his fleet and the legions in Britain, that by degrees he disposed both the one and the other to a revolt in his favour. The Britons submitted without difficulty to a sovereignty which seemed to *reflect a sort*[5] of dignity on themselves. Carausius humbled the Picts by several defeats; he repaired the frontier wall, and supplied it with good garrisons. He made roads and cut canals with vast labour and expense. Whilst he thus laboured to promote the internal strength and happiness of his kingdom, he contended with so much success against his former masters, that they were at length obliged not only to relinquish their right· to his acquisition, but to *admit*[6] him to a participation of the imperial titles.

1. barbarians. 2. sibi conciliare. 3. that part of Britain which is opposite to (*e regione*) Gaul. 4. tam. 5. aliquid referre. 6. adsciscere.

261. *Caligula's Madness.*

As soon as he had reached the camp *he made a great parade*[1] of the discipline of earlier days, degraded general officers who *were late in coming*[2] with their troops, and dismissed centurions from the service on trifling grounds, or none at all. Little came of all this show. A princely refugee from Britain asked for shelter. The Rhine was crossed, a *parody*[3] of a night attack was acted out, and imposing letters were written to the senate to describe the submission of the Britons and the terror of the Germans. Then he hurried with his legions to the ocean, with all the pomp and circumstance of war, while none could guess the meaning of the march. At last, when they could go no further, he bade his soldiers pick up the shells that lay upon the shore, and carry home their trophies, as if *to show in strange burlesque the vanity of schemes of conquest.*[4] Before he left the camp, however, the wild fancy seized him to avenge the insult offered to his majesty in childhood, and he resolved to *decimate*[5] the legions that had mutinied long years before. He had them even drawn up in close order and unarmed before him, but they suspected danger, and confronted him so boldly that he feared to give the word, and slunk away to Rome. On his return he seemed ashamed to celebrate the triumph for which he had made costly preparations, forbade the senate to vote him any honours, but complained of them bitterly when they obeyed.

1. ostentator. 2. minus diem servare. 3. species. 4. to mock the vain schemes of warriors. 5. to execute every tenth man.

262. *A good-tempered Emperor.*

The Emperor *stood little*[1] on his dignity, and could *waive*[2] easily enough the claims of rank, could *take in good part*[3] a friendly jest, or even at times a rude retort. In the house of an acquaintance he was one day looking at some *porphyry*[4] columns which he fancied, and asking where his host had bought them, but was unceremoniously told that under a friend's roof a guest should know how to be both deaf and dumb in season. Long before, when he was governor of

Asia, and had visited Smyrna *in the course of a judicial circuit*,[5] he was quartered by the magistrates in the mansion of the sophist Polemon, who was away upon a journey at the time. At the dead of night the master of the house came home, and knocked with impatience at the doors, and would not be pacified till he had the place entirely to himself, and had closed the doors upon his unbidden guest. The great man took the insult quietly enough, and when years afterwards the sophist came to Rome to show off his powers of eloquence, the Emperor welcomed him to court, without any show of rancour at the past, only telling his own servants *to be careful*[6] not to turn the door upon him when he called. And when an actor came with a complaint that Polemon, as *stage director*,[7] had dismissed him without warning from a *company*[8] of players, he only asked what time it was when he was so abruptly turned away. 'Midday!' was the complainant's answer. 'He thrust me out at midnight!' said the prince, 'and I lodged no appeal!'

1. did not much consult. 2. exuere. 3. in bonam partem accipere, *or*, boni consulere. 4. made out of porphyry. 5. conventus agere. 6. operam dare. 7. rector scenae. 8. grex.

263. *Charles the Fifth's Decision of Character.*

As Charles was the first prince of the age in rank and dignity, the part which he acted, whether we consider the greatness, the variety, or the success of his undertakings, was the most conspicuous. It is from an attentive observation of his conduct, *not from*[1] the exaggerated praises of the Spanish historians, or the undistinguishing censure of the French, that *a just idea of Charles' genius and abilities is to be collected.*[2] *He possessed qualities so peculiar that they strongly mark his character*,[3] and not only distinguish him from the princes who were his contemporaries, but account for that superiority over them which he so long maintained. In forming his schemes he was by nature, as well as by habit, cautious and considerate. Born with talents which unfolded themselves slowly and were late in attaining maturity, he was accustomed to ponder every subject that demanded his *consideration*[4] with a careful and deliberate *attention*.[5] He bent the whole force of his mind *towards it*,[6] and dwelling upon it with a serious application, undiverted by pleasure, and hardly relaxed by any amusement, he revolved it in silence in his own breast. He then communicated the matter to his ministers, and after hearing their opinions, took his resolution with a decisive firmness, which seldom follows such slow and seemingly hesitating consultations.

1. than if one believes. 2. we shall judge Charles' genius and abilities more correctly. 3. summo viro illa ipsius propria et prorsus singularia inerant. 4. deliberatum (participle). 5. intentio. 6, hither,

264. *Difficulties in the way of an Invasion of England.*

He felt that it would be madness in him to imitate Monmouth, to cross the sea with a few British adventurers, or to trust to a general rising of the population. It was necessary, or it was pronounced necessary by all those who invited him over, that he should carry an army with him. Yet *who could*[1] *answer for*[2] the effect which the appearance of an army might produce? The Government was indeed justly odious. But would the English people, altogether unaccustomed to the interference of continental powers in English disputes, be inclined to look with favour on a deliverer who was *surrounded*[3] with foreign soldiers? If any part of the royal forces resolutely withstood the invaders, would not that part soon have on its side the patriotic sympathy of *millions?*[4] A defeat would be fatal to the whole undertaking.

1. questions in the first and third persons to be rendered by the infinitive in oratio obliqua. 2. praestare. 3. stipare. 4. as this is an indefinite number, and the Latin for a million is awkward in form, use 'thousands.'

265. *The Athenian and Corcyraean Alliance.*

To a great extent the speech of the Corcyraean envoys placed the Corinthian ambassadors at a disadvantage. By rejecting arbitration under conditions which were undoubtedly fair, the Corinthians had put themselves in the wrong; and to get rid of this difficulty they could only resort to *hair-splitting.*[1] The arbitration, they urged, was proposed too late: it should have been offered before the Corcyraean blockade of Epidamnus was begun. This plea might have been reasonable if arbitration were a means for preventing the commission of wrongs, rather than of *redressing*[2] them when committed. With more of truth they dwelt on *the selfish isolation*[3] of the Corcyraeans, who, having kept aloof thus far, now wished to obtain the alliance of Athens only because they needed help; and with even more force they reminded the Athenians of the service which they had done them in the recent synod by refusing to interfere between an imperial city and her free and subject allies, demanding that this principle should be observed by the Athenians in their turn. The fear of suffering a navy as powerful *as that*[4] of Corcyra, and second only to their own, to be absorbed by a hostile confederacy, constrained the Athenians, somewhat against their will, to enter into a defensive alliance with the Corcyraeans; and the son of Cimon was despatched in command of ten ships only, with strict injunctions *to remain neutral,*[5] unless the Corinthians should attempt to land on Corcyra or on any Corcyraean settlements.

1. cavillari. 2. lucre. 3. for their own advantage. 4. omit, 5. to join neither side.

266. *Pisander's Proposals.*

At Athens the proposals of Pisander and his fellow-envoys were met by vehement opposition, some protesting against the constitutional change, others exclaiming against the restoration of a man who had defied the laws, while *the officers of*[1] the Eleusinian mysteries denounced it as an insult to the gods. Disregarding the clamour, Pisander went up to each speaker, and quietly asked him how he proposed to carry on the war if the whole weight of Persia *should be thrown into the scale*[2] against them. The speakers were silenced; and Pisander went on to assure the assembly that the *change of constitution*[3] would win for them the confidence of the Persian king ; *that constitutional forms were matters of small moment compared with the safety of the state;*[4] and that if after fairly trying *oligarchy*[5] they found that they did not like it, it would be easy for them to restore the democracy. He spoke to a people worn down by a series of disasters coming upon a struggle which had now lasted for nearly a generation ; and the dulness which is the common result of long-protracted anxiety led them to believe the mere word of a man who told them that the resources for carrying on a struggle in which they could not make up their minds to confess themselves beaten would be supplied by Persia. No one asked what reason there might be *for ascribing to the great king so strange a hankering after a good understanding*[6] with a state which had destroyed Persian fleets and armies, had effectually checked the course of Persian conquest, and taken away for more than half a century the tribute which would have found its way into the royal coffers at Susa.

1. those who presided over. 2. do not translate this metaphor literally. 3. res novae. 4. that in time of peril to the state it was unimportant what laws they used. 5. the power of the few. 6. why the great king should be so anxious for a good understanding (*gratiam inire*).

267. *Columbus checks a Mutiny.*

Columbus was fully sensible *of his perilous situation.*[1] He had observed with great uneasiness the fatal operation of ignorance and of fear in producing disaffection among his crew, and saw that it was now ready to burst out into open mutiny. He retained, however, perfect presence of mind. He affected to seem ignorant of their machinations. Notwithstanding the agitation and solicitude of his own mind he appeared with a cheerful countenance, like a man satisfied with the progress he had made, and confident of success. Sometimes he employed all the arts of insinuation to soothe his men. Sometimes he endeavoured to work upon their ambition or avarice by magnificent descriptions of the fame and wealth which they were about to acquire. On other occasions he *assumed a tone of authority,*[2] and threatened them with vengeance from their sovereign if by their dastardly behaviour they should defeat this noble effort to promote the glory of God, and to exalt the Spanish name above that of every other nation. Even with seditious sailors the words of a man whom they had been accustomed to reverence were weighty and persuasive, and not only restrained them from those violent excesses which they meditated, but prevailed with them to accompany their admiral for some time longer.

1. in what great danger he was involved.   2. in severitatem mutatus.

268. *Evathlus.*

Evathlus, a rich young man, desirous of learning *oratory,*[1] paid a visit to Protagoras, a highly celebrated sophist, and after promising a large fee, paid half of it on the spot, and said he would pay the other half when he had won the first case he should have pleaded in court. His abilities were highly respectable, yet he decided not to *practise*[2] much, although his progress had been rapid. So his master, suspecting that his pupil was putting off the day for paying the balance he owed, adopted this plan, which he thought would infallibly compel him although unwilling. He summoned Evathlus, and after setting forth his case before the judges, he spoke as follows : ' You foolish fellow, don't you see that I must be successful. If the judges are for me, you will have to pay *in accordance with the verdict,*[3] while, if I be defeated, in accordance with your *stipulation,*[4] for you will have won by argument, you will be unable to avoid paying *the balance.*'[5] Evathlus' reply was as follows : ' Most sapient master, I could have evaded even this argument had I not pleaded my cause in person. Don't you see, even letting slip this opportunity, that I am safe whichever way the judges decide. If I win, I shall be acquitted by their verdict; if, on the other hand, *I am cast in my suit,*[6] as I shall have failed to win my case, the stipulated conditions will not *affect*[7] me.' The judges being of opinion that the arguments of both *were unassailable,*[8] put off the further hearing of the case to *a distant date.*[9]

1. avoid an abstract noun.   2. caussas agere.   3. ex iudicio.   4. pacta conditio.   5. debitum.   6. cadere.   7. attingere.   8. refelli non posso.   9. longus dies.

269. *Alexander and Diogenes.*

Soon after, the Greeks, being assembled at the Isthmus, *passed a vote*[1] for joining with Alexander in the war against the Persians, and proclaimed him their general. While he stayed here many statesmen and philosophers came to visit and congratulate him, and among them he expected to see Diogenes of Sinope, who then was living at Corinth. Diogenes, however, thought so little of him, that he never stirred out of the Cranæum, where Alexander (who went to see him) found him *lying along in the sun.*[2] When he saw so much company near him, he raised himself a little, and *vouchsafed to look upon*[3] Alexander; and when he saluted him, and asked him whether he could do anything for him, 'Yes,' said he, 'will you stand from between me and the sun?' Alexander, it is said, was so struck with this answer, and surprised at the greatness of the man, who had taken so little notice of him, that, as he went away, he told his followers, who were laughing at the moroseness of the philosopher, that if he were not Alexander he would choose to be Diogenes. Then he went to Delphi, to consult Apollo concerning the success of the war he had undertaken, and happening to come on one of the *forbidden*[4] days, when it was esteemed improper to give any answers from the oracle, he sent messengers to desire the priestess to do her office; and when she refused, on the plea of a law to the contrary, he went up himself, and began to draw her by force into the temple, until, tired and overcome with his importunity, 'My son,' said she, 'thou art invincible.'

1. determined. 2. humi apricare. 3. respicere. 4. nefastus.

270. *The alleged Offences of the Ameer of Afghanistan.*

About this time the Ameer refused to receive a British embassy at Cabul. A rumour soon got abroad that, *in spite of his*[1] rejection of our embassy, some Russian envoys had been received with *hospitality*[2] and *distinction*[2] by the Ameer. In consequence of this Major Cavagnari rode to the fort of Ali Musjid, at the entrance of the Khyber Pass, to inquire what the Ameer *meant.*[3] He was politely received by the commandant, who informed him that he had received no letter, and that his only orders were to prevent any one entering the pass. A council was held at Simla, and on the *Viceroy's*[4] motion it was resolved to send an ultimatum to the Ameer, threatening him with war, unless he signified his readiness within twenty days to receive the embassy. Major Cavagnari *sent a message*[5] to the *headmen*[6] of the hill tribes, informing them that he wished to confer with them, and requesting them to come into Peshawur. War, he told them, would be declared against Shere Ali, and he recommended them not to assist him against the English, who were their friends and not their foes, and had no desire to draw the sword before reaching the Ameer's territory. The headmen came into Peshawur, and being won over by gifts, promised to pass the English forces through their territories.

1. though he had, etc. (concessive use of relative). 2. adverbs. 3. sibi velle. 4. proconsul. 5. throw what follows into the or. obl. ; no other verb of stating or commanding will be required. 6. reguli.

271. *Caligula.*

Tiberius had nominated as his heir Caligula, the son of Germanicus, his grandson by adoption, and joined with him Tiberius the son of Drusus, his grandson by blood. The former enjoyed on his father's account the favour of the people ; and the senate, to gratify them, set aside the right of his colleague, and conferred on him the empire *undivided*.[1] The commencement of his reign was signalized by a few acts of clemency and even of good counsel. He restored the privilege of the comitia, which had been suspended by his predecessor, and *abolished arbitrary prosecutions for crimes of state*.[2] But, tyrannical and cruel by nature, he substituted military execution for legal punishment. The provinces were loaded with the most oppressive and before unheard-of taxes, and daily, cruel and capricious *confiscations*[3] helped to fill the national coffers. The follies and absurdities of Caligula were equal to his vices, and were they not well attested, would exceed all belief. It is hard to say whether he was most the object of hatred or contempt to his subjects. But they submitted to him too long. Seneca's reflection that nature seemed to have brought him forth to show what was possible by the greatest vice supported by the greatest authority, is but a faint description of matters.

1. integer. 2. and forbade that in future any one should be prosecuted arbitrarily for crimes of state (*arcessiri ex arbitrio maiestatis*). 3. publicare.

272. *Refinement no check to Valour.*

Nor need we fear that men by losing their ferocity will lose their martial spirit, or become less undaunted and vigorous in defence of their country or of their liberty. *The arts*[1] have no such effect either in enervating the mind or the body. On the contrary, industry, *their inseparable companion*,[2] adds new force to both, and if anger, which is said to be the whetstone of courage, loses somewhat of its asperity by *politeness*[3] and *refinement*,[4] a *sense of honour*,[5] which is a stronger, more constant, and more governable principle, acquires fresh vigour by that elevation of genius which arises from knowledge and a good education. *Add to this*[6] that courage can neither *have any duration*[7] nor be of any use when not accompanied with discipline and martial skill, which are seldom found among a barbarous people. The ancients remarked that Datames was the only barbarian that ever knew the art of war; and Pyrrhus, seeing the Romans marshal their army with some art and skill, said *with surprise*,[8] 'These barbarians have nothing barbarous in their discipline.' It is observable, that as the old Romans, by *applying themselves wholly*[9] to war, were almost the only uncivilized people that ever possessed military discipline, so the modern Italians are the only civilized people among Europeans that ever wanted courage and a martial spirit.

    1. artes egregiae.   2. adjectival clause.   3. humanitas.   4. cultus.
    5. appetitus famae.   6. to this (*hac*) is added (impersonal).
    7. durare.   8. mirabundus.   9. totus incumbere.

273. *Dissatisfaction of the Cavaliers.*

The feeling of the *cavaliers*[1] was widely different. (*Or. obl.*) During eighteen years they had, through all vicissitudes, been faithful to the Crown. Having shared the distress of their prince, were they not to share his triumph? Was no distinction to be made between them and the disloyal subject who had fought against his rightful sovereign, and who had never concurred in the restoration of royalty till it appeared that nothing else could save the nation from the tyranny of the army? *Grant that such a man*[2] had by his recent services fairly earned his pardon, yet was he to be ranked with men who had no need of the royal clemency—with men who in every part of their lives merited the royal gratitude? Above all, was he to be suffered to retain a fortune *raised*[3] out of the substance of the ruined defenders of the throne? Was it not enough that his head and patrimonial estate, a hundred times *forfeited*[4] to justice, were secure, and that he shared, with the rest of the nation, in the blessings of that mild government of which he had long been the foe? Was it necessary that he should be rewarded for his *treason*[5] *at the expense of men*[6] whose only crime was *the fidelity with which they had observed their oath of allegiance?*[7] And what interest had the King in gorging his old enemies with prey torn from his old friends?

What confidence could be placed in men who had opposed their sovereign, made war on him, imprisoned him, and who even now vindicated all they had done, and seemed to think that they had given an illustrious *proof*[8] of loyalty by just stopping short of regicide? It was true that they had lately assisted to set up the throne, but it was not less true that they had previously pulled it down, and that they still avowed principles which might impel them to pull it down again.

1. eques. 2. such a man (*iste*) perhaps had, etc. 3. conflare (metaphor from the melting down of metal). 4. owed. 5. perduellio. 6. the property being plundered of men who, etc. 7. that they had faithfully obeyed the King. 8. specimen.

274. *Epicurean Philosophy.*

But as the Stoics *exalted human nature too high,*[1] so the Epicureans depressed it too low; as those raised it to the heroic, these *debased it to the brutal state:*[2] they *held*[3] pleasure to be the chief good of man, death the *extinction*[4] of his being, and placed their happiness consequently in the secure enjoyment of a pleasurable life, esteeming virtue of no other account than as it was a handmaid to pleasure, and *helped*[5] to preserve the possession of it by preserving health and conciliating friends. Their wise man therefore had no other duty but to provide for his own ease, to decline all struggles, to retire from public affairs, and to imitate the life of the gods by passing his days in a calm, contemplative, undisturbed repose, in the midst of rural shades and pleasure-gardens.

1. de natura humana altiora disputare. 2. made it equal to the nature of brutes. 3. velle. 4. translate by verb. 5. conducere.

275. *Statesmanship hampered by Philosophy.*

This[1] was the *scheme*[2] that Atticus followed: he had all the talents that could qualify a man to be useful in *society*[3]—great parts, learning, judgment, candour, benevolence, generosity, the same love of his country and the same *sentiments in politics*[4] as Cicero, whom he was always advising and urging to act, yet determined never to act himself, or never, at least, so far as to disturb his ease or endanger his safety. For though he was so strictly united with Cicero, and valued him above all men, yet he managed *an interest all the while with the opposite faction,*[5] and a friendship with even his mortal enemies Clodius and Antonius, that he might secure *against all events*[6] the grand point which he had in view, the peace and tranquillity of his life. Thus, then, two excellent men, *by their mistaken notions of virtue*[7] drawn from the principles of their philosophy, were made in a manner useless to their country, each in a different extreme of life; the one always acting and exposing himself to dangers, without the prospect of doing good, the other, without attempting to do any good, resolving never to act at all.

1. If 'this' has any reference to what has gone before, use a link. 2. ratio. 3. civilis vita. 4. voluntas. 5. diversis partibus gratiosus esse. 6. whatever kind of fortune might appear (*ingruere*). 7. aberrare avia (plural; cognate accusative) virtutis.

276. *The Battle of Plassey.*

Next day Clive *reviewed*[1] his army, and then moved by forced marches against the enemy. On reaching the neighbourhood of a village called Plassey, Clive, who had only 3000 men, saw some 60,000 cavalry and infantry in the enemy's camp. As it was growing late he chose a suitable spot for a camp, and intrenched *himself.*[2] Battle was joined at daybreak. For some hours *it was confined to a double cannonade.*[3] Meanwhile Clive, who had spent a sleepless night in consequence of the noise of drums and cymbals in the native camp, managed to get a short nap, nor could even the din of battle disturb him. The struggle was long *doubtful.*[4] At last *the war was put an end to*[5] by the treachery of Meer Jaffier, who joined us *towards*[6] nightfall, thereby throwing the enemy into confusion. Heavy losses were inflicted on them, and the Nabob, mounted on a swift camel, was one of the first to fly. When a *list*[7] of the slain was *prepared,*[8] it was ascertained that seventy had fallen. *Such was the cost*[9] of a victory which put the empire of India in English hands !

1. lustrare. 2. the camp. 3. it was fought on both sides from a distance (*eminus*). 4. anceps. 5. debellare. 6. sub. 7. ratio. 8. habere. 9. at such (*tantillus*) price stood.

277. *Cicero's Vanity.*

So many things happen at Rome, that what is done in the provinces is scarcely heard of. I do not fear that I am taking too much on myself if I speak of my quaestorship. I certainly make this assertion : I was at that time perfectly confident that my quaestorship was the sole topic at Rome. At a time of great scarcity I had sent a great *quantity*[1] of corn. Polite to *financiers,*[2] equitable to tradesmen, generous to *contractors,*[3] *easy with*[4] allies, in every *dealing*[5] I was considered most *thoroughgoing:*[6] the Sicilians had devised unheard-of honours for me. So I retired, under the idea that the Roman people would *unasked*[7] confer any favour on me. Well, chancing at that time to leave my province to make a tour, and coming to Puteoli at a time when it is a *favourite resort of people of distinction,*[8] I nearly *collapsed*[9] when some one asked when I had left Rome, and whether there was any news? When I replied that I was leaving my province, he rejoined, ' *Oh yes,*[10] Africa, I presume?' ' *No,*[11] Sicily,' said I, *drily,*[12] with a feeling of annoyance. Then some one, *with the air of*[13] being completely informed about everything, remarked, ' What ! don't you know that this gentleman was quaestor at Syracuse?' *Enough on this head:*[14] I ceased to feel annoyed, and made myself one of the company who had come to the waters.

1. numerus. 2. negotiator. 3. manceps. 4. abstinens. 5. officium.
6. diligens. 7. ultro. 8. many people of distinction (*lautissimi*) are wont to be there. 9. concidere. 10. etiam mehercule.
11. immo. 12. fastidiose. 13. as if. 14. quid multa?

278. *The Effect of Cortes' Victories.*

But notwithstanding *the fortunate dexterity*[1] with which he had eluded this danger, Cortes was so sensible of the precarious *tenure*[2] by which he held his power, that he despatched deputies to Spain, *with a pompous account*[3] of the success of his arms, with further specimens of the productions of the country, and with rich presents to the Emperor, as *the earnest*[4] of future contributions from his new conquests ; requesting, in recompense for all his services, the approbation of his proceedings, and that he might be intrusted with the government of those dominions which his conduct and the valour of his followers had added to the crown of Castile. The juncture in which his deputies reached the court was favourable. The internal commotions in Spain which had disquieted the beginning of Charles' reign were just appeased. The ministry had leisure to turn their attention toward foreign affairs. The account of Cortes' victories filled his countrymen with admiration. The extent and value of his conquests became the object of vast and interesting hopes. Whatever stain he might have contracted *by the irregularity of the steps which he took*[5] in order to attain power, was so fully effaced by the splendour and merit of the great actions which they had enabled him to perform, that every heart revolted at the thought of inflicting any censure on a man whose services entitled him to the highest marks of distinction.

1. adverbs. 2. ius. 3. augere in magnificum. 4. spes. 5. per illicita.

279. *The Relief of Orleans.*

But this treacherous conspiracy was detected and disappointed; Orleans had been strengthened with recent fortifications, and the assaults of the Huns were vigorously repelled *by the faithful valour* [1] of the soldiers or citizens who defended the place. *The pastoral diligence* [2] of Anianus, a bishop of primitive sanctity and consummate prudence, exhausted every art of religious policy to support their courage till the arrival of the expected succours. After an obstinate siege the walls were shaken by the battering-rams; the Huns had already occupied the suburbs, and the people who were incapable of bearing arms lay prostrate in prayer. Anianus, who anxiously counted the days and hours, despatched a trusty messenger to observe from the rampart the face of the distant country. He returned twice without any intelligence that could inspire hope or comfort; but in his third report he mentioned a small cloud which he had faintly descried at the extremity of the horizon. 'It is the aid of God!' exclaimed the bishop, in a tone of pious confidence; and the whole multitude repeated after him 'It is the aid of God.' The remote *object,* [3] on which every eye was fixed, became each moment larger and more distinct; the Roman and Gothic banners were gradually perceived; and a favourable wind, blowing aside the dust, discovered in deep array the impatient squadrons of Aëtius and Theodoric, who pressed forwards to the relief of Orleans.

1. adverbs. 2. as became a diligent guardian of his people. 3. cloud.

280. *Cruel Treatment of the Jews.*

The Jews came bowing to the ground before him, but despaired when they saw *the look of sarcasm on his face,* [1] and were accosted with the words, 'So you are the impious wretches who will not have me for a god, but worship one whose name you dare not mention,' and to their horror he pronounced the *awful* [2] name. Their enemies, overjoyed at the rebuff, showed their glee with words and looks of insult, and their spokesman charged the Jews *with wanton indifference* [3] to the Emperor's health and safety. 'Not so, Lord Caius,' they protested loudly, 'for thrice we have sacrificed whole *hecatombs* [4] in thy behalf.' 'May be,' [5] was the reply, 'but ye sacrificed for me, and not to me.' This second speech completed their dismay, and left them all aghast with fear. But almost as he spoke he scampered off, and went hurrying through the house, prying all about the rooms upstairs and down, cavilling at what he saw, and giving orders *on his way,* [6] while the poor Jews had to follow in his train from *place to pace,*[7] amid the mockery and ribald jests of those about them. At length, after some direction given, he turned and said in the same breath to them, 'Why do you not eat *pork?*'[8] They tried to answer calmly that national customs often varied : some people, for example, would not touch the flesh of lambs. 'Quite right, too,' he said, 'for it is poor *tasteless stuff.*'[9] Then the insults and the gibes *went on again.*[10] 'At last,' says Philo, 'God in His mercy to us softened his hard heart, and he let us go alive, saying as he sent us off, "After all they are to be pitied more than blamed, poor fools, who cannot believe I am a god."'

1. vultum in risum componere. 2. verendus. 3. prorsus negligere. 4. a hundred oxen. 5. be it (so). 6. obiter. 7. quoquoversus. 8. porcina. 9. insulsus. 10. de integro ingeri.

281. *Devonshire Lanes.*

An anecdote is told of a gentleman who, in riding through the deep and shady Devonshire lanes, became entangled in the intricacies of their numberless windings ; and not being able to obtain a sufficiently wide view of the country to know whereabouts he was, trotted briskly on, in the confident hope that he should at length come to some house whose inhabitants would direct him, or to some more open spot from which he could take a survey of the different roads, and observe whither they led. After proceeding a long time in this manner, he was surprised to find a *perfect uniformity in the country*[1] through which he passed, and to meet with no human being, nor come in sight of any habitation. He was, however, encouraged by observing, as he advanced, the prints of horses' feet, which indicated that he was in no unfrequented track ; these became continually more and more numerous the further he went, so as to afford him a still increasing assurance of his being in the immediate neighbourhood of some great road or populous village ; and he accordingly paid the less anxious attention to the bearings of the country, from being confident that he was in the right way. But still he saw neither house nor human creature ; and, at length, the recurrence of the same objects by the roadside opened his eyes to the fact, that all this time, misled by the multitude of the turnings, he had been riding in a circle ; and that the footmarks, *the sight of which had so cheered him,*[2] were those of his own horse, their number, of course, increasing *with every circuit he took.*[3] Had he not fortunately made this discovery, *perhaps,*[4] he might have been riding there now.

1. the same character (*natura*) of country (*locus*). 2. which he had seen with delight. 3. the (*quo*) oftener he rode round. 4. nescio an.

282. *The Ability of Charles V.*

His promptitude in *execution*[1] was no less remarkable than his patience in *deliberation.*[1] He did not discover greater *sagacity*[1] in his choice of the measures which it was proper to pursue than *fertility*[1] of genius in finding out the means for rendering his pursuit of them successful. Though he had naturally *so little of the martial turn,*[2] that during the most ardent and *bustling*[3] period of life he remained in the Cabinet inactive ; yet when he chose at length to appear at the head of his armies, his mind was so formed for vigorous exertion *in every direction,*[4] that he acquired such knowledge in the art of war and such talents for command as rendered him equal in reputation and success to the most able generals of the age. But Charles possessed in the most eminent degree the science which is of the greatest importance to a monarch, that of *knowing men,*[5] and of adapting their talents to the various departments which he allotted to them.

1. use verbs : avoid the use of abstract nouns as much as possible ; thus, turn 'sagacity' and 'fertility' in some other way if you can.
2. militiae adeo incuriosus. 3. trepidus. 4. quoquoversus.
5. knowing the differences (*discrimina*) between men.

283. *A Perfect Gentleman.*

In his domestic and social life[1] his *behaviour*[2] was very amiable. He was a most indulgent parent, a sincere and zealous friend, a kind and generous master : his letters are full of the tenderest expressions of love for his children, in whose *endearing conversation,*[3] as he often tells us, he used to sink all his cares, and relieve himself from all his *troubles*[4] in the *House*[5] and *law courts.*[6] The same affection to an inferior degree was extended also to his servants, when by their fidelity and services they had *recommended*[7] themselves to his favour. In his clothes and dress, which the wise have usually considered as an index of the mind, he observed a modesty and decency adapted to his rank and character. A perpetual cleanliness without the appearance of pains, free from the affectation of singularity and avoiding the extremes of rustic negligence and *foppish precision,*[8] both of which are equally contrary to true dignity, *the one implying*[9] an ignorance or illiberal contempt of it, the other a childish pride and ostentation of proclaiming our pretensions to it.

1. as a father and friend. 2. use a verb. 3. dulce colloquium.
4. contentio. 5. senatus. 6. forum. 7. probare. 8. inepta concinnitas. 9. as the one is (a mark of).

284. *What is Humanity?*

Human nature appears a very deformed or a very beautiful object *according to the different lights in which* [1] it is viewed. When we see men of inflamed passions or wicked designs tearing one another to pieces with open violence, or undermining each other by secret treachery; when we observe base and narrow ends *pursued* [2] by ignominious and dishonest means; when we behold men mixed in society as it were for the destruction of it; we are either ashamed of our species or *out of humour* [3] with our own being. But, in another light, when we behold them mild, good, and benevolent, full of a generous regard for the public prosperity, compassionating each other's distress and relieving each other's wants, we can hardly believe they are creatures of the same kind. In this view they appear gods to each other, in the exercise of the noblest power—that of doing good; and the *greatest compliment we have ever been able to make* [4] to our own being has been by calling this *disposition* [5] of mind 'humanity.' We cannot but observe a pleasure arising in our own breast upon the hearing or seeing of a generous action, even when we are wholly disinterested in it. I cannot give a more proper instance of this than by a letter from Pliny, in which he recommends a friend in *the most handsome manner;* [6] and methinks it would be a great pleasure to know the success of this epistle though each party concerned in it has been so many hundred years in his grave.

1. prout hinc vel illinc. 2. keep to the active. 3. poenitet. 4. and nothing more complimentary (*honorificus*) can be said. 5. affectus. 6. enixissime.

285. *Prestige a great assistance to a General.*

Since *prestige* [1] is a most *powerful factor* [2] in the conduct of a war and in military commands, no one can doubt that in respect of this this same celebrated general *carries the greatest weight.* [3] No one is unaware of the fact that in the management of a war the opinions held by enemies and allies of our generals are of the highest moment. In affairs of such importance men are led to despise and fear, like and dislike, by *what people think and say,* [4] no less than by any fixed *standard of judgment.* [5] What name was ever more celebrated in the whole world? Who ever achieved like exploits? About what other general have you *expressed your opinion* [6] *in such complimentary terms,* [7] a thing that in itself especially gives a man influence? Can any one imagine that a general who has effected so much by mere prestige will fail of success through want of valour?

1. auctoritas. 2. multum valere. 3. plurimum posse. 4. use substantives to express this. 5. ratio. 6. iudicia facere.
7. use adjectives to agree with iudicia.

286. *An Acknowledgment of a Gift.*

I am perfectly sensible *of the very flattering distinction*[1] I have received in your thinking me worthy of so noble a present as that of your History of America. I have however suffered *my gratitude to be under some suspicion*[2] by delaying my acknowledgment of so great a favour. But my delay was only to render my obligation to you more complete, and my thanks, if possible, more merited. *The close of the session*[3] brought a great deal of troublesome though not important business on me at once, so I could not *go through*[4] your work at one breath at that time, though I have done so since. I am now enabled not only to thank you for the honour you have done me, but for the great satisfaction and infinite variety and compass of instruction I have received from your incomparable work.

1. how you have honoured me. 2. you to suspect that I was rather forgetful. 3. rerum prolatio. 4. use *haurire*, keeping up the metaphor contained in 'one breath.'

287. *An admirable History.*

Everything has been done which was to be expected from the author of the History of Scotland and the Age of Charles XII. I believe that few books have done more than this towards clearing up dark points, correcting errors, and removing *prejudices.*[1] You have too the rare secret of *rekindling an interest*[2] in subjects *that have so often been treated,*[3] and in which everything which could have fed a vital flame appeared to have been consumed. I am sure I read many parts of your History with that fresh concern and anxiety which attend those who are not previously apprised of the event. You have besides thrown quite a new light on the present state of the Spanish provinces, and furnished both materials and *hints*[4] *for a rational theory*[5] of what may be expected of them in future.

1. opiniones praeiudicatae. 2. of applying a fresh torch; this metaphor harmonizes with the expression 'to feed a vital flame.' 3. iam decantatus. 4. argumentum. 5. whence we may infer by a probable theory (*coniectura*).

288. *Victory stained by Rapine.*

Meanwhile Charles, satisfied with the easy and almost *bloodless*[1] victory which he had gained, and advancing slowly with the precaution necessary in an enemy's country, did not yet know the whole extent of his good fortune. But, at last, a messenger despatched by the slaves acquainted him with the success of their *noble effort*[2] for the recovery of their liberty ; and at the same time deputies arrived from the town in order to present him with the keys of their gate, and *to implore his protection from*[3] military violence. While he was deliberating concerning the proper measures for this purpose, the soldiers, fearing that they should be deprived of the booty which they had expected, rushed suddenly and without orders into the town, and began to kill and plunder without distinction. It was too late to restrain their cruelty, their avarice, or their licentiousness. All the outrages of which soldiers are capable in the fury of a storm, all the excesses of which men can be guilty when their passions are heightened by the contempt and hatred which difference in manners inspires, were committed. Above thirty thousand of the innocent inhabitants perished on that unhappy day, and ten thousand were carried away as slaves. Hassen took possession of a throne surrounded with carnage, abhorred by his subjects, on whom he had brought such calamities, and pitied even by those whose rashness had been the occasion of them. The Emperor lamented the fatal accident which had stained the lustre of his victory, and amidst such a scene of horror there was but one spectacle that afforded him any satisfaction. Ten thousand Christian slaves, among whom were several persons of distinction, met him as he entered the town, and falling on their knees thanked him and blessed him as their deliverer.

1. on this side (*citra*) of blood. 2. egregium ausum. 3. deprecari.

289. *Pandora's Box.*

Beside these several advantages which rise from hope, there is another, which is none of the least, and that is, its great efficacy in preserving us from setting too high a value on present enjoyments. The *saying*[1] of Caesar is very well known. When he had given away all his estate *in gratuities*[2] amongst his friends, one of them asked what he had left for himself ; to which that great man replied, Hope. His natural magnanimity hindered him from prizing what he was certainly possessed of, and turned all his thoughts upon something more valuable than he had in view. I question not but every reader *will draw a moral*[3] from this story, and apply it to himself without my direction. The old story of Pandora's box (which many of the learned believe was formed among the heathens upon the tradition of the fall of man) shows us how deplorable a state they thought the present life without hope. To set forth the utmost condition of misery, they tell us that our forefather, *according to the pagan theology*,[4] had a great vessel presented him by Pandora. Upon his lifting up the lid of it, says the fable, there flew out all the calamities and distempers *incident to* [5] men, from which till that time they had been altogether exempt. Hope, who had been enclosed in the cup with so much bad company, instead of flying off with the rest, stuck so close to the lid of it, that it was shut down upon her.

    1. vox.   2. in giving largess.   3. will so interpret for himself.
    4. a thing which had been handed down by the priests
          of old.   5. which could happen to.

290. *The Disaster at Isandula.*

Next day Lord Chelmsford, hearing from his scouts that considerable numbers of *Zulus* [1] were lurking in the *bush*,[2] determined to reconnoitre in person, in order to be more fully informed of the enemy's movements. He accordingly sent on Major Dartnell with a small force, intending to follow shortly in person. He was soon informed that the Zulus were visible in force and that reinforcements were wanted. Accordingly he set out with a tolerably strong force, leaving the 24th regiment, with some companies of the auxiliary troops, to guard the camp. While still on the march, towards nightfall, Commandant Lonsdale came up *at a gallop*,[3] and brought word that the Zulus were in possession of the camp, and that our men who had been left to guard it had been slain to a man. Hastily, *yet all too late*,[4] returning to the camp, everything was found *ransacked*,[5] and a *night of apprehension was passed* [6] amid the corpses of the slain. At dawn a movement was made on *Rorke's Drift*,[7] to ensure a retreat, if necessary, within our frontier. On reaching it the troops who had been left to guard the Drift were found in a state of great exhaustion from wounds and exertion. Lieutenant Chard, *R.E.*,[8] the officer in command, reported that the enemy had but just retired, after incessant attempts to storm the camp throughout the whole night, which had been repulsed with heavy loss by the devotion of the British troops, and that our loss amounted to *some* [9] sixteen men, that of the Zulus to nearly four hundred. Thus, by the resolution and skill of a lieutenant of engineers and a handful of men, the Zulus were prevented from seizing the Drift, depriving our forces of all hope of retreat, and cutting off *the survivors*.[10]

    1. Afer.   2. tesqua.   3. admisso equo.   4. sero demum.   5. compilare
      6. they spent the night in great apprehension.   7. the ford.
      8. praefectus fabrum.   9. ad.   10. adjectival clause.

291. *The Protector's Manifesto.*

The Protector, before he opened the campaign, published a *mani- festo,*[1] in which he *exposed*[2] all the arguments for that measure. He said that nature seemed originally to have intended the island for *an*[3] empire, and having cut it off from all communication with foreign states and guarded it from the ocean, she had pointed out to the inhabitants the road to happiness and security. That the education and customs of the people *concurred*[4] with nature, and by giving them the same language and laws and manners *had invited*[5] them to a thorough union and coalition. That fortune had at last removed all obstacles, and had prepared an expedient by which they might become one people, without leaving any place for that jealousy, either of honour or interests, to which rival natures are naturally *exposed.*[6] That the crown of Scotland had devolved on a female, that of England on a male, and happily the two sovereigns as of a rank were also of an age the most suitable to each other. That the hostile dispositions which prevailed between the nations, and which arose from past injuries, would soon be extinguished after a long and secure peace had *established confidence*[7] between them : that the memory of former miseries, which at present inflamed their mutual *animosities,*[8] would then serve only to make them cherish with more passion a state of happiness and tranquillity so long unknown to their an- cestors.

1. libelli. 2. confirmare. 3. remember that 'a' or 'an' is sometimes emphatic. 4. variety may be often given by negativing the opposite to what you wish to express : so here you can say 'did not disagree.' 5. again, for the sake of variety, you can make this a question. 6. obnoxius. 7. fidem conciliare. 8. simultas.

292. *A Letter to a Nephew.*

My dear Nephew,—The *tone*[1] of your former letter caused me, I confess, keen distress. You impressed me, *you will allow me to say,*[2] as showing a weak desire to return to the refinements of city life. I thought too that I read in some of them *a want of soldierly courage,*[3] in others of energy, in others a lack of modesty, strangely at variance with your true modesty. However, I have made your acknowledg- ments to the minister in pursuance of your last instructions, which have caused me unspeakable satisfaction, and I am glad to be able to compliment you on having at last come to some settled resolution. For myself, if I *consulted*[4] my own convenience, I should be most anxious to have you by my side, as few things could afford me more pleasure than your society, and more advantage than your assistance. But as you sought my friendship and confidence from earliest youth, I have always thought it incumbent on me not only to defend your interests, but to promote and favour them in every possible way ; and you have, I daresay, not forgotten the *unsolicited* [5] offers which I made you when on the point of *accepting a colonial appointment.* [6] No sooner did I change in my plans, than, perceiving that my successor treated me with great distinction and friendship, I recommended you to him in the strongest terms. Good-bye ; let me hear where you are to pass the winter, with what position or prospects.— Your affectionate uncle.

1. omit.   2. pace tua dixerim.   3. translate these abstract ideas by adjectives.   4. rationem ducere.   5. ultro.   6. in provinciam exire.

293. *An Obstacle to ambitious Designs.*

But the punishment of Rabirius was not the thing aimed at, nor the life of an old man worth the pains of disturbing the peace of the city : the design was to attack that *prerogative* [1] of the senate by which, in the case of a sudden tumult, they could arm the city at once, by requiring the consuls to take care that the republic received no detriment ; which vote was supposed to sanction anything that was done in consequence of it, so that several traitorous magistrates had been cut off by it, without the formalities of a trial, *in the act of* [2] stirring up sedition. This practice, though in use from the earliest times, had always been complained of by the tribunes *as* [3] an infringement of the *constitution,* [4] by giving the senate an *arbitrary power* [5] over the lives of the citizens, which could not be taken away without a hearing and judgment of the whole people. But the chief grudge of it was from its being a perpetual check to the designs of the ambitious and popular who aspired to any power not allowed by the laws. It was not difficult for them to deceive the multitude, but the senate was not so easily managed, who by that single vote of committing the republic to the consuls could frustrate at once all the effects of their popularity when carried to a point which was dangerous to the state ; for since in virtue of it the tribunes themselves, whose persons were held sacred, might be taken off without sentence or trial when engaged in any traitorous practices, all attempt of that kind must necessarily be hazardous and desperate.

1. ius.   2. cum maxime.   3 make this clause indirect (saying, etc.).
4. respublica.   5. arbitrium.

'We shall next be told,' exclaims Seneca, 'that the first shoe-maker was a philosopher.' For our own part, if we are forced to make our choice between the first shoemaker and the author of the three books ' On Anger,' we *pronounce for* [1] the shoemaker. It may be worse to be angry than to be wet. But shoes have kept millions from being wet ; and we doubt whether Seneca ever kept anybody from being angry. It is very reluctantly that Seneca can be brought to confess that any philosopher had ever paid the smallest attention to anything that could possibly promote what vulgar people would con-sider as the wellbeing of mankind. He labours *to clear Democritus from the disgraceful imputation of having made* [2] the first arch, and Anacharsis from the charge of having contrived *the potter's wheel.* [3] He is forced to own that such a thing might happen ; and it may also happen, he tells us, that a philosopher may be swift of foot. *But it is not in his character of philosopher* [4] that he either wins a race or invents a machine. *No, to be sure.* [5] The business of a philosopher was to declaim in praise of poverty with two millions *sterling* [6] out *at usury,* [7] to meditate *epigrammatic conceits* [8] about the evils of luxury in gardens which moved the envy of sovereigns, to rant about liberty while fawning on the indolent and pampered freedmen of a tyrant, to celebrate the divine beauty of virtue with the same pen which had just before written a defence of the murder of a mother by a son.

1. prefer. 2. that no one should prove that Democritus made. 3. rota figularis. 4. but it has nothing to do with wisdom. 5. scilicet. 6. sesterces. 7. in fenore ponere. 8. frigidae sententiolae.

295. *Nothing certain.*

'A man's ransom !'—who was it that had said five hundred florins was more than a man's ransom ? *If now, under this mid-day sun,* [1] on some hot coast far away, a man somewhat stricken in years —a man not without high thoughts and with the most *passionate* [2] heart—a man who long years ago had rescued a little boy from a life of beggary, filth, and cruel wrong, had reared him tenderly, and been to him as a father—if that man were now under this summer sun toiling as a slave, hewing wood and drawing water, perhaps being smitten and buffeted because he was not deft and active. If he were saying to himself, 'Tito will find me : he had but to carry our

manuscripts and gems to Venice; he will have raised money, and
will never rest till he finds me out.' If that were certain, could
he, Tito, see the price of the gems lying before him, and say, 'I will
stay at Florence, where I am fanned by soft airs of promised love
and prosperity; I will not risk myself for his sake'? No, surely
not, if it were certain. But nothing could be further from certainty.
The galley had been taken by a Turkish vessel on its way to Delos:
that was known by the report of the companion galley, which had
escaped. But there had been resistance, and probable bloodshed; a
man had been seen falling overboard: *who were*[3] the survivors, and
what had befallen them amongst all the multitude of possibilities?
Had not he, Tito, suffered shipwreck, and narrowly escaped drown-
ing? *He had good cause for*[4] feeling the omnipresence of casualties
that threatened all projects with futility.

1. supply a verb, and break up the long period that extends to 'active'
    into short sentences; as it stands it is involved,   2. loving.
       3. how small (*quotus*) a part.   4. esse cur.

296. *The Execution of the Conspirators.*

After the senate had *voted in favour of Cato's motion*,[1] the consul,
deeming the wisest course of action was *to make good use of*[2] the
approaching night to prevent any fresh occurrences within that time,
ordered the triumvirs to get ready all things *necessary for*[3] the
execution, and in person escorted Lentulus to the prison *between rows
of soldiers;*[4] the remainder were served in like manner by the praetors.
In the prison there is a place called the Tullianum, after you *descend*[5]
a short way towards the left, sunk in the ground to a depth of twelve
feet or thereabouts; it is enclosed by party walls on all sides, and
overhead by a *vaulted roof*[6] with stone arches: the whole *effect*[7] is
disgusting and appalling from its darkness and evil odours. When
Lentulus had been sent down to this place the appointed officers
dislocated[8] his neck with a halter. Cethegus and the rest of the
conspirators were *dealt with*[9] in like manner.

1. discedere in Catonis sententiam. 2. antecapere. 3. use an adjectival
clause. 4. dispositis praesidiis. 5. shall have descended. 6. camera.
    7. facies. 8. frangere. 9. punished (*supplicium sumere &c*).

297. *A City Churchyard. I.*

Situated in an unfrequented part of the town, away from any habitation, and totally unknown to hundreds of the inhabitants; its only approaches long, sullen-looking, sombre lanes, which even by day *have a cut-throat look*[1] about them, and by night present the *beau ideal of a ghost walk*,[2] is the disused, forgotten burial-ground. Unwholesome, *blear-eyed*,[3] rotting walls of eight or ten feet high on either side bound the dark lane leading to it, and in the crumbling carcase of one of these is a low-browed doorway, the door of which would be a disgrace to the meanest outhouse. Such is the entrance to this place of sepulture. Within, an oblong *slip of earth*,[4] bounded on either side by *allotment grounds*,[5] and divided from them by low frowsy walls, near relations to the outer ones, forms the burial-place.

1. sicarii nescio quid sapere. 2. sedes prorsus Tartareae. 3. introduce this metaphorical idea by some qualifying expression, 'so to speak,' etc. 4. agellum. 5. the gardens of the poor.

298. *A City Churchyard. II.*

The last occasion on which *we visited*[1] the place was in the summer time. The old rickety door had been left unfastened, and was swinging to and fro on its rusty hinges with a melancholy sound as we entered. A wretched-looking *pony*[2] was blundering among the unkempt graves, and lifted up its head as in mute protest at such sorry fare and ghostly quarters. *Hassocks*[3] of coarse rank grass had blotted out all traces of a path, if there ever had been any. One of the tombs is fenced in with tottering palisades, near which a tree had been planted, but had sickened and died, and its skeleton rattled *ominously*[4] in the low summer wind. Other mementoes and tablets stand or lie about in all directions; the flat ones seemed to be the favourite promenade of snails, for their surfaces were covered with slimy hieroglyphics left by their trail. Others lie about and stand at *all*[5] angles, while some again are panelled into the rotting walls, down which green stains run from the humid stones, and all have that peculiar mildewed appearance which *gathers about*[6] things and places seldom visited.

1. do not make this the principal verb; it is a subordinate idea. 2. caballus. 3. iuba. 4. omine ferali. 5. unequal. 6. proper to.

299.

If the Italians *have a genius for music above the English*,[1] the English have a genius for other *performances*[2] of a far higher nature and capable of giving the mind a much nobler *entertainment*.[3] Would one have believed that it was possible (at a time when an author lived capable of writing the Phaedra and Hippolytus) for a people to be so *stupidly*[4] fond of the Italian *opera*[5] as *scarcely to give a three days' hearing*[6] to that admirable tragedy? Music is certainly a very agreeable entertainment; but if it would take the entire possession of our ears, if it would exclude arts that have a much higher tendency to the refinement of the human race, if it would make us incapable of hearing sense, I must confess I would *allow it no better quarter*[7] than Plato has done, who banished it out of his commonwealth. At present our notions of music are so very uncertain that we do not know what it is we like: only in general we are transported with anything that is not English, so it be of a foreign growth; let it be Italian, French, or High Dutch, it is the same thing. In short, our English music is quite rooted out and nothing yet planted in its stead.

1. excel the English as regards music. 2. do not translate such a word as this. 3. cibus: notice the concrete Latin for the English abstract. 4. perdite. 5. mimus. 6. almost to neglect when acted (*recitare*) for the third time. 7. proceed (*animadvertere*) against it not more gently.

300. *The End of Ximenes.*

Ximenes did not bear[1] this treatment with his usual fortitude and spirit. *Conscious*[2] of his own integrity and merit, he expected *a more grateful return from a prince*[3] to whom he delivered a kingdom more flourishing than it had been in any former age, together with authority more extensive and better established than the most illustrious of his ancestors had ever possessed. He could not therefore on many occasions *refrain from*[4] giving vent to his indignation and complaints: he lamented the fate of his country, and foretold the calamities it would suffer from the insolence, the rapaciousness, and the ignorance of strangers. While his mind was agitated with passion, he received a letter from the king, in which, after a few cold and *formal*[5] expressions of regard, he was allowed to retire to his *diocese*,[6] that, after a life of such continued labour, he might end his days in tranquillity. His haughty mind, it is probable, could not survive disgrace, perhaps his generous heart could not bear the prospect of a misfortune *ready to fall*[7] on his country. Whichever of these opinions we embrace, certain it is that he expired a few hours after receiving this letter. The variety, the grandeur, and the success of his schemes during a *regency* [8] of only twenty months leave it doubtful whether his sagacity in *counsel*,[9] his prudence in conduct, or his boldness in execution, deserve the greatest praise.

1. To Ximenes was wanting, etc. 2. sibi conscius. 3. that the prince would be of more grateful feeling. 4. sibi temperare quin. 5. tralaticius. 6. provincia. 7. imminens. 8. tutela regni. 9. use gerunds of corresponding verbs.